Black and Blue Horizons
DAVID GOULET
A Kanu Culture publication, published by Batini Books

Jacob, a troubled teenager, wakes to find himself on a plane bound for the South Pacific island of Samoa and a reform school camp dubbed 'Black and Blue Horizons'. His parents have had enough of his defiant attitude and behaviour. His life up until this point in California is one of surfing, gaming, fights and family conflict.

The secluded camp serves to reform wayward youth who have lost their place in the world, where camp staff ground the youth in the family and community-centered Samoan culture. It's a shock to the system for Jacob, who dreams of escaping the spartan camp.

That outlook takes a new turn when a teacher introduces him to the unique paddle sport of outrigger canoeing. More than a sport, outrigger canoeing serves as a cultural touchstone bonding many indigenous cultures of Oceania through its physicality, teamwork and spiritual connection to the seafarers of ancient Pasifika.

Black and Blue Horizons follows Jacob's story as he embarks on the most challenging journey of his young life, paddling towards the discovery of his better self.

Black and Blue Horizons
DAVID GOULET
A Kanu Culture publication, published by Batini Books

published by

BATINI BOOKS Est 1994

Black and Blue Horizons
DAVID GOULET
A Kanu Culture publication, published by Batini Books

Disclaimer - Copyright Issues

This art by
Sunny Pau'ole
of Kona Hawaii

Publishing Information

© David Goulet, Batini Books 2020
www.kanuculture.com

ISBN 978-0-9574664-6-3

DAVID GOULET

David Goulet is a Canadian voyageur who spent several formative years as a volunteer in Samoa where he was introduced to Outrigger Canoeing, Polynesian culture And his future wife, Tina.

Fast forward to today where David is a freelance writer and creative dynamo. He lives in Toronto with Tina and their two children, Leah Moana and Justin Manu. He still dreams of the blue horizons of the South Pacific.

"I wrote this novel as a way of capturing some of my experiences as a volunteer in Samoa. Perhaps I was inspired to be a 'teller of tales' after sleeping one night on the tomb of Robert Louis Stevenson that rests atop Mt. Vaea. Like the characters in this story, I see the Samoan people navigating the big waters of change, facing waves that threaten to overwhelm the canoe. But when a team pulls together, believes in each other, and has faith in the stars...they can overcome the storm. That's the message of this book and my hope for the young people of the world."

DEDICATION
To all those I was blessed to share a paopao with. When our adventures are done, may the waves carry us to restful waters.

SAMOA

Samoa, formerly called Western Samoa, is famed for its natural beauty and friendly people. The large islands of Savaii and Upolu are mountainous (volcanic in origin) and are covered with heavy forests. Both are ringed by coral reefs.

Originally settled by the Tongan Polynesians, it was the European explorers and missionaries that transformed these islands for better or for worse. Christianity was introduced to the natives and many local customs soon disappeared. At the conclusion of World War I and for 42 years, New Zealand occupied and administered the islands. Then, in 1962, Samoa became the first Polynesian nation to reestablish its independence in the 20th Century.

The local population is mostly indigenous Samoans. The port city of Apia is the centre of local government and trade, and the economy revolves around agriculture, timber and tourism. American Samoa, a neighbouring group of islands, shares the same culture, and much of the same history.

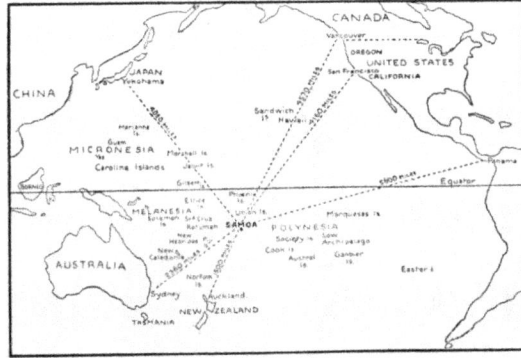

OUTRIGGER CANOEING

Photo by JOSS

Outrigger Canoeing, is not simply another sport but in fact a cultural touchstone. Within the Pacific, from the islands of Melanesia, Polynesia and Micronesia collectively called Oceania, Outrigger Canoeing ties together the connection shared between its peoples as surely as the ropes and lashings tie together the canoes they paddle.

The Outrigger Canoe and is an artefact of great cultural significance, the voyaging canoes of which, served to populate the Pacific Islands so as every indigenous person is the result at least one great canoe journey, recorded in folklore and mythology.

Outrigger Canoeing's cultural significance cannot be over-stated. While desecration of cultures of the Pacific have been widespread, participation in Outrigger Canoeing, serves to keep alive a sense of identity and connection with a seafaring, canoe based culture.

The sport is active in Samoa under the Samoan Outrigger Canoe Association and participation levels are increasing as youth take to the sport, seeing it not just as a healthy, social activity, but indeed as a way of connection with their brothers and sisters of the Pacific Islands, be it in Fiji, Tonga, Tahiti or New Zealand - the connection is real. Blue Horizons touches on this connection and the passion by which it is participated.

PRELUDE

"Relax kid, in a few more hours you'll be in your new home; Samoa."

Darkness.

A roaring wind.

Jacob Michaels' head throbbed with pain, his lean teenage body sore and limp. All the strength had been drained from him. He opened his eyes groggily and looked around. He was sitting in a dimly lit airplane, the loud engines overpowering the other sounds in the cabin.

He tried to rub his bleary eyes, only to realize that his hands were tied behind his back. He turned his head to the left and looked out the tiny window. The moonlight reflected off a vast expanse of water. As far as he could see, there was only ocean beneath them.

Was this a dream, he wondered. It must be; it felt like one. He slowly turned to the right; his head felt like it weighed a hundred pounds. Sitting next to him was a huge, brown-skinned man dressed in sweatpants and a San Diego Chargers t-shirt. The big man was asleep.

Jacob leaned forward and tried to stand up. The seat in front of him was too far back and blocked his momentum. He needed his hands. As he repositioned his legs he made another discovery. His feet were taped together. A wave of panic shot through him. Why were his hands and feet bound? Why was he on this plane?

He saw a flight attendant making her way down the aisle, checking the sleeping passengers. He tried to call out to her.

"Please . . . help," but his voice was too weak to be heard over the engines. He began rocking his body side-to-side in his seat, hoping she would see him.

Suddenly two heavy hands grabbed his shoulders from the seat behind.

"Mika! Wake up fool. The kid's coming out of it," hissed a deep voice.

The big man beside Jacob stirred to life.

"What should we do?" he asked.

"Give him another shot - a half dose."

Jacob watched the big man pull a syringe from a black leather bag. He stuck it into a small bottle and filled the syringe half full. He leaned over towards Jacob, the needle aimed at his arm.

Jacob struggled against the powerful hands gripping him, trying to break free. It was futile; he couldn't budge them. He felt a sharp pain in his upper arm as the needle punctured his skin. Within seconds his eyes began to fog over again and his muscles went dead. "Relax kid, in a few more hours you'll be in your new home . . . Samoa."

Samoa? What was he talking about? This can't be real, thought Jacob. As a drug-induced tiredness overcame him, his mind drifted away from the airplane and back to the last things he could remember.

CHAPTER 1

"A pig wouldn't want to live in this mess."

In a dark room, a computer screen cast an eerie glow as heavy metal rock music blared from an iPhone deck.

On the screen, a ninja crept toward an unsuspecting guard outside a warehouse. With a quick flick of his wrists, the ninja threw two sharp metal stars at the guard. The projectiles slashed into his neck, blood spurting from the throat, as the victim dropped dead to the ground.

"Gotcha!" smiled Jacob, as he used his control-pad to move the ninja into the warehouse. "Three more kills to go."

His eyes were bloodshot from staring at the screen. He knew he was close to finishing this level of the game. His ninja character flashed a samurai sword and another guard was eliminated, this time beheaded.

"Yes! Two left." Jacob could smell the victory now. He manoeuvred his ninja through a hallway toward the next target, a guard in front of a steel door. Jacob had to be careful here, the guard was well armed. One wrong move and . . .

Knock, knock! Jacob was startled by a tapping on his bedroom door.

"Jacob? Are you up? Time to get ready for school," called a muffled female voice from the other side.

Jacob tried to ignore the voice. He refocused on his game and attacked the guard. The guard fired, but missed the ninja. Jacob quickly pressed three buttons on his controller and the ninja leapt into the air and slashed down with the samurai sword. The guard's head was sliced in two.

"Sick!" laughed Jacob. This was it, the last target. His ninja slowly opened the steel door and entered. A well-dressed man stood looking out a large window. Jacob moved the ninja forward, silently. But this seemed too easy; he had to watch for a trap.

Knock, knock.

"Jacob?! Are you getting dressed?" the voice now louder.

Jacob frowned, he needed to concentrate on . . .

The bedroom door opened and a hand switched on the light. Brightness lit up the room and half-blinded Jacob's tired eyes. Through his squinting, he could just see his ninja stepping across infrared security lasers. An alarm sounded and the man at the window turned around, a huge machine gun in his hands.

Jacob jerked the controller, pressing buttons. Too late, his ninja's evasive actions were useless as the machine gun bullets tore into his body. The screen went red and a sign flashed on: Mission Failure, Restart Level?

Jacob spun around. His mother stood in the doorway.

"Thanks a lot," he growled. "Now I have to redo the whole damn level!"

Heather Michaels looked at her son in shock. He looked like he hadn't slept. "You haven't been playing that game all night, have you?" she asked, "You have school today. How can you possibly pay attention in class with no sleep?"

"That's my problem," he replied as he switched off the computer.

"Jacob, you know your father doesn't appreciate that attitude. You better get washed up and downstairs for breakfast."

"Fine, whatever," he grumbled. He walked over to a dresser and looked for some clean underwear.

His mother looked around the disheveled room. The walls were covered with movie posters, as well as those of rock stars and professional surfers. In the corner leaned two surfboards and a boogie board. The bed wasn't made; shorts and t-shirts littered the floor.

She stepped in and reached for the iPhone, turning it off.

"I don't know how you can listen to that noise," she said as she picked up a small empty pizza box. "And I want to see this room cleaned up by tomorrow. A pig wouldn't want to live in this mess.

Jacob didn't answer her. He stepped past her toward the bathroom.

"Did you hear what I said, Jacob?"

"Yeah, I'll get to it." He slipped into the bathroom shut the door.

He leaned over the sink and took a good look at himself in the mirror. He ran a hand through his greasy brown hair. He noticed a new pimple under his chin and popped it. He touched the dark bags under his eyes. He had to admit he did look rough. But so what, he thought, it was his life. He was seventeen, old enough to make his own decisions. Why did his parents have to nag him so much? Why couldn't everyone just leave him alone?

CHAPTER 2

As he headed for school, he replayed the confrontation with his parents in his mind.

Jacob found a faded t-shirt in his musty closet and put it on. It had "Leave Me the F*#! Alone" written on the back. He slipped on a pair of ripped jeans and his high-top running shoes. He grabbed a worn-out school bag off a chair and headed downstairs.

He jumped over the last three steps and marched into the kitchen. His parents were sitting at the table. Ben Michaels put down the newspaper he was reading and glared at Jacob. His mother looked at his shirt and sighed, "Can't you wear something half-decent to school?"

Jacob shrugged, grabbed a bagel and proceeded toward a side door.

"Sit down," commanded his father.

Jacob stopped and turned around, "But I'm late, I better get . . ."

"I said, sit down!"

Jacob rolled his eyes and sat down at the table. His father leaned forward.

"Your mother says you were up all night playing a computer game. On a school night, are you crazy?"

Jacob tried to look innocent, "I lost track of the time. It's no big deal."

Ben shook his head, "If it happened once in awhile, it wouldn't be a big deal. But it seems to be happening most of the time. When you're not on that

4

computer all night, you're at the beach surfing all weekend. Your grades are dropping, you haven't been to church in three weeks and you're becoming disrespectful to your mother and me. What's wrong with you?"

Jacob just stared blankly at the walls. His father sat back, frustrated.

"Jacob," began his mother, "we're worried about you. You seem to be cutting yourself off from us, from everyone. You don't have any friends around; you just close yourself up in that 'cave' of yours or take off alone to the beach without telling us. Is something bothering you?"

He remained silent, hoping they'd get tired of asking dumb questions.

She patted his hand, "You don't have . . . a drug problem?"

Jacob's jaw dropped. "A drug problem! If that's what you think, then you must be the one sniffing glue!"

"Don't you talk like that to your mother," warned Ben.

Jacob shook his head in disbelief. How could his parents be so unfair?

"Can I go now?" he asked.

"Just one more thing," added his father. "This Sunday is the church's youth picnic. I've already told Pastor Rodriguez that you'll be there."

Jacob stood up and slammed a fist onto the table.

"I'm not going to that stupid picnic. All they do is play kids games and sing lame church songs!"

Both parents were surprised at Jacob's angry outburst. Ben stood up and looked his son in the face.

"Don't you raise your voice to me, young man. You will go or . . ."

"Or what?!" barked Jacob, "I'm not a kid. You're not bossing me around anymore. I can make my own decisions!"

Adrenaline shot through Jacob's body. He could feel his heart pounding. He had never openly defied his father like this. He was scared, but it also felt good seeing the confusion in his father's face, and the shock in his mother's. Jacob felt a sense of power. He didn't wait for them to respond. He slung his bag over his shoulder and made for the door. He pointed his thumb to the message on the back of his t-shirt, and then slammed the door shut behind him.

His mountain bike was leaning against the garage; he jumped on and pedaled hard down the street. As he headed for school, he replayed the confrontation with his parents in his mind. It felt weird to disobey them, but it also felt liberating. He didn't need them or their rules. It felt like he had just caught a perfect wave on his surfboard. Just him and his fastest board gliding over the deep blue sea, alone and as free as the wind. He smiled. No one was going to get in his way any more.

CHAPTER 3

"You want me to sell drugs for you? You've got to be joking!"

Jacob rolled into the school parking lot at the rear of the building.

"Gee, I'm late," he chuckled sarcastically to himself. He coasted to the heavy iron bike rack and hopped off. He unwound the cable and lock from under his seat and was about to secure it when he heard footsteps behind him.

"Nice wheels, Michaels. Is that a Schwinn?"

Jacob stood up and turned around. Five well-dressed teens, smoking cigarettes, were watching him. He recognized the oldest, nicknamed Dice, a popular athlete and a senior. He wore baggy jeans that hung well below his waist over a muscle shirt with the Oakland Raiders logo on the front. A long gold chain hung around his neck, two small solid dice dangling from the end. The rest of the boys, a mix of seniors and sophomores, were dressed in a similar fashion, imitating Dice.

All five of them had their hair dyed blond and glistening with gel. They kept spitting onto the pavement, in between puffs on their cigarettes. Jacob stifled the urge to laugh at them.

"Yeah it's a Schwinn," he answered coolly.

Dice inspected the bike. He noticed the back of Jacob's shirt.

"Sick shirt, even sicker bike. How about a test ride?" grinned Dice.

Jacob resisted the obvious pressure to say "yes."

"Sorry, I'm late for class, maybe some other time." He went to click the lock shut. Dice grabbed his arm.

"What's the rush?" Dice's tone had a growing hint of menace.

"I've been watching you, Michaels," he continued, "You don't say much. You've that lone wolf vibe going, a loaded gun ready to go off. I like that."

Jacob was surprised by the remark. Dice took his hand off Jacob's arm.

"How'd you like to hang with me and my crew?" offered Dice.

Jacob's surprise turned to bewilderment. Why would Dice think he'd want to join his moronic posse? He looked at the four other boys, all trying hard to look tough, and then back to Dice.

"And why would I want to hang with you guys?" challenged Jacob.

The other boys bristled at the slight. Dice just turned to them and smiled.

"You see, I told you the kid had balls." He turned back to Jacob.

"Michaels, high school can be a great place if you're friends with the right people. For example, my friends enjoy certain privileges, we get invited to the best parties, hell . . . we are the party!"

The others laughed and high-fived each other. They looked like total goofs, thought Jacob.

"Now when it comes to the ladies," continued Dice, "it's a booty buffet. Take your pick, hot cheerleaders, spicy numbers from the jazz band, or even a certain guidance counselor."

The boys whooped and nudged each other at the reference to the counselor. Jacob wanted to roll his eyes at the exaggerated boasting. Were these guys for real?

"So what's the catch?" asked Jacob.

Dice shrugged, "No catch. Of course, friends do things for friends."

"Like let them ride their bike," replied Jacob.

Dice smiled, "Yeah, but that's hardly much of a favour. I had something else in mind."

He flicked his cigarette away and moved closer, pulling a small package from his pocket. Inside were small white crystals. Now Jacob understood what Dice was after.

"You want me to sell drugs for you? You've got to be joking!"

"Hey, keep it down," hissed Dice, "I thought you'd be into this."

Jacob turned his back and bent over to lock his bike, "You thought wrong. Sell your own garbage."

Dice's face instantly turned angry. He grabbed Jacob by the arm and swung him up and around.

"I don't think you get the picture, Michaels. I was trying to be nice, cut you in on some fun. But the bottom line is that you don't disrespect me, or my offer. Like I said, high school is a great place to be if you have the right friends, or it can be real hell. So you will do what you're told, got that?"

Jacob felt Dice's grip on him tighten. From the corner of his eyes he saw the other boys moving closer. He felt trapped, once again being told what to do. Well, he wasn't going to be pushed around by a bunch of losers. He yanked his arm free from Dice and pushed him back. Not expecting the push, Dice lost his balance and fell. He immediately reached into his sock and pulled out a short, mean-looking knife. He waved the others forward.

"Grab him!"

The others rushed Jacob. He felt the reflex to run, but he also felt the steel cable with the lock still in his hand. An inner rage exploded from within and he whipped the cable upward. It caught the first boy just above the eye, opening a gash over his brow. He fell to the ground holding his head, blood oozing through the fingers.

The assault caught the others off-guard, Jacob used the hesitation to whip the cable around again and it caught another boy on the kneecap. He buckled to the pavement, clutching his knee.

The other two boys backed off, but Dice was now coming forward with his knife. The three of them surrounded Jacob.

"Now," yelled Dice.

The two boys tried to tackle Jacob. The one on the right took the swinging lock square on the jaw and was knocked unconscious. The other one did manage to get a hold of Jacob's leg. Seeing his chance, Dice lunged forward.

Jacob gave the cable a quick spin and launched it at Dice. It caught him right in the groin. He dropped to his knees. Jacob turned his attention to the boy trying to up-end him. He brought his other knee up and around quickly, smashing it into the boy's nose. The boy clutched his face and rolled on the pavement. Blood flowed from under his hands.

Jacob looked at the blood on the ground. He couldn't believe it, in less than a minute, he had viciously beaten Dice and his gang. He saw the knife lying on the ground and kicked it away. He looked at his hands; they were shaking. Where had this ferocious rage come from? He suddenly felt very cold.

"Arrrrr!" a body slammed into Jacob. It was Dice. The two boys hit the pavement hard. The sharp pain rekindled Jacob's anger. He rolled over and locked his arms onto Dice, who outweighed him by at least twenty pounds. Dice threw several punches, two of them landing on Jacob's head. But Jacob hardly felt them. He flung his elbow around and smashed it into Dice's face. It dazed him, allowing Jacob two quick jabs into Dice's ribs, knocking the wind out of him.

Jacob knelt over Dice. He cocked his fist back ready to ground-and-pound him senseless, when two hands grabbed his shoulders and pulled him away. He was driven to the ground and his arms pinned behind him. He couldn't move. With his face on the hot pavement he could see a pair of polished shoes and a uniform. It was the school security guards.

"Better call for a paramedic!" called a voice, "And the police. There's a bag of crystal meth here. Looks like we broke up a little drug war."

CHAPTER 4

Intervention? Now what was his father talking about?

"Those weren't my drugs, I swear! Dice and his boys started the whole thing," moaned Jacob sitting in the back of his parent's car. Ben and Heather Michaels sat in the front grim-faced.

His father looked at him in the mirror. "Do you really expect us to believe that story you gave the police?"

"Well they didn't charge me, did they?"

"Only because they couldn't prove the drugs were yours, or the knife. And if that custodian hadn't seen those boys ganging up on you, you'd be facing assault charges. Their parents could still take us to civil court."

"Thank God none of them was seriously hurt," added his mother.

"None of them?" blurted Jacob, "What about me? I'm jumped by five goons but I'm the one that's suspended from school! That's bull."

"You're lucky you weren't expelled," answered his father.

Jacob leaned back in his seat and rubbed his temples, head aching. Why wouldn't they believe him?

The car pulled into their driveway, his mother turned to look at him.

"Son, your father and I have been talking and we think we need to take drastic measures to help you."

Jacob rolled his eyes. "Now what?! Let me guess, you're taking away my computer and I'm grounded. And no surfing for a month. Right?"

"It's gone way past that," his father replied, "We're enrolling you in a special school. Pastor Rodriguez recommended it. It's outside the city. They have a drug rehab and behavior modification program. It's expensive, but they have a good success rate."

Jacob sat there in stunned silence. This can't be happening, he thought. His mother began to cry.

"We don't know what else to do with you. You've become so . . . violent. We just want to help you."

"If you really want to help me, just leave me alone!" shouted Jacob as he opened his door and began to walk across the lawn toward the street. As he passed by their two aluminum garbage cans that sat on the curb, he kicked them both over. Garbage spilled onto the sidewalk.

His father got out of the car, but didn't chase after him, "Mister, you better get back here and pick that up! You're going to do as you're told."

Jacob kept walking. "Pick it up yourself!"

His father slammed his fist on the roof. "I'm warning you Jacob, if it's a full intervention you want, that's what you'll get."

Intervention? Now what was his father talking about? Jacob looked back; his mother was still in the car crying. His father had pulled out his cellphone. Probably calling a lawyer, thought Jacob.

As he turned the corner and could no longer see the driveway, his anger started to ebb. It had been a long hard day; he just needed to relax for awhile. He decided to head to his favorite cyber-cafe a few blocks away. He'd unwind with a few hours of online gaming. At least a computer couldn't accuse him of anything.

CHAPTER 5

"Don't worry kid,
this is for your own good."

The sun was beginning to set when Jacob stepped out of The Blue Dragon Cyber-cafe. He stretched his arms and back. His muscles were stiff and sore, sitting hadn't helped his war wounds, but he felt calm and clear. Nothing like three hours of gaming to clear the head.

He started walking home. He hoped his parents had cooled down and come to their senses. He'd sit down and have a good talk with them. He'd promise to buckle down on his studies if they dropped the silly idea of sending him to that special school. Where did they ever come up with that plan anyway? Well, there was no way he was going to some holy-roller, share-your-feelings reform school. He felt his stomach grumble. He'd have to raid the fridge before the conference with his folks.

A black mini-van pulled up beside him on the street. The driver, a brown-skinned man, leaned out the passenger window.

"Excuse me, buddy, do you know if there's a McDonald's anywhere around here?" asked the man.

Jacob nodded, "Yeah, at Fairmount Plaza, three blocks south."

The man held up a map, "Do you think you could point it out on this map? We're not from around here."

"Sure," replied Jacob and he walked over to the vehicle.

"Thanks, it's appreciated," said the man as he stepped out of the van. He laid the map on the hood. The guy was big. Jacob guessed he was Mexican.

Jacob looked over the map as the big man kept scanning the street. Jacob pointed to a spot on the map.

"We're here," he traced his finger south," there's Fairmount Plaza."

The big man watched a car drive by and turn at a corner. The street was quiet. He looked down at the map. Jacob pointed again at the spot.

"Right here. Think you can find it now?" he asked.

"I don't think that will be a problem, Jacob," replied the man.

Jacob froze. How did this guy know his name? Suddenly the big man grabbed him and swung him toward the rear door, which was opening.

"What the hell!" shouted Jacob as he was forced into the van. A second brown-skinned man reached out from the rear seat and pulled Jacob inside headfirst. A thick, rough hand clamped over his mouth. He kicked furiously with his feet, but the two monsters quickly pinned them down. He couldn't move.

"Don't worry, kid, this is for your own good," grunted one of the men.

Jacob felt something prick him in his left hip. What were they doing to him? He began to feel weird. His arms and legs were soon going numb. He felt his eyelids growing heavy. His head began to spin. He heard the van doors shut and felt the van moving. As he drifted into unconsciousness, the last thing he heard was the driver speaking to the other man.

"Call his parents. Tell them we're on our way to the airport."

CHAPTER 6

"Welcome to Faleolo Airport, boy."

Jacob felt someone shaking his body.

"Are you sure you just gave him a half dose? Don't tell me we're going to have to carry his butt all the way to Lotofaga!"

"I think he's coming around."

Jacob opened his eyes a fraction. He was still in the airplane, though the roaring sound had stopped. He leaned forward; a pair of hands grabbed his arm and helped lift him up. He tried to walk but his legs didn't move.

"Untape his feet. He's not running any marathons for a while."

One of the brown-skinned men bent down and unwound a long strip of duct tape from Jacob's feet. Jacob tried again to move, and this time his feet obeyed. Though his legs were stiff and weak, Jacob gladly trudged into the aisle. It seemed like days since he had blood flowing through his body.

Strong hands gripped his arm again and led him forward. Jacob realized his own hands were still tied behind his back. He shook his head, trying to shake away the fuzz on his brain.

A flight attendant waited at an open door. She looked at him as he reached the door and frowned. Was it pity or disgust? Jacob couldn't tell.

As he stepped out of the plane onto the metal steps, Jacob's senses reawakened. A hot humid breeze, smelling of dirty diesel fumes, blew across his skin. Though it was night, the tarmac was lit up by strong floodlights and a large building glowed with activity.

"Welcome to Faleolo Airport, boy," announced a voice behind him.

Jacob turned around. The two brown-skinned men stood in the plane's doorway. The big man wore a black aloha shirt. The smaller man had a noticeable scar on his neck. They both looked tired. One of them stepped forward and took him by the arm.

"Well, c'mon. We still have a couple of hours driving ahead."

Jacob let the man guide him down the steps to the tarmac. So this wasn't a dream. He really had been abducted. But where in the world was he? And who were these people? He decided to take the direct approach.

"Where am I?' he asked the big man, the driver of the van.

The man pointed to a colorful sign at the entrance of the terminal: Talofa lava - Welcome to Samoa.

"Suh-mow-eh?" blurted Jacob, "Are we in Mexico?"

"Mexico!" the big man growled, "Do we look like Mexicans to you, boy? Do we sound like Mexicans?"

The other man laughed, "Oi sole, we've been flying for ten hours. We could have driven to Mexico in 30 minutes. You're in Samoa, brother, the heart of Polynesia."

The big man shook his head, "They don't call it that anymore. The tourist bureau says it's Samoa . . . the Treasure Island."

"That's right," noted the other man as he patted Jacob on the shoulder, "And we got us our own little treasure right here."

Now Jacob understood what was going on. They were kidnappers! For a brief second he panicked, and then a wave of anger flowed through him. Finally, he started laughing.

"What's so funny, boy?" asked the big man.

Jacob shook his head, "You picked the wrong kid to kidnap."

"Is that so?"

"Afraid so." There was a confident smirk on his face. "There's no way my parents are going to pay you any ransom. My dad has enough money to buy a small army to come here, to this Suh-mow-eh, and wipe you out. You guys are dead meat."

The two men looked at each other and smiled.

"I'm not joking," warned Jacob.

"Actually," chuckled the big man, "the joke's on you, boy. Your father's the one who paid us to bring you here."

"Blue Horizons. It's where we run our behavior modification school, and the place you'll be calling 'home' for the next year."

Jacob was led by his captors through the airport terminal. His senses absorbed the sights, sounds and smells, but his mind was still trying to process what the big man had told him. Had his parents actually arranged his abduction by these goons? Why?

The big man handed a set of papers to an immigration officer who quickly flipped through them. He nodded and stamped them.

"Another palagi bad boy, eh?" grinned the officer.

"We're just doing our part for Samoan tourism," winked the big man.

All three men chuckled at the remark. Jacob didn't understand what was so funny. He stepped in front of the officer.

"Sir, these men kidnapped me. I'm an American citizen; I need to be taken to a United States Embassy!"

The officer stared at Jacob then broke out laughing. The big man pushed Jacob towards the exit doors.

"Let's go. We wouldn't want to create an international incident," he said sarcastically.

Jacob turned around and confronted the two men, "I demand to contact my parents. I want my one phone call, I've got rights."

The man with the scar rolled his eyes, "That's only if you're arrested. We aren't cops, so forget your rights. Besides . . ." he pulled a piece of paper from his pocket, "this document, signed by your parents, puts you into our protective custody."

Jacob grabbed the paper and scanned it. It was all legal mumbo-jumbo which he couldn't make sense of, but he did recognize his parents' signatures on the bottom.

"How do I know this is what you say it is? I want to talk to my parents," ordered Jacob.

The big man led him outside, where dozens of cars and buses were busy loading passengers and luggage. A few people noticed Jacob and pointed him out to others. They stared at him with a mix of curiosity and ridicule. Jacob hated all these brown-skinned people staring at him, like he was some kind of freak. What kind of savage place had they brought him to? He glared back at the onlookers and then turned to his captors.

"Listen you idiots, you can't just tie people up, pump them full of drugs and take them to . . . God knows where . . . and treat them like prisoners! Who the hell do you think you are?"

Despite his cursing them, the men ignored him as they spotted a lanky brown-skinned man waving to them from a parking lot on a small hill.

"There's Sanele," noted the big man, "I hope he brought some barbecue. I'm starved."

They walked up the short incline to where Sanele leaned on a large Toyota Land Cruiser. He shook hands with the men. "Malo Mika," he said to the scarred man.

"Malo Peter," he nodded to the big man. They responded in kind. Sanele then looked at Jacob and smiled.

"So this is our new guest. Talofa Jacob, welcome to Samoa."

Jacob's patience finally snapped. He pointed a finger at Sanele, "Look, I don't know who you people are, but I want to be taken to a phone and allowed to contact my parents. Now!"

Sanele frowned, "That won't be possible. You won't be allowed to talk to your folks for a few weeks. That's the rule. They knew that when they signed the contract."

"What contract?" asked Jacob, more confused by the minute.

Sanele looked at the men; "You haven't explained anything to him?"

Mika shook his head, "He was out most of the flight. We had to keep him sedated and bound, because of the violence problem."

Sanele nodded, "Yes, I read his file. Well, hopefully we can do something about it."

Peter chuckled, "I'm sure Big Sefo has a few ideas."

Mika also laughed but not Sanele. He looked away, pulling a set of keys from his pocket.

"Well, we better get moving." He opened the cruiser door, "Oh, I picked up some . . ."

"Barbecue!" cheered Mika and Peter together.

Sanele laughed, "I knew you boys from the States would be craving some sosisi, mamoe, fai, sapasui and . . . "

"Kalo? Please say kalo," begged Mika.

"Kalo? On my salary?" countered Sanele, "How about kaamu?"

Peter nodded. "Okay, as long as it isn't alaisa!"

Jacob stared at them bewildered. What were they talking about? Food? Were they insane? They had just turned his entire life upside down, and all these jerks could think about was their stomachs. Things couldn't possibly get any worse, he thought.

Sanele opened the rear door of the cruiser, then led Jacob over and helped him in. Jacob eased back into the seat, his shoulders stiff and aching.

"Can you at least untie my hands?" he pleaded.

"Sorry," replied Sanele, "not until we get to camp. It's procedure."

"Camp? What camp?"

"Blue Horizons. It's where we run our behavior modification school, and the place you'll be calling 'home' for the next year."

Jacob's spirit sank. Things had just gotten worse.

CHAPTER 8

Jacob closed his eyes and wished he was home at Gibson's Point, sitting alone on his surfboard, waiting for a juicy wave.

As the land cruiser sped along the coastal road, the pungent smell of roasted meat made Jacob nauseous. He looked over at Mika who sat beside him, a bowl of woven leaves on his lap, chewing on a bone. He made loud smacking noises as he sucked out the marrow. In the front of the car, Peter did the same.

Just looking at Mika's greasy hands and face made Jacob's stomach flutter. He turned away and looked out his half-open window. The bright moon illuminated the coastline, which the road followed religiously. The sea was calm, though the branches on the coconut trees swayed in a light breeze. Jacob could smell the salty air. He wondered if they had good surf here.

Every half-mile they passed small houses and what looked like beach huts. The houses had slatted windows and tin roofs, while the beach huts were topped with thatching. Some houses had odd concrete slabs in front of them, though what purpose they served Jacob could only guess.

There were certainly a lot of dogs roaming around. One or two even slept on the side of the road. Apart from a car or two that they passed, there was no human activity to be seen. If a place could be said to be unconscious, then this was it, thought Jacob.

"Want a piece?"

Jacob was startled back to his immediate reality. He looked to his right where Mika held a large chunk of gray potato in front of Jacob's mouth.

"It's taamu, swamp taro, in coconut cream. Try it, it sticks to the ribs."

Jacob gazed at the glistening lump and wrinkled his nose, "No, thanks."

"Suit yourself," replied Mika as he bit into the taamu, "but you might as well get used to it, you'll be seeing plenty of it."

Peter turned to them and chuckled. "That's right. You won't be eating french fries and pizza for awhile. Just lots of canned herring, mutton soup and . . .

"And rice, lots of rice!" added Sanele. "I have to admit our cook isn't the most imaginative man in a kitchen."

Mika nodded. "He burns everything too, especially his koko esi. He tries to fix it by dumping bags of sugar into it."

Sanele laughed. "That's why we call him, Suka the Kuka."

Peter raised a sausage in the air as a salute. "To Suka the Kuka."

Mika grabbed a piece of mutton and did the same. "To Suka, please don't make us piuka." The three men roared with laughter at the joke. Jacob closed his eyes and wished he was home at Gibson's Point, sitting alone on his surfboard, waiting for a juicy wave. He could almost see the big breaker as it rolled in over the reef. He'd feel his board hook onto it and pull him along, then lean into the wave as it curled over itself, and slash across its crest. Like a dart he'd sail swiftly, smoothly down the wave, the wind flowing over his body and . . .

"Look out!" someone yelled.

Jacob was knocked forward as the cruiser's brakes slammed on. Almost at the same time there was a jarring thump on the right side of the vehicle. The car skidded for a second then came to rest. A sharp-pitched squeal could be heard. Jacob looked out the rear window. A huge black pig scampered through a ditch and into the bush.

"The damn thing," gasped Sanele. "Lucky it just caught the fender. That monster would've wrecked the front end."

Peter stuck his head outside the window inspecting the damage, leaned back inside. "Just a small dent. No big deal."

Sanele pulled back onto the road and continued on, though his speed was noticeably slower, more cautious, now.

"What would you have done if you'd killed it?" asked Jacob.

The men glanced at him, a little surprised by the question. Then Mika smiled.

"Taken it back to camp. The boys would have enjoyed a good feed of pork." By the gleam in Mika's eyes, Jacob knew he wasn't kidding.

CHAPTER 9

As they descended the mountain toward another coastal road, Jacob experienced a growing sense of dread.

The land cruiser wound its way further inland and began to climb upwards. As it strained against the steep incline of the road, chugging higher and higher, Jacob was refreshed by the brisk air flowing through the open window. Mika and Peter breathed deeply and yawned. The cool, comfortable air was very relaxing, and allowed the jet lag to catch up with them. Both men leaned against their doors and closed their eyes. Within minutes they were snoring.

Sanele also yawned but kept his concentration on the road ahead. The cruiser crested the top of the mountain and the road became rougher. Potholes pockmarked the pavement. Sanele did his best to avoid most of them, but in the dark it was difficult to catch them all. Every few seconds the vehicle vibrated as it hit another hole. Between the bumps and the cold mountain air, Jacob became aware of something. He needed to go to the bathroom. He hadn't gone since he left the cyber-cafe and was abducted. And even though he hadn't had a drop to drink and the long plane ride had dehydrated him, he now felt his bladder pinching to be released.

"Hey, driver, can we stop for a minute," he called.

Sanele looked at him in the rear view mirror, "What's the matter?"

"I gotta take a leak, man. You know, drain the vein."

"Can't you wait? We'll be there in another twenty five minutes."

"I can't wait another twenty five seconds!"

Mika opened a sleepy eye. "What's the problem now?"

Sanele slowed the cruiser, "He needs to pee, can't hold it til camp."

Mika scratched his head. "I guess it has been a good twelve hours for him. But we're not supposed to take the cuffs off him until camp. And I sure ain't unzipping or holding anything for him."

"But I gotta go!" pleaded Jacob.

Mika pointed a finger at him, "You'll just have to hold it. And don't even think about letting it go in here. I'll make you mop it up with your tongue."

Sanele shook his head and stopped the vehicle.

"What are you doing?" asked Mika.

Sanele got out and opened Jacob's door. He helped him out.

"This is ridiculous. The cuffs should have come off when you landed," he murmured as he fiddled with a small key ring. He found the key he wanted and unlocked the cuffs. Jacob slowly brought his arms in front of him. They were painfully stiff, as if needles were exploding through the muscle tissues. His wrists were barely able to bend and his fingers were cramped shut.

"Hurry up," ordered Sanele.

Jacob walked over to the side of the road and unzipped. The floodgates opened and he sighed as he relieved himself. A long minute later, he zipped up again and returned to the cruiser.

Sanele placed the cuffs back on him and helped him in. Mika smirked as he shook his head.

"Sanele you're getting soft. Sefo isn't going to cut him slack in camp."

Jacob saw a brief flash of disdain on Sanele's face as he closed the door.

"I know," he nodded. His eyes met Jacob's; there was a sense of apprehension in them.

Sanele jumped in and they drove on. As they descended the mountain toward another coastal road, Jacob experienced a growing sense of dread. He chewed nervously on his lip. As bad as it had been up until now, were even worse things waiting ahead?

CHAPTER 10

"This is your worst nightmare, my friend. You're in Samoa. . . a pile of rock and sand, in the middle of the Big Empty, five thousand miles from home. . . surrounded by people who make Planet of the Apes look like Sesame Street."

The long grass whipped against the side of the cruiser, forcing Sanele to roll up his window. They had pulled off the main road ten minutes ago and were now bouncing along little more than a dirt path. Finally the dense bush gave way to an open area, beyond which lay the ocean. The dirt path turned parallel to the sea and continued on. Coconut trees lined the shore, edging a wide swath of white-sand beach. In the fading moonlight, it was a beautiful sight. For a moment Jacob lost himself in the picturesque panorama. Then he saw the camp lying just ahead.

Fringed with pandana trees, six large concrete and tin-roof buildings dominated the scenic area. Jacob wasn't sure what was uglier: the drab, cream-coloured buildings themselves or the idea of building a reform school in this otherwise unspoiled paradise.

Sanele parked the cruiser a few yards from the buildings. The men got out of the vehicle and stretched. Sanele let Jacob out. They all walked quietly into the compound. As they approached the corner of the nearest building, there came the sound of dogs growling.

"Hush!" commanded a voice.

The growling stopped. A flashlight turned on, held by someone in the shadows under the building overhang. Sanele held up his hand to shield his eyes.

"Malo Solofa," he hailed quietly.

An old man wearing a sarong and sweatshirt came walking towards them. Three large dogs joined him. The dogs, a mix of mutt and German Shepherd, quickly ran ahead, sniffing the visitors. Their tails wagged madly when they saw Sanele. They surrounded him and he began petting their bouncing heads.

The dogs then cautiously sniffed the other two men, not exactly sure who these familiar smelling humans were. Then as if realizing they were friends, the tails again wagged excitedly.

Finally the dogs trotted over to Jacob, but their ears immediately flattened. One of the dogs growled.

"Rambo!' hissed the old man.

Mika picked up a stone and playfully tossed it at the dogs, which scampered off. The men greeted the man and spoke a language that Jacob thought sounded like they were choking on vowels.

The old man shone his light in Jacob's face. He nodded and said something to the others. He then turned around and headed back into the shadows. Sanele walked over to Jacob.

"That's Solofa, our watchman. Don't be fooled by his age. He's as strong as a bull and has the night sight of a flying fox, as well as the keen ears and noses of his three friends: Rambo, Saddam and Osama."

Jacob got the hint. "I take it that wandering away from the camp at night isn't a good idea."

Sanele smiled and nodded. He led Jacob across a grass and sand courtyard to another building. Mika and Peter followed silently behind. Sanele peaked into a window then turned to Jacob.

"This is the dorm," he said softly. "The first bed nearest the door is yours. There's a sheet and a pillow for tonight. You'll be given the rest of your kit tomorrow morning. I suggest you try and sleep, you'll need it."

Sanele reached around and uncuffed Jacob.

"Oh, and in case you need to use the toilet tonight, there's one at the far end of the dorm. The sink water is from a rain tank, so it's okay to drink. Just don't be wasteful with it."

He opened the door and let Jacob in. In the half-light Jacob could see a row of beds on either side of the long dorm room. He noticed the one that was empty and tip-toed over to it. He heard the sound of many people breathing heavily in their sleep, as well as the occasional snore.

He reached the bed and sat down. It wasn't much of a bed, just a hard wooden frame and a thin foam mattress on top of it. He looked to the door and saw Sanele gently closing it. He heard them talking quietly as they walked away.

Jacob sat on the end of the bed, once again wondering if this was all really happening to him. For the first time since he was a kid, he felt like crying.

"Pssst!"

Jacob spun around. Someone in the bed next to him was waving at him.

"So you're the new guy they told us was coming in," he whispered.

Jacob strained to see a face, "I guess. What the hell is this place?"

The kid got up and edged over onto Jacob's bed.

"This is your worst nightmare, my friend. You're in Samoa . . . a pile of rock and sand, in the middle of the Big Empty, five thousand miles from home . . . surrounded by people who make Planet of the Apes look like Sesame Street."

Jacob wasn't exactly comforted by the kid's reply.

"Where are you from?" asked the kid.

"San Diego, just outside of it actually. How about you?" replied Jacob.

"Salt Lake City, Utah. The City of God," chuckled the kid. He reached down and grabbed a plastic water bottle. He opened it and took a sip. He offered it to Jacob, who took it gratefully.

"Thanks. I haven't had anything to eat or drink for hours." He handed it back, but the kid refused it.

"Finish it. You gotta keep hydrated in this place or you'll be dead on your feet. And you better catch a few zee's while you can. We'll be getting up in a couple of hours."

The kid got up to return to his bed, but then stopped and turned.

"Almost forgot . . . what's your name?"

"Jacob."

The kid held out his hand, Jacob shook it.

"I'm Brigham. I'm named after the great Mormon saint, Brigham Young," he laughed, "But then, what's in a name right? Well, Jacob, welcome to Blue Horizons, or as we like to call it: Black and Blue Horizons."

"Why do you call it that?"

"You'll see."

Brigham lay down on his bed, Jacob did likewise on his. He felt the sweat drip off his forehead onto the musty pillow. He didn't think he'd be able to fall asleep, but it wasn't long before the swirling worries in his head began to blur together. As he drifted off into a hot, uneasy slumber there was a final dreamy wish - that when he woke up again, all this would be gone.

CHAPTER 11

A door opened in the building and out stepped a humongous Samoan man. He was over six feet tall. His arms were bigger than most men's thighs, his legs like tree trunks.

Bong!

Silence.

Bong!

A dull murmur. Bong!

Voices.

Bong!

Someone was shaking Jacob. He opened his eyes groggily.

"Didn't you hear the bell? Time to rock and roll newbie," said Brigham, putting on a light blue t-shirt and a pair of navy blue shorts.

Jacob sat up and looked around. In the half-light of a dawning sun, he could see thirty or forty boys making their beds or getting dressed. Most of them kept looking over at him, curious.

"What time is it? The sun isn't even up yet," grumbled Jacob.

"Don't worry about time here," replied Brigham. "It doesn't matter."

Jacob got up and stretched. He noticed the other boys neatly folding their sheets and tidying their beds. He felt their eyes staring at him, so he busied himself by making his bed too. As he glanced around, he noticed all the boys wore the same blue t-shirts and navy shorts. On their feet they wore blue flip-flops. He looked down at his own shoes, which he just realized he hadn't taken off for over twenty-four hours. His feet must reek, he thought; as did the rest of his body no doubt. He hadn't showered for at least two days.

"Any place I can shower and get a blue t-shirt you guys are wearing?"

Brigham shook his head, "No showers except in the evening and on Sunday morning. And they'll give your fatigues . . . after."

"After what?"

"You'll see," grinned Brigham, "If you need to pee, better go now."

Jacob did need to pee. As he walked toward the back of the dorm, every face turned to watch him. He wished he were invisible. He tried to look cool, as if he didn't even see the others, but his eyes betrayed his nervousness.

He slipped around the corner into the open bathroom. There were four sinks along one wall and four toilet stalls along the other. Two boys were brushing their teeth. They froze when they saw Jacob, toothpaste dripping from their mouths.

Jacob hopped into the closest stall. He sat down on the seat and was about to relieve himself when he felt something crawling on his bum cheek.

"Whoa!" he yelled as he jumped up and brushed the thing off onto the floor. The biggest brown cockroach he'd ever seen skittered back around the toilet base.

His heart pounding, Jacob zipped up and left the stall. The two boys were rinsing their mouths and giggling. Jacob headed for the stall at the far end and went in. He carefully checked the toilet for bugs then went about his business.

When he finished and left the stall, he saw another boy at the sink, combing his hair. He was a tall, lanky brown-haired kid, very tanned and with a bit of stubble for a goatee. He ignored Jacob.

Jacob turned on the hot water knob to wash his hands. Only cold water came out. He tried the other knob; it too had only cold water. He moved to the adjacent sink and tried those knobs . . . cold water again.

"Like there's only cold water in the morning dude," said the goatee kid as he pointed to the ceiling. "Solar heaters."

Jacob nodded, not fully understanding at first. He washed his hands with the cold water and his face too. He wished he could have a shower, even a cold one. He felt sticky and his hair looked like a wire brush.

He walked to his bed. The boys were beginning to file out of the dorm. Brigham was talking to two boys. One had Asian features and the other, olive skinned. As Jacob approached, they stopped talking. Brigham motioned him over.

"Meet your fellow cons. This is Jet Li and Antonio Banderas."

Jacob nodded, not sure how to react to the Hollywood nicknames.

"Nice to have some movie stars in the place," he offered cautiously.

They smiled. The Asian kid struck a karate pose. Brigham rolled his eyes.

"His real name is Corey Li and he couldn't chop a paper towel in two."

He pointed a thumb at the other boy. "Desperado here is Chico Perez."

Chico noticed the last of the boys were exiting the dorm. "Hey man, let's go," he said with a slight Latino accent. "I don't want to be scraping pots for being late again."

The boys marched out, Jacob following their lead. The sun was obviously up, although he couldn't see it yet, as the ocean was reflecting the warm orange of the sky. It was a spectacular vista to start the day.

The boys made for another long building on the other side of the compound. As they entered, Jacob smelled meat and eggs frying and his stomach growled. He was so hungry he could eat his shoes. The boys sat down on benches at long wooden tables. Jacob sat next to Brigham and Li. Chico sat across from them, next to a chubby redheaded kid. At the head of the room was a shorter table with four men sitting on the one side of it. There was a fifth seat, but it was unoccupied. The men were watching the boys. Jacob recognized one of the men as Sanele.

When all the boys were finally seated, Sanele stood and rang a small dinner bell. It went totally silent and everyone stood up. Jacob did likewise, curious as to what ritual was about to be performed.

Sanele opened a small book.

"Heavenly Father, we thank you for granting us breath for another day. May we use it wisely for the good of our brothers and sisters and for your greater glory. We thank you for the food you have provided for us this morning, we ask you to bless it, so that it may give us the strength to do your work. We ask this in Jesus' name."

"Amen," replied everyone, except Jacob.

Sanele and the three men sat down. A boy, wearing an apron over his blue fatigues, brought over a tray and served their plates to them. Seeing the men had been served, the rest of the room began filing toward a long serving counter that divided the mess hall from the kitchen. Other boys stood behind it, dishing out the food.

Jacob followed Brigham over to the counter. The boys had all began talking quietly again. Brigham grabbed two plates and gave one to Jacob.

"Load up; you won't be eating again until lunch."

Jacob was eager to pile up his plate, but as he looked at the food he was quickly disappointed. There was hardly much to choose from. There was a big stack of limp looking pancakes, an open can of cabin biscuits, a couple of bunches of over-ripe mini-bananas and wedges of unripe papaya.

"Where were the eggs and sausage I smelled?" he asked Brigham.

Brigham looked at him as if he was crazy, "That's the staff's chow. Dream on, buddy."

Jacob's spirits sank, but he was so famished he had to eat something. He grabbed a couple of biscuits, they felt rock hard, and spread butter and jam on them. He took two mushy bananas and moved down the counter. An African American boy across the counter was dishing a bowl of something hot from a pot.

"What's that?" inquired Jacob.

"Koko esi. It's not bad. Pretty sweet, but it's got cocoa in it. It's kind of like chocolate porridge."

That sounded much more appetizing to Jacob.

"Give me two big bowls," he said to the boy, who looked surprised.

"Uh, I don't think . . ."

"C'mon Tariq," said Brigham. "Jacob's hungry. Give him two bowls."

Tariq grinned. "Yeah, sure, okay."

He filled two bowls to the brim with the rich, brown porridge. He looked at Brigham and grinned. Jacob wondered what the joke was.

He grabbed a spoon from the counter and walked carefully back to his bench. He sat down and took a bite out of his biscuit. It snapped off in his teeth like a piece of wood. He tossed it back onto the plate. He took his spoon and tried the porridge. It was delicious! A little on the sweet side, but the cocoa had blended nicely with some kind of tapioca and fruit. He quickly finished the bowl and started on the second one.

"Found something you like, did ya?" asked the grinning red-headed kid sitting across from Brigham. "That's a food you can really run with."

Brigham gave the kid a kick under the table.

"Don't mind Torch," he said to Jacob. "He's psycho."

The kid frowned. "Screw you Brigham. I'm not psycho. I have issues."

Brigham nodded. "Whatever." He turned to Jacob. "Just don't lend him any matches. There's a reason we call him Torch."

Torch pointed his fork at Brigham angrily. "I haven't torched anything since my second month here, and you know it."

Brigham held up a hand, "Okay, okay, take it easy. It's still a cool nickname, or would you prefer the one B.S. gave you?"

Torch shook his head emphatically. Brigham leaned closer to Jacob.

"Pig-belly, "he whispered.

Jacob was about to laugh, but noticed Brigham wasn't smiling. There was obviously something behind the nickname, something much crueler than the name itself.

"Who's B.S.?" asked Jacob.

The other boys looked at him, a mix of fear and hatred in their eyes.

Bing-bing.

Sanele was ringing his dinner bell. Breakfast was over. The boys gulped down the rest of their food, picked up their plates and filed toward the door. They placed their dishes in plastic tubs as they left. The sun was already heating the air. Jacob felt sweat forming on his underarms. Everyone was marching toward the center of the courtyard. He tapped Brigham on the shoulder.

"You didn't answer my question, who is B.S.?"

"Big Sefo, he's the warden here."

"Was he one of the guys sitting at the staff table?"

"Sefo doesn't eat breakfast, just lunch and supper. He thinks breakfast is for wimps."

The boys began lining up in front of a set of steps leading into a building that was divided into two classrooms. One of the boys stepped forward and grabbed a big seashell sitting on a table. He blew into the shell and it made a loud, resonating sound like a horn.

"What's that?" asked Jacob.

"Shhh," hushed Brigham,"no talk during morning commencement."

Jacob stood silently like the others, who all suddenly seemed to have straightened their posture.

A door opened in the building and out stepped a humongous Samoan man. He was over six feet tall. His arms were bigger than most men's thighs and his legs looked like tree trunks. He wore a short sleeved white shirt and what Jacob assumed was a blue kilt.

The man was slightly bald and had a blunt nose that looked like it had been broken a dozen times. His eyes burned with an inner hellfire. He scanned the boys and grinned, the meanest grin Jacob had ever seen.

He knew this man-monster could be only one person . . . Big Sefo.

CHAPTER 12

"Your parents are expecting a lot from both of us. It's our job to help you change your attitude; turn you from undisciplined punk into an honest young man . . ."

All eyes were focused straight ahead. None of the boys dared look right at Big Sefo. Only Jacob, fascinated by the raw toughness of the huge man, stared directly at him. Big Sefo held up a small clipboard in his thick hands.

"Good morning maggots! I hope you ladies slept well last night." From the tone of his voice it was clear he hoped they all had insomnia.

"I have two announcements for you this morning. The first is to tell you that because of the lack of rain, your water is being rationed. The toilets are not to be flushed unless there is crap in them and your evening showers will be cut from seven minutes to five."

The boys grumbled to themselves.

Big Sefo frowned, "Is there a problem with that?" Silence. "Good! Secondly, I want to introduce our newest arrival. Jacob Michaels, why don't you step up here."

Jacob's heart was pounding so hard he feared he might pass out. He took a deep breath and walked to the steps. Big Sefo beckoned him to come up further.

"C'mon, don't be shy. I want everyone to see you."

Jacob stepped up to the step below Sefo's. The man looked even bigger at close range. Sefo took a step to the side so he could read Jacob's vulgar t-shirt.

"So you want to be left alone? I see you have an attitude. Well, it might help you to know that SO . . . DO . . . I!" The words spit from his lips, like venom. He took a hold of Jacob's shirt.

"We have a few simple rules here. Rule #1: every maggot wears his uniform unless told otherwise. Civvies from your old life have no place here."

In one powerful yank, he ripped the shirt right off Jacob's body. Jacob almost lost his footing and fell, but recovered and stood perfectly still.

"Take off your shoes and socks!" commanded Sefo.

Jacob did so. Sefo grabbed the shoes and socks and threw them aside.

"From now on you wear sandals or go barefoot."

Jacob wondered if he would ever see his Reeboks again.

"Drop your shorts!"

Jacob looked at him thinking he was kidding. It was no joke. He unbuckled his shorts and let them drop. He was standing in his underwear in front of all the camp. It was completely humiliating. Sefo smiled.

"The rest of the rules are simple," he continued. "Rule #2: Do what you're told, as soon as you're told to do it. Rule #3: If you are caught with any contraband . . . liquor, drugs, tobacco, pornography, or prohibited food items . . . you will be severely reprimanded. Rule #4: You will show total respect to your teachers and supervisors at all times, or you will be severely reprimanded. Rule #5: If you are caught using foul language, you will be severely reprimanded. Rule #6: Anyone caught fighting or threatening violence will be severely reprimanded."

He stepped onto the same step as Jacob and eyeballed him.

"And the most important rule of all: Don't you ever think you can get something by me, because I will make you pay, maggot!"

Sweat rolled down Jacob's temples, and it wasn't because of the heat. Big Sefo was the scariest human being he had ever met. The big man saw the fear in Jacob's face. He grinned and stepped back up.

"But I'm sure we won't have trouble with you, will we, Mr.Michaels?"

Jacob cleared his tight throat, "No, sir!"

"Good. Your parents are expecting a lot from both of us. It's our job to help you change your attitude; turn you from undisciplined punk into an honest young man. All you have to do is get with the program. If you do, you'll make my job easy. And believe me, that will make things a whole lot easier for you."

He pointed at his watch, "Well, stop staring and get ready for class!"

The boys dashed back to the dorm. Sefo looked at Jacob.

"Give your clothes to Mr. Sanele. He'll give you a uniform."

Jacob began gathering his stuff. Big Sefo wrinkled his nose.

"Hurry up! You stink worse than a dead pig."

Jacob picked up his shoes and rushed toward the dorm, still in his underwear. His emotions were raging within him. He was afraid, yet mad at himself for being afraid. He had never been so intimidated by anyone. He was embarrassed at the way he had been ridiculed in front of the others. He hadn't done anything to deserve this kind of treatment.

But if there was an emotion that cut through the others it was a burning hate for Big Sefo.

CHAPTER 13

"Exactly where are we?" he inquired. Sanele pointed to a map of the Pacific Ocean on the wall. "Do you see the United States coast on the map?" Jacob located it and nodded. "Now look south and west for a red circle."

"Two pairs of shorts, one pair of swim trunks, three t-shirts, one dress shirt for Sundays, three pairs of underwear, a lavalava, and your sandals."

Sanele handed the pile of clothing, wrapped up in the lavalava, to Jacob who was still undressed. They stood in a small storage room, the walls lined with shelves of boxes and bags.

"You can pick up a fresh towel and soap at the laundry room. There's a wash day every second day. You'll be taking a turn of duty there once every two weeks. You also do kitchen duty once a week. These are in addition to your daily clean up duties after classes. I'll show you where the showers are, you can get dressed there."

Sanele locked the door and led Jacob to a concrete block building. Inside, it was almost bare; except for a counter, one toilet stall and several showerheads along both walls. Jacob put his bundle on the counter and opened it. He pulled out a t-shirt and shorts and hastily put them on.

"Shower time is six o'clock. Lotu, or prayer time, is 6:20 sharp in the mess hall, followed by dinner."

They walked out the courtyard again and over to a smaller building with offices. They were the only buildings with air conditioners.

"This is the staff building, computer lab and counseling rooms," Sanele noted as he ushered Jacob into his office. There was a computer on a small desk and stacks of file folders sat in trays. Sanele motioned for Jacob to sit down on a chair next to the desk. He opened a drawer, pulled out a small plastic bag and gave it to Jacob.

"There's your toothbrush, paste and shampoo. If at any time you feel ill, you can speak to Mr. Tuala or me. We are the only people with keys to our small dispensary. If it's worse than that, we'll take you to a clinic in the village or to the hospital in town."

He took thin brown notebooks from atop a short file cabinet and passed them to Jacob.

"Here are your notebooks for your classes. This term it's History, Economics and Calculus, as well as the weekly Personality Adjustment sessions and Samoan culture. You're fortunate that we're only a week into the new term, so you should be able to catch up quickly."

Jacob looked at the books. "Are you a teacher?" he asked.

Sanele smiled. "Just for Economics. My full time role is that of Bursar. I look after the money."

"And how much money did my parents pay to put me here?"

Sanele looked uncomfortable with the question.

"It was a significant amount. Obviously you mean a lot to them."

Jacob rolled his eyes, "Yeah, sure."

"Jacob, don't think it was easy for them to have you abducted and flown halfway around the world to Samoa. It's very hard for them. That's why we do not allow any direct contact with them for two months. Too often parents change their minds the first week after an intervention. It also gives you a chance to better accept your current situation and make the most of it. But we do give parents weekly reports and in a few weeks you will be able to speak with them on the phone or via email."

Jacob sighed. So there was no way out.

"Exactly where are we?" he inquired. "Where is Samoa?"

Sanele pointed to a map of the Pacific Ocean on the wall.

"Do you see the United States coast on the map?"

Jacob located it and nodded.

"Now look south and west for a red circle."

Jacob strained his eyes, he could see Hawaii marked. He scanned south from there. He spotted New Zealand, but knew that they couldn't be that far south. He looked back to the northeast. He saw the circle, inside it was a small dot marked Samoa.

"How big is this island?" he asked.

"Not very. There's actually more than one island in our group. But you'll learn all about Samoa and our culture in your Samoan classes. I think right now you best go ahead to History class."

Jacob stood to leave. Sanele held up his hand.

"Jacob, this can be a time of change for you, positive or negative. It's up to you. The first few weeks are the toughest and will take some adjusting. An old New Zealand missionary told me his secret to success whenever he got dropped into a strange new culture: 'Keep your mouth shut and your bowels open.' I think it's good advice."

Jacob considered the odd suggestion as he exited the office. He took his clothing and sundries to his bed, grabbed one of the notebooks and rushed over to the classrooms. On one side several students appeared to be reading and doing homework. On the other side a teacher was talking about World War II. He guessed this must be the History class he was supposed to attend.

He slipped quietly in through the rear doorway and found an empty desk. Some of the boys looked at him, but then turned back to the blackboard where the teacher was writing notes. He recognized the teacher as one of the men from the breakfast staff table.

Jacob looked to the right and saw Brigham, who gave him a quick thumbs-up. Jacob nodded back. He opened his book and started copying the notes from the board. It was a relief to be able to rest and gather his thoughts without someone shoving a new rule down his throat. Maybe if he could just play it cool, fly under everyone's radar . . . especially Big Sefo's . . . he might just get through those two months and then he'd convince his folks to get him out of here. There might just be a light at the end of this tunnel after all.

Suddenly he heard a gurgle in his stomach. It was followed by a movement of liquid through his gut. He rubbed his stomach and tried to concentrate on the notes. But the gurgling continued and this time they were accompanied by sharp cramps. He clutched his side. The cramps stopped. He breathed a sigh of relief.

More gurgling. A massive cramp wrenched his guts. He had to bend over it was so painful. He felt a growing pressure in his bowels. Whatever was ripping through his stomach was now trying to rush out his rear end. He pinched his butt cheeks tight. Maybe it would pass.

Gurgling. Cramps. Jacob thought he was about to void his bowels on his seat. He couldn't hold it much longer. He rushed from the classroom, across the courtyard toward the shower block. Out of the corner of his eye he saw someone watching him from the staff building. Jacob didn't care; this was an emergency.

He leapt into the shower block and into the toilet stall. He barely got his shorts down before the contents of his bowels exploded into the toilet. He winced with cramps as wave after wave hit the bowl. When it finally stopped, he felt completely drained - but very relieved.

He cleaned up, flushed and left the stall. He went over and turned on a showerhead to wash his hands. He gave them a good rinsing, turned the water off and turned to go back to class. He froze . . . Big Sefo was standing in the doorway.

"What do you think you're doing, maggot?"

Jacob shrugged, "Uh, nothing. I just had to go to the bathroom."

"I know that! You think I can't smell the mess you left in there? Who gave you permission to use this toilet or use the shower water? Didn't you hear what I said at commencement?"

"Yes sir," began Jacob, "But I had cramps and . . ."

"I don't care what your problem is, maggot. You don't leave a classroom without permission, you don't use this block unless it is shower time and you don't run across the compound like it's a rugby pitch."

Jacob bit his lip with frustration. He hadn't done anything wrong!

Sefo kicked open the door on the toilet stall and looked in. He shook his head angrily. "Disgusting! You have no respect for the other people using these facilities. A pig wouldn't leave a mess this bad."

Jacob couldn't take it anymore. Was this ogre that stupid?

"Would you prefer if I had shit all over my desk? I think that would've been worse than a dirty toilet bowl, don't you!"

Big Sefo's face twisted with fury. Jacob instantly regretted what he said. Sefo marched over to him, grabbed him by the neck and hauled him outside. He led him over to the front of the classrooms. The boys in both rooms buzzed anxiously, tempted to rush to the windows but thinking better of it.

Sefo stopped and jerked Jacob forward, "Here's a little revision for you maggots. Michaels decided he didn't need to ask permission to leave his desk. He also feels our rules about respect and foul language don't apply to him. Perhaps you can tell him what the punishment is for these offenses?"

"The Cooler," murmured the boys.

"I can't hear you!"

"THE COOLER," they all shouted with one voice.

"That's right. Now get back to work," he growled yanking Jacob away.

Sefo took Jacob behind the kitchen and over to a small box made from roofing iron that sat under a tree. There was just one square hole on the side, covered with chicken wire and a screen. It looked like a doghouse or a maybe a pigpen. Sefo opened the hinged door on the front.

"Get in."

Jacob hesitated. The inside of the box was filthy and smelled of urine. There was no floor, just the rough ground. Sefo gave him an open-handed smack on the back of the head.

"I said get in!"

Jacob kneeled down and crawled into the box. The smell was even more pungent inside. He gagged. Sefo closed the door. Jacob heard a lock being placed on the latch and clicking shut. Sefo leaned down and looked through the hole.

"Twenty fours, maggot. It'll be more if I hear so much as a peep out of you. But feel free to pee or a have a crap, you have my permission." The big man laughed as he walked away.

Jacob shifted his position to get more comfortable. He tried sitting up, but the top of the box was so hot he quickly lay down on his side against the cooler ground. He couldn't believe this was actually happening. Wasn't this against the law? Child abuse?

As he wiped the sweat from his brow he thought back to the advice Sanele had given him. Jacob had certainly kept his bowels open, but he should have kept his big mouth shut!

CHAPTER 14

Jacob thought about it. Brigham had to be exaggerating his chances of getting away. How was he going to get back to the States . . . swim?

A jug full of ice cold Pepsi was all Jacob could think about. His tongue was a dry piece of cardboard that kept sticking to the roof of his mouth. It was at least eight hours since he'd been put into this oven. He prayed for a torrential rain, but the sky remained clear and blue. He rolled over, trying to find any spot on the ground that might be cooler.

Footsteps! Someone was outside. A face peered through the hole.

"Jacob, it's me Brigham. There's a half inch space between the roof and the walls, put your hand near the back left corner."

Jacob sat up and slid his hand along the wood toward the corner. The heat radiating from the metal roofing was intense. He touched something and thought at first he had burned himself, but quickly realized the object wasn't hot - it was very cold. He pinched the end of it and pulled it in. It was a foot long ice-freezie. He gripped the frozen treat with both hands, letting the ice cool his hands. Then he pressed it against his feverish forehead.

He bit the plastic off the end and sucked on the refreshing flavored ice. Sweet, cold juice flowed into his parched mouth and soothed it. He let pieces of slush slide down his throat. This must be how heaven tastes, he thought.

"Easy buddy, don't down it all at once . . . you'll get cramps," warned Brigham from outside.

Jacob looked at the freezie; he'd already gulped half of it down. He'd wait a minute or two before finishing it. He looked through the hole.

"Where'd you get the freezie?"

"We usually get one each on Fridays, after we cut the grass around the camp. I saved mine for you."

Jacob was touched by Brigham's generosity, "Thanks, you might have just saved my life."

"Well, it's kind of my fault you're in here. If I hadn't let you eat all that koko esi, you wouldn't have had to cut class like that."

"What is that stuff? I thought my guts were dropping out my ass."

Brigham chuckled. "It's made with papaya, which is a natural laxative. Normally it's safe to eat half a bowl."

Jacob punched the wire meshing. "You let me eat two full bowls!"

"Sshhh," warned Brigham, "if B.S. catches me here there'll be two of us in this box."

"Sorry," whispered Jacob. "But that was a dirty trick."

"I know, but we catch a lot of the new guys with that one. I didn't figure on you getting into it with Sefo. What did you say to him to set him off so bad?"

Jacob recounted to Brigham exactly what happened in the shower block. Brigham shook his head and smiled.

"Dude, you sure know how to make an impression. I knew when I first saw you, you had radical attitude . . . unlike most of the wimps around here."

Brigham moved a little closer to the screen and lowered his voice.

"Listen, I've been working on a way to get of this hell hole. How'd you like in on it?"

Jacob was surprised by the offer. "You mean escape from the camp? But where would you go, we're on a friggin island!"

Brigham tapped his head, "I got it all worked out. I just need some help putting the pieces together. Are you interested?"

"What's your big plan?"

"Rather not say until I know you're in or not. I can't take any chances."

Jacob thought about it. Brigham had to be exaggerating his chances of getting away. How was he going to get back to the States . . . swim? Jacob thought about his own plan: he'd wait it out for two months and then talk his parents into bringing him home. If he did try and escape now and got caught, it could blow his chances later on. He was better off on his own, staying out of Brigham's scheme.

"No thanks, man. I'm working on an angle of my own."

"Whatever," replied Brigham, sounding annoyed. "But do yourself a favor; when you get out of here tomorrow morning, sign up on the recreational board for the paddling outing."

Jacob didn't quite follow him, "What recreational board?"

"It's outside Sanele's office. Every Saturday we can sign up for sports and stuff in town. Most of the guys sign up for basketball, soccer or volleyball. But there's a bunch of us doing outrigger canoeing."

"So why should I sign up for that?"

"If you do, I'll show you how we can get off this island."

Brigham looked away then back again, "I better get back to the dorm. Relax, the day's almost done. It's not so bad at night. I'll see you tomorrow. And hide the wrapper from the freezie or Sefo will know you had a visitor."

He disappeared from view. Jacob sat back and drank the rest of his melting freezie. He sucked every last drop from it, then put the wrapper in his pocket and lay down. His stomach growled with hunger. Now in addition to a jug of cold Pepsi, he was mentally picturing a full bucket of Kentucky Fried Chicken with a box of crispy fries. He was so hungry he'd eat anything right now. Anything except koko esi. He hated koko esi. Just like he hated this place.

Patience, he reminded himself. Be smart, get back under Sefo's radar and wait it out. In the end he'd get the last laugh.

CHAPTER 15

.... most of the camp was signed up for basketball, volleyball and soccer. He took hold of the pen tied to a string on the board. He signed his name under the outrigger canoeing title.

Jacob heard someone laughing. He propped himself up inside the box. His muscles were stiff and he ached all over. He had somehow managed a few hours sleep during the night. He guessed it must be an hour after sunrise now. He heard the lock on the box being clicked open. The door opened, Jacob squinted as the morning light blazed in.

"Get out!"

There was no mistaking the voice. Jacob crawled out and tried to stand. His back and legs so stiff, he could barely straighten up. Big Sefo glared at him.

"Sole! You sure stink boy. You're a filthy mess."

Jacob kept his gaze on the ground.

"So, Michaels, what do you think of our Cooler? It's a nice place to sit and think, isn't it?"

Jacob had to fight the urge to tell Sefo where he could stick his damn cooler. But he bit his tongue.

"And this was just a brief introduction. Now that you have a clearer understanding of how we do things here, I won't be so lenient next time."

Sefo leaned down to close the door. He stopped, spotting something inside. He reached in and picked up a small piece of plastic. Jacob's heart missed a beat. It was from the top of the freezie!

Sefo looked at the tiny shred, looked again inside, then shrugged. He closed the door. Jacob's heart beat regularly again.

"All right, maggot," he growled, "the rest of us have been smelling your stench long enough. Hit the showers . . . I'll even give you ten minutes to wash up. It'll take that long to scrub the crap out of your rear end. So get moving!"

Jacob dashed for the dorm. He rushed in, went right to his bed. Some of the other boys were hanging out, enjoying their Saturday free time. Brigham looked at Jacob and winced.

"I hope you feel better than you look."

"And smell," added Torch, lying on his bed reading a book.

Jacob grabbed his towel, soap and fresh clothes. "Gotta run, Sefo gave me ten minutes to shower."

He raced out again then stopped. No running in the courtyard, he remembered. He marched calmly to the shower block. He didn't bother to take off his clothes as he slipped under a showerhead and turned it on. The cool water cascaded over him. He stood, mouth open, letting the water flow over his face. He swallowed gulp after gulp of the sweet rainwater. He stripped off his clothes and lathered his soap up. It had a strong pure smell. He rubbed the suds all over his body and scrubbed the grit from his skin. He felt his greasy hair.

"Damn, I forgot my shampoo."

He lathered up more soap and put it in his hair. He repeated the process three times. He wondered how much time he had left. He didn't want to get nailed for going overtime. He lathered up one more time and rinsed. He raised his right leg out to let the water wash away the soap from around his crotch. He froze. There was a raw red patch on his skin. When he inspected more closely he discovered his whole groin area was covered in a red rash. He held back a sense of panic. He turned off the water and grabbed his towel to dry off.

He swabbed his groin dry and looked at the rash. He realized now that it was heat rash. He'd had it before; on those times he'd stayed in his wet surf trunks all day. But he'd never had it this bad. Maybe Sanele would have some anti-fungal cream in the dispensary.

He slipped on his fresh clothes. A clean pair of underwear had never felt so good. He was still hungry and tired, but the shower had lifted his spirits immensely. It was as if he had washed away the past three nightmarish days with the dirt.

As he exited the shower block, Sefo watched him from the staff building. The big man looked at his watch, frowned, but nodded. Jacob could tell he was disappointed that he hadn't overrun his time limit. Now he'd have to go find someone else to pick on for awhile.

Jacob walked back to the dorm. The boys gave him a thumbs-up. The Asian boy, Li, tossed him a banana.

"Here . . . that's for joining the club," he said.

"What club?" replied Jacob.

"The Cooler club. We're all members."

Torch reached over to his bed stand and grabbed a granola bar. He threw it over to Jacob.

"And here's your prize."

"Why? What did I do?"

"You beat the record," laughed Brigham. "You're the only one to ever get tossed in the Cooler on his first day."

Jacob ripped open the wrapper on the granola bar and wolfed it down.

"Who had the previous Cooler record?" he asked through a mouth full of granola.

Torch held up his hand. The others chuckled.

"Torch went in on his second day," Brigham explained. "He set fire to a roll of toilet paper and threw it into the mess hall."

Torch looked away, a pained expression on his face, remembering the incident. Jacob imagined the price he must have paid for that act of defiance.

"He did three days in the box, only a bottle of water a day," Brigham continued. "But you did lose some weight didn't you Torch?"

Torch flipped his book back open, ignoring Brigham's comment. Jacob felt sorry for Torch. The kid was such an easy target for Brigham's verbal jabs. He tried to change the subject.

"Hey, thanks again for the emergency ration yesterday," he said quietly to Brigham.

Brigham winked. "Glad to help. Now, are you going to sign up for paddling this afternoon?"

Jacob shrugged, "Yeah, I guess so. If only to get away from here for awhile. You said the sign up sheet is outside Sanele's office?"

"Yeah, on the bulletin board."

Jacob slipped on his rubber sandals and headed out. "I'm going there now anyway. I need something for my . . . skin."

"Jock rash?" guessed Brigham.

"How did you know?" replied Jacob, surprised.

"We've all got it, buddy. He'll give you the calamine lotion. It won't cure it, but it helps the itching. Don't worry, you'll get used to it. And the boils. And bug bites. And . . ."

"Okay, okay," said Jacob, "I get the idea."

He marched over to the staff building. He found the bulletin board. There were some announcements, duty rosters and sheets for the various sports. Brigham was right; most of the camp was signed up for basketball, volleyball and soccer. He took hold of the pen tied to a string on the board. He signed his name under the outrigger canoeing title.

"Going to try paddling are you?" Sanele, standing in his office doorway, startled Jacob.

"I surf back home, so this seemed the closest activity to that."

Sanele nodded, "You'll like it. I told the boys if they can put together a half-decent team, they might even be able to race in the Teuila Festival races. You know, we Samoans came to these islands two millennia ago in canoes. In fact, Polynesia was settled by canoe-going navigators. They were master sailors."

Jacob nodded, trying to look very interested. He remembered his rash.

"Uh, Mr. Sanele, could I get some calamine lotion, I have . . ."

"Jock rash. I figured you'd need some after three days without a shower – one of which was spent in the Cooler."

He shook his head at the mention of the word "Cooler" and went back into his office. Jacob could tell he didn't approve of the harsh punishment. Sanele opened a large metal cabinet and took out a small plastic bottle, then put it back and removed a larger one, stepped back outside and handed the bottle to Jacob.

"If you're going to do the paddling you'll probably need the big bottle."

Jacob thanked him and headed back toward the dorm. This place wouldn't be half-bad if everyone was like Sanele, he thought. He wondered if all Samoans were like Sanele, or were they more like Sefo. He hoped he wouldn't be on this island long enough to find out.

CHAPTER 16

Jacob looked around the van at the rest of the outrigger sign-ups. On his right was Brigham, leaning against the open window hogging the breeze.

Sweat dripped from Jacob's face. It was almost as hot inside the back of the Blue Horizons van as it was in the Cooler. Sanele sat in the front passenger seat, chatting with another teacher who was driving.

Jacob looked around the van at the rest of the outrigger sign-ups. On his right was Brigham, leaning against the open window hogging the breeze. Doing the same on his left was Tariq. In the seat behind them sat Torch, Li and Chico. Everyone was wearing their swimsuits and sat on a towel, trying to keep the sweat from forming between their skin and the vinyl seat covers.

In the half seat in the very rear was the tall, scruffy kid Jacob had last seen in the washroom when he first arrived. He had to scrunch in his long legs just to fit in the tight spot. His knobby knees were almost in front of his face.

"You all right back there, Shaggy?" asked Brigham to the tall kid.

The kid scratched his goatee beard and nodded. "Like it's fine, man."

Jacob laughed and turned to Brigham."He looks and sounds like . . ."

". . . Shaggy from Scooby Doo? Why do you think we call him that?"

"Okay, stupid question, but is he a pothead or what?"

"No, worse, a skater!" warned Brigham with a grin.

Jacob didn't understand. "Why would his folks send him here if he's just a skateboard freak?"

"Because ole Shaggy and his pals used to sneak onto people's property when they were away and drain their swimming pools. Then they used the empty pool as a skateboard park. It was a cool gig until one of the pool owners came back from vacation early and found twenty kids tearing up the sides of his pool with their boards. Unfortunately for Shaggy, that pool owner was a captain with the LAPD. He was not amused."

"Ouch! Tough break!" said Jacob.

The van descended the cross-island road. Jacob looked out the windows. Samoa looked a lot busier in the daytime. Hotter, but busier. They passed several vividly painted buses, a few taxis and dozens of pick-up trucks. The traffic increased as they pulled into town. They passed several small shops, a cemetery and a hospital.

"So, this is Ap-ya?" asked Jacob.

"Not 'Ap-ya', dufus," corrected Tariq. "It's Ah-pee-ah. As in 'Ah pee ah' lot at night."

The others laughed. Jacob could see the harbor ahead. There was a big container ship at a wharf and several small yachts moored closer to the shoreline. The van pulled onto the road that hugged the harbor.

"This is Beach Road," noted Tariq. "This is where the action is!"

"What action?" wondered Jacob.

"Night clubs, restaurants, Aggies, everything."

"Not that we see any of it," moaned Li. "Other than the odd barbecue and the market."

The van headed toward the wharf area. There was a high concrete seawall and trees on the left, shops and a church on the right. They passed an elegant hotel facade.

"That looks pretty fancy, what is it?" asked Jacob.

"Aggie Greys," replied Brigham, "where all the bigshots stay. They sure have some sweet looking girls working there, let me tell you."

The boys nodded and grinned in agreement.

Jacob raised an eyebrow. "And how do you know that?"

"They come and watch us paddle after they've done their shift. Although I'm not sure if it's because they think we're cute, or if they think we're freaks."

Torch puffed out his chest and flexed a bicep. "I'll tell you why they come and watch. It's to take a look at this sexy white boy."

"Dream on," scoffed Tariq as he ran his hand through his curly hair.

"They're diggin' this beautiful black homeboy."

"Nah, you're both wrong" said Chico. "Torch you is undercooked, and Tariq you is overcooked. They want ole Chico, toasted just right!"

The others laughed and Li gave Chico a high five. Brigham rolled his eyes and leaned toward Jacob.

"See what I have to put up with."

The van pulled in toward the end of the seawall. A group of Samoan youth sat on the seawall, facing the harbor. The boys jumped out of the van and hopped onto the seawall. Two outrigger canoes were racing each other to shore. The canoes cut through the water, as the six paddlers in each vessel dug their paddles into the sea. It was a close race until the end, when the one canoe seemed to kick into another gear and launched into a clear lead. By the time they passed a small red buoy, they had gained over a canoe length on the other canoe.

The paddlers in the winning boat, all young men, raised their paddles in victory. Someone called out something in Samoan and the paddlers let out a victory cheer. The two canoes then eased to the sandy shore as another group of paddlers jumped off the rocks they were sitting on and headed to replace them.

Jacob was immediately struck by the size of the young men. Though not extremely tall, they were massive in the muscle department. They looked like professional bodybuilders. But one paddler stood out above the others. He was the steerer of the winning canoe. He was a little taller than the rest and his body looked like it had been carved from a side of beef. It was pure muscle. He walked out of the water, sweat shining on his body. His eyes were calmly intense.

"Who's the Incredible Hulk?" asked Jacob.

"That's Toa, captain of the Matagi Canoe Club," replied Brigham. "His name means 'warrior'."

Jacob nodded. "I believe it."

CHAPTER 17

He turned and saw the two canoes edging toward the buoy. The one canoe, purple in color, was pouring it on. The other canoe, pure white with green trim, was losing steam.

Jacob and the others scampered over the seawall onto large boulders at the shoreline. Toa noticed the visitors then spotted Sanele waving from the wall.

"Malo cuz!" called Toa.

"Malo foi!" replied Sanele.

Surprised, Jacob turned to Brigham. "They're related?"

"Cousins," nodded Brigham," I swear everyone in Samoa is related. But that's how we got hooked up with the paddling. Sanele and Toa are aiga."

"Ae-inga?" asked Jacob.

"It means family. In Samoa your aiga is your support system. It's kind of like the mafia, without the guns."

Toa walked over to the boys, sizing them up. Jacob noticed black markings on the upper halves of Toa's legs. It looked like a pattern. As the stocky Samoan got closer, Jacob realized the markings were part of one large tattoo. He'd never seen anything like it.

"So our palagis are here for their training," remarked Toa.

Sanele smiled, "Try not to drown them."

Jacob hoped Sanele was just kidding.

"Do you mind keeping an eye on them for a bit?" Sanele asked. "Maselino and I have to pick up some supplies from Farmer Joe's."

Toa nodded. "No worries, but you have to bring some ice pops for my crew. That's my babysitting fee."

"Fair deal," laughed Sanele as he got in the van.

Jacob bristled at the way they were talking about them. Babysitting! He folded his arms, trying to look tough.

Toa eyed Jacob, "You're a new face. When did you get here?"

"Two days ago," answered Jacob curtly.

"Sole, no wonder you still have fat on you. Have you ever paddled?"

Jacob didn't like Toa's tone.

"No, but I surf . . . a lot."

Toa grinned. "Is that so? Well, paddling isn't surfing. It requires muscle. You don't have the waves doing all the work. You're not that big, I hope you can at least pull your own weight in my canoe."

Jacob wasn't going to let this guy laugh at his expense.

"Sure, luckily I don't have to pull as much weight as you."

The other boys held their breath in shock. Was Jacob nuts? Toa frowned, not expecting the comeback. He crossed his arms, his biceps looking like coconuts. Jacob wondered if he might have bitten off more than he could chew. Then Toa smiled.

"Okay surfer man, we'll see how you do on the water. Maybe you're a real superstar."

Toa looked at the seawall. A group of eight girls were approaching. Some walked on top the wall, the others along the road. Jacob noticed one of the girls on the road appeared to be limping. As they got closer he was a bit surprised to see how pretty she was. She had long black hair, twisted into a thick ponytail. She had big brown eyes, full lips and a cute blunt nose, typical of most of the people here. From what Jacob could see of her upper body, she had powerful shoulders.

"You're late!" yelled Toa.

The pretty girl rolled her eyes, "You said to be at the va'a at four."

Toa shook his head, "I told Tala yesterday to tell you three o'clock."

The girl grit her teeth, "She didn't give us the message!"

"That's your problem. You'll just have to wait your turn now."

The girls shook their heads in frustration. As they reached the end of the wall, Jacob cast a glance at the muscular girl, curious to see if her legs were as sexy as the rest of her. She stepped into full view, and Jacob's eyes went wide. The girl had an artificial leg! No wonder she was limping. The girls trudged over to a large tree along the shoreline and sat in the shade, pouting.

Toa turned his attention back to the boys. "You boys are next up, so start stretching. And since there's seven of you, someone has to sit first."

He walked back to the water's edge to watch the race unfolding on the water. The two canoes were charging back in. Jacob touched his toes, limbering up his back. He was actually looking forward to proving a thing or two to Toa. He noticed the others doing their stretching but Brigham was scanning the harbor.

"What are you looking at?"

"See that small boat coming in?" pointed Brigham.

Jacob spotted a small red dinghy coming toward them from the direction of the yachts. Two thin, long-haired blond men sat in it. One of them handled the tiny outboard engine.

"A couple of guys off the yachts," said Jacob unimpressed. "So what?"

"Exactly. They came in last week at this time, for happy hour at Paddles."

"Where's that?"

Brigham pointed to a large sign across the road, obscured by tall trees.

"I still don't see . . ." began Jacob, but was cut off by the paddlers who were suddenly cheering. He turned and saw the two canoes edging toward the buoy. The one canoe, purple in color, was pouring it on. The other canoe, pure white with green trim, was losing steam. As the purple canoe passed the buoy, the spectators let out a whoop. As with the first race, the winning team held their paddles up in victory.

"Good race!" noted Jacob, but Brigham wasn't paying attention. He was watching the dinghy. The blond men were almost at the seawall, angling for a metal peg on the wall used for mooring small boats.

"I'll sit out first," said Brigham with a sly smile.

Jacob didn't have a clue as to what Brigham was up to. He was about to ask, when the canoes slid onto the shore. Toa looked at the boys.

"Okay, palagi boys! Let's go."

The boys headed toward the canoes, except for Brigham who scooted over to the rocks and sat down. He was only about twenty yards from the peg where the blond men were about to arrive.

Jacob and the others were handed the paddles from the paddlers exiting the canoes. The paddles were bent on the ends. Jacob had never seen paddles like this. Toa handed a straight paddle to Tariq.

"You remember how to steer?" he asked.

Tariq nodded, "I think so."

"Do as I showed you," said Toa, "keep your weight on the ama side."

They pushed the canoe into deeper water, about chest level, and then Toa's team started pulling themselves into the white canoe along the left side, that held the long outrigger arms. Tariq and the others hopped up into the purple canoe. Torch had trouble getting into his seat and had to use the arm of the outrigger as leverage to lift himself in. Jacob saw Toa shaking his head.

Jacob decided to show Toa that he wasn't a klutz like Torch. He quickly dove under the canoe and popped up on the right side, which had no outrigger. He grabbed the rim of the canoe and pulled himself up in a swift, smooth motion. For a second he held himself there, letting his tricep muscles flare. It was a second too long.

The weight of the canoe shifted completely onto the right and the outrigger ama began to rise off the water. In a flash the arm and canoe flipped completely over, spilling everyone into the water. The ama came slapping down into the water, splashing Toa and his crew.

The boys' heads popped up in the water. Torch retched up a mouthful of seawater. The girls on the shore were laughing hysterically. Toa and the others quickly hopped out of the white canoe and picked the overturned canoe up into the air. The water drained from it and they flipped it back over and set it down. Toa grabbed a bailer, made from a plastic bottle, from the white canoe and tossed it to Li. He immediately began bailing out the residual water still sloshing in the canoe. Toa glared at Jacob.

"Stupid palagi! Didn't you see the others getting in on the ama side?"

Jacob shrugged. Toa slapped the water.

"If that's how you surf, you must spend a lot of time underwater."

Jacob felt like telling Toa where he could stick his precious outrigger, but bit his tongue. Toa pointed to one of the Samoan boys standing on the beach.

"Kiuga, sau. Come and take this palagi's seat," he waved Jacob away. "Go sit on the rocks surfer boy. Practice your balance there first."

Kiuga rushed out and hopped in the purple canoe with the boys. Toa and his crew jumped into their canoe and paddled out into the harbor. Jacob watched them, angry and humiliated. Finally he waded back to shore, trying to not look at the girls, who were still giggling. He sat down on a boulder and stewed. He glanced to the seawall and saw Brigham talking to the blond men with the dinghy. For a moment he forgot his embarrassment and wondered what was going on.

Why was Brigham so eager to talk with those guys?

"It's happened to all of us," said a voice.

Jacob, startled, turned to find the pretty girl sitting next to him.

"Sorry, what was that?" he stammered.

She smiled, "It's happened to us all, fuli le va'a, you know, capsizing."

"Oh yeah, I didn't realize it was so easy to tip over," replied Jacob.

"You're one of the bad boys, right?" she asked.

"If you mean one of the lucky guys to win an all expense paid trip to the Blue Horizon health spa, then yes I am a bad boy."

She gave him a confused look then laughed. "Pepelo oe!"

"What's that mean?" he asked with a serious face.

"It means you're a good liar."

Jacob smiled. "You don't believe me?"

"I know what goes on at your camp. Your cook is my Mom's cousin."

"Suka the kuka!" remembered Jacob. "Everyone here is related!"

"It seems like it sometimes. What did you do to get sent to our island?"

He hesitated, not sure if he should reveal anything too personal to this girl. But her smile melted his distrust.

"I'll tell you," he began, "if you'll answer a question of mine."

She nodded, "Sure, but you go first."

"I killed a man," he said very gravely. The girl's eyebrows jumped. Jacob lowered his voice as if he didn't want anyone to hear.

"I stuck a balloon up his ass and blew him up."

She punched him hard on the shoulder. "Pepelo!" she laughed.

He rubbed his shoulder, "Okay, for real, I got in a fight with some guys at my school who wanted me to sell drugs for them. I refused and they jumped me. I laid them out and then I got accused of starting the whole thing. My parents didn't trust me so they had me kidnapped and sent here, to get rehabilitated. So I guess I'm not much of a bad boy."

The girl listened intently. She shook her head, "Parents! They always take everyone else's word before their own kids."

They both were silent for a moment. Jacob looked at her.

"It's my turn. I'd like to know how you lost your leg?"

"I fell out of the boat in the harbor and a shark bit it off."

Jacob's eyes nearly popped. He looked at the harbor. He had been standing up to his chest in shark infested water. The girl looked at his shocked face and burst out laughing. Jacob didn't understand what was so funny; then he slapped himself on the forehead.

"You got me, ha ha. Very funny, a shark, yeah right."

She wiped a tear from her face, she had laughed so hard. But then she calmed down and tapped her artificial leg.

"It was an accident. I was riding my bike home after a netball game. A pick-up didn't see me and smashed into me. I got pinned between the pick-up and a light post. The doctors couldn't save my leg, but said I was lucky to be alive."

She stared at her leg. Jacob could sense her inner pain.

"You don't sound like you feel too lucky."

She gave him a half-hearted smile, "Before the accident I was getting ready to go to New Zealand on a netball scholarship program at Grey Lynn. The accident changed that. My netball career was over before it began. The only sport I can do now is outrigger . . . but they don't give scholarships for that."

Jacob listened quietly, trying to imagine how her world must have fallen apart because of someone else's stupidity. It wasn't fair.

"So, are you still studying here?" he asked.

She nodded. "I'm starting a commerce course at National University. I'll probably end up with some boring desk job."

"That's rough. I hope they locked up those who caused the accident."

"Not exactly," she replied as she let out her long hair and re-tied it. "The family of the guy who was driving did an ifoga and my folks dropped the charges."

Jacob wasn't following her. "What do you mean they did an 'ee-fonga'? What's that got to do with anything?"

"An ifoga is our Samoan way of asking for forgiveness. The family of the accused covers themselves in fine mats and sits in front of the victim's house in the hot sun, begging forgiveness. How long they sit there, depends on how bad the crime was. In my case it was only one full day."

Jacob was stunned by the custom. "But what if the victims don't want to forgive the accused?"

She smiled. "Then it's war!"

"So the guy who caused the accident walked away without any penalty."

She shook her head. "No, his family did pay my family a fine, mostly money but other stuff too. And he'll always carry the shame that he brought onto his family. Plus, I'll never forget what he did."

Jacob didn't think the Samoan justice was very just.

"Well, I hope the guy gets hit by a truck himself."

She laughed. "Why don't you tell him that? Here he comes now."

Jacob looked at her, thinking she was pulling another joke. She pointed at the two canoes.

"I'm serious. There he is, steering the white canoe." Pointing at Toa.

CHAPTER 18

Jacob flashed a look at Toa. The big captain was storming towards them. Now what, wondered Jacob. "You here to paddle or chat up the palagis?" Toa growled to Moana.

Jacob tried to figure out why this girl would want to paddle for a team captained by the guy who cost her a leg. He was about to ask her, when Brigham appeared suddenly beside him. He had a grin from ear to ear.

"What are you so pleased about?" asked Jacob.

Brigham looked over at the girl suspiciously, then back to Jacob. "I'll tell you later."

"Whatever," Jacob shrugged. He turned back to the girl. She was removing her artificial leg. She massaged the stump, just below her knee.

"I better get warmed up," she said. "Sometimes it cramps if I don't loosen the leg up."

The two canoes had just pulled in to the shore. Jacob noticed Toa staring intensely at him and the girl. Jacob ignored him and inspected the girl's leg.

"It healed nicely. You still have a very attractive leg."

She looked at him, surprised by the compliment. Jacob thought she might even be blushing under that brown skin.

"Thanks. No one's ever said that before."

He held out his hand. "By the way, my name is Jacob."

She shook his hand. "I'm Moana."

She continued massaging her leg. Jacob flashed a look at Toa. The big captain was storming towards them. Now what, wondered Jacob.

"You here to paddle or chat up the palagis?" Toa growled to Moana.

She barely gave him a glance. "What's it to you?"

He pointed an angry finger at her, "If you're here to train, then train! This is a racing club, not a social club! I don't want you talking with these dumb palagis."

Jacob's anger flared. He stood up. "She can talk to whoever she wants to, it's a free country."

Toa's eyes narrowed as he faced Jacob.

Brigham grabbed on Jacob's t-shirt and tugged.

"Uhh, Jacob buddy. Maybe you should just sit down."

Jacob pulled away. Moana watched, fascinated. Toa took another step toward Jacob.

"Listen white boy, this isn't America. You better watch your step."

Jacob's adrenaline was pumping like crazy. He knew he should back off, but he wasn't going to let this guy intimidate him.

"Hey, have you got a problem with the colour of my skin or what?"

Toa sneered, "Yeah, you look like an uncooked piece of fasi moa."

The other Samoan boys laughed. Jacob's crew watched nervously from their canoe. Jacob didn't know what a "fasi moa" was, nor did he care. He knew he'd been insulted and he didn't like it.

"I may be white, but at least I'm not yellow," he shot back. Part of Jacob hoped Toa wouldn't understand the insult, but he had. He took another step towards Jacob, this time he wasn't going to stop. Jacob spread his legs into a martial arts stance. No turning back now, he thought.

But before Toa could make a move at Jacob, Moana jumped in between them. She glared at Toa.

"Leave him alone. You've done nothing but pick on him. And if you don't want me sitting around talking to palagis then give me a canoe to train in."

Everyone held their breath, waiting to see Toa's reaction. He clenched his fists tightly. His eyes burned with fury, but something held him back. He stepped backwards and looked at Jacob.

"You're lucky she stopped me."

Jacob scoffed at him, "So are you."

Toa laughed. No one had ever taunted him like this, not sober anyway.

"You have no idea who you're messing with, boy."

Jacob was sick of listening threats. He flipped his middle finger at him.

"Bite me!"

"Jacob!" yelled a voice from the seawall.

Everyone looked around. Sanele stood there with a bag of ice freezies. He hopped onto the boulders then to the sandy shore and stormed toward Jacob.

"What's going on here? We give you the privilege of coming to town to paddle and you're making trouble already?"

"But I didn't . . . "

"Get in the van," he turned to the other boys in the canoe. "All of you! Mr. Michaels has decided to cut your afternoon short."

The boys moaned with disappointment but trudged toward the van. Jacob looked at Toa, who flashed him a gloating smirk. He looked to Moana, but she turned away. Sanele gave him a push on the shoulder.

"I said get in the van."

Jacob pushed Sanele's arm away and headed for the van.

"I heard you the first time," he shouted. As he climbed up the boulders to the top of the seawall, he could hear Sanele apologizing to Toa for the rude American's behavior. Jacob spat onto the ground. He felt like spitting on the whole damn island. He caught up to the others as they reached the van.

"Way to go, Einstein," said Tariq.

"You spoiled it for all of us," added Li.

"Yeah, like what's your problem dude," asked Shaggy.

Jacob didn't answer. What was the use? No one ever took his side anyway. He looked at Brigham.

"You were there; you know I didn't start it. It was that lunkhead Toa."

Brigham shrugged, "I guess, but it doesn't matter what I think. When we get back to camp, the only thing that matters is what Big Sefo thinks."

Jacob considered the remark; the bottom of his stomach felt like it dropped out.

CHAPTER 19

"Sure, they said the weather is looking good this month. By the time the sun came up, we'd be half way to Tonga. I'm telling you it's foolproof!"

Bang! Jacob bumped his head on the aluminum roofing iron inside the Cooler. The door slammed shut and the lock clicked shut.

"But it wasn't my fault. He started it!" yelled Jacob.

Big Sefo looked in through the screened hole.

"Shut your mouth or I'll make you sleep two nights in there!"

Jacob wanted to scream but instead bit his tongue and slammed his fist into the ground.

Sefo laughed.

"Don't like the Cooler do you, maggot? Maybe next time you'll show some respect for your elders."

Sefo smiled sadistically at Jacob then walked away.

Jacob lay on the ground, fighting the urge to cry. He hated this place! He wished Torch had burned it to the ground. He looked out the small hole. It was getting darker out and he could feel a definite breeze picking up. At least he wouldn't roast this time. But he hadn't eaten since breakfast and his stomach was grumbling. He needed a drink too. He closed his eyes and tried to imagine he was laying in his bed back home, his mom cooking up a Saturday morning meal of pancakes, sausages and fresh squeezed orange juice. Then he remembered that it had been a few years since he'd joined his folks for a weekend meal. He was too busy with his surfing nowadays. I guess things change, he thought. But he sure wished he was sitting at that kitchen table now.

"Psst," came a voice from outside. Jacob sat up and looked outside. It was Brigham.

"I was hoping you might show up," smiled Jacob.

"I owe you, man," replied Brigham. "You created a hell of a distraction today, and that let me hook up with my yachtie friends without anyone noticing."

He passed an ice freezie through the corner slit of the Cooler. Jacob took it and ripped it open and sucked on the ice.

"So what exactly is the deal with those guys?" asked Jacob.

"They're from Sweden. They're sailing across the South Pacific to Australia. They're a cool bunch of guys. They smoke a little hash, sail to a new island, smoke a little hash, check out the ladies, smoke a . . . "

"Okay I get the idea," cut in Jacob, "So what, are you trying to score some dope? Count me out."

Brigham laughed, "Would you shut up and listen. I thought you would have figured this out by now."

"Figured what out?"

"Those Swedish meatballs are our ticket out of here."

Jacob pressed closer to the box. "How?"

"I told them about how badly we want to get out of here . . . how Sefo treats us like dirt. They're willing to take us with them to Australia."

Jacob was stunned. A way out! This was incredible.

"But how do we get to town and onto their boat without getting caught?"

Brigham held up a finger. "First we have to make sure our paddling team can race in the Teuila Festival."

Jacob tried to think ahead.

"Okay that gets us into town and to the harbor, but there's no way we'll just walk away without anyone seeing us. Or are you crazy enough to think we can jump onto their yacht during the race."

Brigham rolled his eyes. "Give me some credit, I'm not stupid. Sanele told us that if we raced at Teuila we could camp with the rest of the Matagi Club."

Jacob wasn't following, "Camp? What do you mean?"

"Whenever there is a big race, each Samoan club sets up a camp somewhere. All the members of the club eat, sleep and train together. During Independence Day, Matagi spent two nights camped at a church hall. It's a team bonding thing. Sanele thinks it would be a good way for us to experience Samoan culture. Whatever, it's perfect for us."

Jacob was catching on now. "So on the night we camp in town, we sneak out and swim out to the yacht."

Brigham nodded. "The Swedes will wait and we'll leave immediately."

"Can they sail in the dark?"

"Sure, they said the weather is looking good this month. By the time the sun came up, we'd be half way to Tonga. I'm telling you it's foolproof!"

Jacob pumped his fist. "Brigham, you're a genius!"

"I know. But you have to do your part. We need a team in that race. That means you have to suck it up and quit making waves with Toa."

Jacob sighed. "Yeah, I see your point. Don't worry; from now on I'll kiss his butt, if it means getting off this psycho island."

"Good," replied Brigham as he slipped something through the corner.

Jacob grabbed it. It was in a wrapper. It was a Snickers bar!

"Right on! Thanks man!"

"Don't thank me. Thank Sanele."

"Sanele?"

"Yup, he asked me to give it to you. I think he felt bad about you getting tossed in here. He had to report the incident, only he just wanted you to have to do extra kitchen or laundry duty. But B.S. wasn't going to let you get off so easy."

Jacob opened the wrapper and took a bite of the chocolate bar. It was soooo good. Jacob made a mental note to thank Sanele when he got out of here.

Brigham stood up. "Better go. Looks like we're going to get some rain."

"Good, I'll be able to sleep."

"If it rains too hard it can get a little wet in there," warned Brigham.

"I don't mind. Better wet than sweat."

"True, but there are other . . . discomforts."

"Like what?"

Brigham shook his head, "It's better if you don't know. I'm sure you'll be fine. See you tomorrow."

Jacob continuing chewing on his chocolate bar. He crunched the peanuts, savoring their flavor. The caramel melted deliciously in his mouth. He finished the bar and stuffed the wrapper in his shorts. He drained the ice freezie; it tasted good after the sweet chocolate.

Tump, tump. Heavy raindrops began landing on the Cooler. Within a few minutes the sound of the pouring rain was almost deafening. Jacob felt like he was inside a drum. Water began to drip in through the nails in the roofing iron. Jacob smelled the moist air through the hole. The wind blew a light mist onto his face. It was refreshing. He lay down on the cool ground. The noise of the rain was very soothing. He closed his eyes and imagined he was lying on his surfboard, thundering surf rolling onto the beach.

Maybe it was the rain, or the no longer empty stomach, or maybe it was the thought of Brigham's ingenious escape plan, but whatever it was, Jacob felt very content. As sleep began to overtake him, he wondered why Brigham had warned him about "discomforts". This was as comfortable as he'd been since he got to this hellhole. He was going to have a good night's sleep . . . take that, Big Sefo!

CHAPTER TWENTY

Jacob began to see white spots before his eyes. His breathing was becoming shallow. He touched his swollen neck; the skin was burning. His whole body felt like it was on fire.

Jacob dreamt.

His little aluminum prison was floating in the ocean, tossed and pitched from wave to wave in the middle of a great dark storm. Jacob watched from his window as the Cooler crested a huge wave and surfed down its side. He shifted his weight in the Cooler, angling it just like a surfboard. The thunder boomed outside and lightning flashed across the sky. Jacob's heart pumped with giddy excitement. He believed he could surf all the way back to California. He laughed and screamed out to the sea.

"Nothing can stop me!"

The sky flashed and a bolt of lightening stabbed down from the clouds and struck the Cooler. The electrical spear pierced the aluminum box and zapped Jacob in the neck. He slammed backwards against the wall. He clutched his neck, a searing pain stabbing through it. The pain increased. Jacob screamed.

His screams woke him. He looked around the dark box. It was still night, and there was indeed a storm outside. Thunder and lightning rattled the area. And his pain was also real. His neck throbbed, he touched it expecting to find blood, he was sure he must have cut himself on a nail. There was no blood. The pain was becoming unbearable. He sat up and felt something slither across his stomach. Something had bit him! He kicked and flayed his arms at the ground, trying to kill whatever was in the box with him. He screamed and pounded on the box. The heavy gauge aluminum wasn't even dented.

A streak of burning pain clawed its way around his throat and into his ear. He realized he'd been injected with some kind of venom. The poison was working its way through his blood. A fever began build in his body and he became dizzy. His throat began to tighten, making it hard to swallow and breathe. He screamed again. "Help! Let me out! I'm going to die in here!!"

But the thunder and rain drowned out his cries for help. He kicked with all his might against the door; it didn't budge. The Cooler was obviously built to withstand violence.

Jacob began to see white spots before his eyes. His breathing was becoming shallow. He touched his swollen neck; the skin was burning. His whole body felt like it was on fire. His mouth was dry and chalky. His head began to spin and he dropped onto his side and vomited. As his body began to convulse, he felt a numbness overcoming him. His last thought before he slipped into blackness was one of disbelief. So this is how I die?

CHAPTER 21

"In English you say centipede. The one dat bit you very big. Make you very sick. But eat my soup. I make with big chicken. Chickens eat centipedes, dis soup scare all poison from you."

A bead of sweat dripped down Jacob's temple. He opened his eyes. He was staring at the ceiling of the dormitory. He turned his head toward the window. It was a hot, sunny day outside. No wonder he was sweating. He raised himself up onto his elbows. He felt weak, but otherwise fine. He felt the skin around his neck. It wasn't swollen anymore, and other than a bit of stiffness he felt no pain. The poison hadn't killed him after all.

"Ah, you are feeling good now."

A thin old man was looking at him from the window. Jacob sat up and squinted to see better. The man walked to the door and entered carrying a tray. He put it down on the end of Jacob's bed.

"Mr. Sanele said it okay to give you someding," the man said with a thick Samoan accent. "Soup and fruit, make you strong again."

Jacob looked to the bowl of thick soup and bananas on the tray. His mouth watered. It seemed like a week since he had last eaten.

"Thank you. I'm starving."

He pulled the tray closer, grabbed the spoon and stirred the soup. A hard-boiled egg popped up, as did a chicken's foot. The old man saw the uncertainty in Jacob's face. He laughed.

"You eat. I make dis soup, special recipe. It is best medicine when atualoa bites you."

"Ah-ta-loa? What's that?"

"In English you say centipede. The one dat bit you very big. Make you very sick. But eat my soup. I make with big chicken. Chickens eat centipedes, dis soup scare all poison from you."

Jacob didn't quite follow the logic, but he was so hungry it didn't matter. He began slurping the thick soup. It was very salty, but it wasn't bad. The old man nodded and grinned.

"See, I am good cooking."

Jacob smiled, now he knew who this man was.

"You're Suka the Kuka, aren't you?"

The man chuckled, "Yes, dey gave me dat name when I am cooking before at Aggie's. But I like work here now, dis camp. Nobody complain here."

I'll bet, thought Jacob. Complain about the food and Big Sefo will make you eat stones for a week. As he downed more soup he remembered something.

"I met one of your relatives paddling," said Jacob, "a girl with one leg."

Suka's eyes lit up, "Moana! Yes, she a good girl."

Jacob nodded, "Yes, very friendly. It's too bad about her leg."

Suka made a "tsk,tsk" sound, "Very bad. She was going New Zealand, to taalo netball. But now . . ."

"Suka, why does she paddle with that guy, Toa? If he was the one that caused the accident that took her leg, I mean, doesn't she hate him for it?"

The old man shook his head sadly, "She can never hate Toa. Their families neighbors in Tauese. When dey were in school, dey be best friends.

DAVID GOULET - WWW.KANUCULTURE.COM

Maybe more." He winked at Jacob.

"You mean they were boyfriend and girlfriend?" asked Jacob, surprised.

Suka giggled, "Yes. When dey little dey always play togeder. When dey got bigger, dey still play togeder . . . only different games. But after accident, no more playing."

Jacob couldn't believe it. What could she ever have seen in that hothead in the first place? He shrugged. What did he care? He was going to be off this island soon anyway. He finished his soup, pushing the chicken feet to the side, and started on the fresh bananas.

Suka took the bowl and tray and got up to leave.

"I go now. Make coco-rice for supper. You rest. Now you better, Sefo will make you working."

Suka left and Jacob lay back on his bed. Yes, Sefo would surely have him cleaning toilets soon enough.

Clang, clang.

The bell rang outside. Jacob heard the sound of desks and chairs scraping the floor in the classrooms. Then he heard the voices of the others as they came across the courtyard. Li was first through the door. He looked at Jacob.

"Well, well, look who's back among the living."

The other boys filed in, the paddling gang all gathered around his bed. Brigham inspected Jacob's neck.

"The little bugger nailed you good - must have pumped a full dose of venom into your artery. No one here's ever been bitten so high up."

Jacob raised an eyebrow. "You guys been stung too?" They all laughed.

"Of course," answered Brigham, "you don't do time in the Cooler and not get stung, especially if it rains."

Tariq held up four fingers. "Four times I got stung, twice in the ass."

Shaggy pointed to his back. "I got it twice in the back."

Chico touched behind his knee joint. "I couldn't bend it for three days."

Torch pointed both his index fingers to his crotch. "Two inches away from my testicles!"

They laughed. Brigham nodded, "He couldn't walk straight for a week."

Jacob rubbed his neck. "How long have I been out?"

"Only a day," replied Brigham. "Actually you were lucky, in a way. Normally Sefo just makes us suffer from the bites. But in your case it was too risky. You had a fever of 104 degrees. Sanele gave you some anti-venom. The stuff really does the trick."

Chico scratched his head. "We were going to make you eat three bowls of coco-esi for screwing up our free time in town, but I guess this was worse."

Li shook his head, "You just keep setting records, Jacob. Quickest into the Cooler, now worst centipede bite. What's next?"

Jacob didn't say out loud what he was thinking: he was going to be one of the first to escape Blue Horizons.

CHAPTER 22

The white canoe was heading like a dart for shore. The Samoan boys' paddles slashed in and out of the water in perfect timing, like a machine. They seemed to be almost floating across the flat sea.

The week couldn't go fast enough for Jacob. Thoughts of escaping filled his head as he sat through boring classes and endured various chores around the camp. Big Sefo wasn't happy that Jacob didn't serve his full time in the Cooler. He accused Jacob of faking the fever, even though Sanele insisted the centipede bite had induced it. Just to be sure Jacob suffered his full punishment; Sefo gave him extra work duties. Jacob cleaned every toilet in the camp, scrubbed every pot at least three times, cut the long grass behind the sheds and washed dirty shirts and underwear all week in the laundry room. In his head he counted down the hours until the next paddling session.

When Saturday finally rolled around, Jacob was the first one in his shorts and waiting at the van. Sanele looked him in the eye as they got into the vehicle.

"Jacob, I hope you've learned your lesson. I'm giving you another chance. So is Toa. I trust you won't disappoint us."

Jacob shook his head, putting on his best innocent look. "I just want to paddle, sir."

Sanele nodded, "Good. Then let's forget about last week and have a fresh start."

As Jacob took his seat next to Brigham, they gave each other a conspiratory wink. The other boys also seemed to have forgotten about the previous week. Everyone was in high spirits, except Torch. He had run afoul of Big Sefo during the week, having been caught taking two helpings of coco-rice one night. Sefo had made him eat the rest of the pot. Torch, to his credit, ate it all without throwing up. But it was way too much and he was sick half the night with cramps. Jacob sensed that Torch didn't mind the stomach pain, as much as the tongue-lashing from Sefo. The big man had called Torch 'pig-belly' and 'hog-gut', among other demeaning words.

When the van reached the seawall in Apia, the boys hopped out excitedly. Jacob was glad to be away from camp and closer to bringing their plan to fruition.

They scampered over the rocks onto the shore. Toa and his boys were just putting the canoes in the water. Toa's eyes immediately fell on Jacob. He walked over. Brigham nudged Jacob in the ribs.

"Play it cool, focus on the plan," he whispered.

Toa stood in front of Jacob, his arms at his sides looking conciliatory.

"You look like you lost some fat since last week. Maybe you can pull your weight now," joked Toa.

The Samoan boys laughed. Jacob grit his teeth, shrugged his shoulders and smiled.

"I hope so."

Toa looked at Jacob, suspiciously. He turned and pointed to the canoes.

"You boys will have to sit. My boys are going to do their trials, to see who paddles what race at Teuila. It may take awhile."

"Do we have to do trials too?" asked Jacob.

Toa laughed, "You? Why?"

"We're racing at Teuila too, aren't we? Mr. Sanele said we could," recalled Brigham.

Toa shook his head. "I told him you could race if we could enter three teams per race, but the Race Committee has cut the heats down to two per division. I can't afford to waste a spot with you bunch. You're not fit."

Jacob and Brigham looked at each other. The whole plan was blowing up in their face.

"We're fit!" argued Jacob. "At least give us a chance!"

Toa laughed at him, "You palagi boys couldn't run to the end of the seawall and back without dropping."

"Wanna bet?" challenged Jacob. "You give us a time to beat and we'll do it!"

The other boys looked at Jacob like he was crazy. Even Brigham was skeptical. Toa laughed.

"Okay, big talker, I'll give you 30 minutes, that's how long it took the girls' team. You and your boys run to the end of the wall at Mulinuu and back, and I'll let you tryout on the water. But you all have to do it in 30 minutes. If even one of you doesn't make it, the whole team is out."

Jacob nodded. "You've got it."

Brigham pulled him away. The other boys surrounded him.

"Are you nuts?" asked Chico. "We'll never make it in these sandals."

Shaggy nodded, "Like man, I just dig being on the water. I don't care if I race or not."

"Me either," agreed Torch. "I'm not killing myself just to race."

"Why didn't you ask for more time?" asked Brigham, frustrated.

Jacob hushed them." Listen, are you guys going to wimp out in front of these Samoans."

They looked at the Samoan boys who were chuckling at them. There was no doubt in their minds; these "bad boys" couldn't win the challenge.

Li frowned. "I'd love to wipe that smile off their faces."

Jacob patted him on the back, "That's right. Let's show these dorks what we're made of."

Just then they heard the sound of girls laughing. They turned and saw Moana and her team making their way to the training. Chico rolled his eyes.

"Oh, man, now we're really going to look stupid. Let's just forget it."

Toa saw the look of anxiety in the boys' faces. He called out to the girls.

"Hey, Moana, the palagis are going to try and beat your girls' record to Mulinuu and back. Think they can do it?"

Moana had a perplexed look. "I hope so. They're boys, not girls, right?"

Torch hung his head. "Can we make this any more humiliating?"

Toa, holding a watch, walked over to the boys. A young boy on a bike was passing by on the road. Toa whistled at him and spoke to him in Samoan. He then looked back to Jacob. "Well, c'mon let's get you started. I've got a training to run here."

Jacob pushed his gang to the wall. "Let's do it. C'mon, we can do this."

The boys lined up at the wall. Brigham still had his sports watch on. He set the timer for 30 minutes. Toa raised his hand.

"Just follow the wall to the end. My cousin Fialua is going to follow you, make sure you don't stop too early or take any shortcuts. So, on your mark . . ."

The boys got into position. Toa brought his hand down.

"Go!"

The boys took off, their flip-flopping sandals whacking madly on the cement. Torch tripped over his sandals. The Samoans laughed. Jacob helped him up and they sprinted off. The first hundred yards went fairly quickly, but then their lungs began crying out for air.

As they rounded a big curve, Li, Tariq and Shaggy were well in front, followed by Brigham, Jacob and Chico. Torch was well behind.

"What's our time?" gasped Jacob.

"5 minutes," gulped Brigham, "not a bad . . . start . . . but . . . can we keep . . . up . . . this . . . pace?"

"We have to," replied Chico.

The boys followed the wall as it snaked around a tall building and through a fish market and bus stand. People waiting for buses turned and stared at the seven runners. Many laughed when they saw poor Torch lagging behind, red-faced and sweating profusely. Jacob pulled back and waited for Torch.

"Time?" shouted Jacob ahead to Brigham.

"12 minutes gone!"

Jacob looked at Torch, "C'mon Torch, keep those legs . . . pumping."

The boys passed an open area with some trees. Just ahead the young boy on the bike was waiting at the end of the wall. Li and Tariq reached it and immediately turned and headed back the way they came. Shaggy was right behind. The boys' shirts soaked with sweat, their toes blistered from the sandal straps.

As they reached Brigham and Chico they urged them on. They then headed toward Jacob who was still running with Torch. Jacob waved at them.

"Don't finish . . . without . . . us. Wait for us."

They passed and Jacob turned to Torch, "Move it! Hurry!"

As Shaggy and Brigham passed by on the return leg, Jacob called out. "Time?!"

Brigham looked at his watch, "16 minutes. He won't make it."

They were behind on time. Jacob and Torch had another 20 yards to reach the end and then the whole way back. And they would have to do it faster than on the first leg. It would be impossible, even if Jacob had the legs to do it . . . Torch was fading off fast.

They reached the end. Torch gasped for air. "I can't do it!"

Jacob pushed him ahead, "You damn well will do it!"

Torch kept going but he looked like he was ready to drop. Jacob knew he had to do something. He pulled up beside Torch. "C'mon pig-belly . . . move it!" Torch shot him a surprised look. "Don't . . . call me . . . that."

"Why not?" shot back Jacob. "That's what . . . Sefo calls you . . . right?"

Jacob could see anger building in Torch's face. He also noticed Torch had sped up a little.

"I can't wait to . . . tell Sefo that . . . your fat ass . . . lost this race," continued Jacob.

"Shut up!" shouted Torch. His speed increased as his face became twisted with rage.

Jacob kept antagonizing him. He called him names, told him what Sefo was going to say to him. It was cruel but there was no denying the results. Torch's fury was propelling him on. They came around the big bend and looked down the straight stretch to the finish. The others were nearly there, but had slowed down - waiting for Jacob and Torch. They waved at them to hurry. As Jacob got closer he could hear Brigham yelling.

"40 seconds!"

They'd have to sprint it. Jacob pushed Torch.

"This is . . . your chance to prove . . . Sefo wrong . . . all of them wrong."

Torch and Jacob chugged down the seawall with all the strength they had left. As they reached the others, the whole team sprinted to the finish . . . sandals slapping on the cement. Toa and the others were watching them. Moana and some of the girls were cheering them on.

Jacob and the boys flashed past Toa, just as Brigham's watch started beeping. They had done it! Victory made their burning muscles feel better and took the edge off their screaming lungs. They walked around, bent over and sucking in as much air as they could. Torch's face had changed from red to pale white. He stumbled to the water and sat down in the water. He cupped water and splashed it into his face. Jacob trudged over to him.

"You okay, Torch?"

Torch nodded, but didn't look up.

"I want to throw up and I may not be able to walk tomorrow . . . but I've never felt so good." He looked up and smiled.

Jacob patted him on the back.

"Sorry I had to say all that crap back there, I didn't mean it."

"I know. It's cool. I wouldn't have made it if you hadn't."

Jacob helped him get up. They rejoined the others who had finally gotten their wind back. They gathered together, proud to have won the challenge as a team. Jacob noticed Moana waving at him. She gave him a thumbs-up. He gave her a thumbs-up back. Toa saw the exchange and immediately headed over to Jacob.

"Okay palagis, you proved you can use your legs well enough, but that's not much good in a canoe. Let's see if you can paddle."

Jacob wiped sweat from his face, "You mean we can try-out now?"

"That's right. If you pass this test, you can race at Teuila."

Jacob stretched his arms nonchalantly. "Let me guess, another time limit we have to beat."

Toa smiled. "Not exactly. You see that canoe coming in . . . " he pointed to the harbor. The white canoe was heading like a dart for shore. The Samoan boys' paddles slashed in and out of the water in perfect timing, like a machine. They seemed to be almost floating across the flat sea.

". . . that's my A2 team. All you have to do is beat them right now in a little race, and then you boys can have their spot in the Teuila races."

Jacob's hopes sank like an anchor.

CHAPTER 23

Jacob felt the canoe jump ahead. He didn't know where the boys were getting their energy but they were pouring it on. He checked behind. The white canoe was closer but they were running out of water to make up distance.

"Game over," moaned Torch.

The boys from Blue Horizons looked at each other anxiously. Tariq shook his head. "Running to beat the clock was one thing, but we can't compete against guys who have been paddling for years! There's no way."

Chico nodded in agreement, "He's right, man, besides I haven't got any energy left anyway."

They all nodded at that comment. Jacob sighed, he couldn't argue with them. What chance did they have against seasoned paddlers? But they had to try, or he and Brigham would lose any chance of escaping with the yachties. He looked back at Toa.

"What exactly is the race?"

Toa pointed again to the harbor. "From our red buoy here, out to the big metal buoy at the far end of the wharf, around it and straight back. You boys have the advantage, your arms are fresh, and my boys have already done it three times."

Jacob could tell by Toa's grin that the advantage was hardly enough to even make it close. Still, they had no other option but to try. He tried to smile coolly at Toa. "Let's do it."

Toa laughed at the bravado and called his boys to ready the purple canoe. Jacob rallied his troops.

"Okay guys, I know this is a million to one shot, but we can't win if we don't try. So let's just go for it. We only need six though, so who wants to sit?"

Everyone looked at Torch, figuring his weight would be a disadvantage. But he punched his open hand with his fist, exuding a newly found confidence.

"I'm going for it, give me number three seat. Don't worry I'll pull my weight . . . all of it!"

Nobody questioned his resolve. Brigham coughed.

"I guess I'll sit, I'm not much good at this paddling stuff anyway."

Jacob looked at their faces. "All right, Tariq's the steerer, who wants to be number one seat?"

"I'll go stroker," volunteered Li. "Just follow my count guys."

Jacob grinned with embarrassment, "You know; I've never actually paddled before. What seat should I be in?"

"Number five," answered Shaggy. "It's like easier to follow the rest of us from there."

"Okay," said Jacob. "Let's show 'em what we're made of."

They tapped each other's fists resolutely and made for the canoe. Jacob made very sure he stayed on the ama side this time.

Toa gave some instructions in Samoan to his A2 squad. They all laughed. This was going to be an easy race for them.

Jacob looked around to Moana. She flashed him the thumbs-up again. Jacob held up his finger like a number one. She smiled.

They eased the canoe into the water and hopped in. Jacob felt the smooth wooden paddle in his hands. The rich greenish brown wood was beautiful, apart from several dings and scratches along the blade, which was angled at 45 degrees. He dipped the blade in the water and pulled. He let his muscles flare and gave a good swish with the paddle. He heard laughing. He looked and saw the A2 team snickering.

"What are they laughing at?" wondered Jacob.

Tariq poked him from the behind. "Your paddle is backwards. The bend should aim outward, not in."

Jacob looked at the others sitting ahead of him, they indeed had their paddles the other way. He sheepishly turned his around and took a deep stroke. What a stupid way to paddle, he thought.

The two canoes lined up at the red buoy. The A2 team looked more than ready as they held their paddles up sharply. Their muscles rippled along powerful bodies, their eyes glared at Jacob's team, trying to intimidate them.

"Eyes front, guys," said Jacob, "Zero in on our target."

The large metal buoy seemed like a million miles in the distance. Toa had hopped up onto some boulders that were parallel to the canoes and held up a stick with a t-shirt tied to it.

"Ready!" he yelled across to them.

The boys aimed their paddles forward, three on each side, all eyes now on Toa. The makeshift flag flashed down.

"Go!"

The two canoes surged forward. Jacob concentrated on matching his strokes with those of the others. It wasn't easy, but he wasn't too bad off the mark. That was until Li called out 'hut', and on the next stroke they changed sides. Jacob completely missed the timing and was momentarily out of synch.

"Listen for the change," urged Tariq, who used a straight paddle like a rudder to steer the canoe. Apart from a few over-steers, Tariq kept the canoe heading directly for the buoy.

"Hut!" called Li. The boys switched sides. Jacob almost got it this time, but he was still too slow.

"Malo palagi!" shouted someone.

Jacob looked across on his right to the A2 canoe. The steerer was smiling at him, obviously amused by Jacob's inexperience. But Jacob noticed something else: the A2 team wasn't paddling nearly as hard as his squad. Their strokes were slower, but very even and synchronized. Yet, despite the slower pace, they were staying even with the purple canoe. Jacob realized what was happening.

"They're showing us up!" he spit.

The A2 squad was deliberately going half speed, trying to make them look bad. Jacob was furious. He didn't mind losing, but this kind of humiliation was uncalled for. He yelled a curse to the other canoe. The Samoan boys just laughed.

Suddenly their steerer veered the white canoe toward the purple one. The outrigger on the white canoe edged up inches from the right side of the purple canoe . . . forcing Torch to pull up his paddle or have it broken.

"Hey!" yelled Jacob, "that's not fair!"

The tactic was forcing all of Jacob's team to paddle on the left side only. They simply couldn't switch back to the right because the white outrigger was blocking them. The A2 squad laughed hysterically at their opponent's predicament. They continued the cat and mouse game, backing off then sliding over again and bumping the right side of the purple canoe.

As the metal buoy approached, Jacob was gripping his paddle with total rage. The A2 team thought this was all a big joke! No doubt as soon as the showoffs turned around the buoy, they'd sprint in to shore and really rub their superiority in.

Thump! The white canoe banged into their right side again and Jacob had to switch his paddle back to the left. His arms were burning from fatigue, and even more so his right shoulder, as it was spending so much time crossed over paddling on the left. The buoy was just a few yards ahead. The A2 canoe had backed off slightly but was now angling to cut right in front of the purple canoe, taking the corner first. Jacob looked at the angle and a flash of hope struck him. The A2 steerer had made a mistake. He was cutting the corner sharp, assuming they would easily speed ahead of the purple canoe. Jacob dug in his paddle.

"Now boys! All you've got for the next 10 yards, we've got 'em."

The others didn't quite understand his excitement, but pulled hard as he commanded. The purple canoe shot ahead just enough that the white canoe was cut off from the inner edge of the buoy.

"Turn hard Tariq!" yelled Jacob.

Tariq stabbed his paddle in on the left, swinging the rear end out to the right. The A2 steerer tried to turn his canoe on the same tight angle but it was so close to the purple canoe, there was no room. The white outrigger skidded along the side of the purple canoe and actually rode up onto it. Torch had to lean to his left to avoid getting hit by it. Jacob saw his chance. He jammed the butt end of his paddle onto the white canoe's ama, right where it was joined to the outrigger. He pushed up with all his might.

The white canoe, already unbalanced due to its outrigger being off the water, was helpless. The ama and outrigger shot skyward and the whole canoe flipped completely over. Jacob let out a whoop of excitement.

"They're in the water boys, let's see them catch us now."

As the others realized what had happened they also let out whoops and paddled with a new found zest. Their arms were sore, they could barely breath . . . but now they had a chance!

The A2 paddlers were in shock, but quickly flipped their canoe over and found their paddles. The canoe hadn't gotten completely swamped, so they quickly used the bailers to empty as much water as possible. They jumped back into the canoe and began paddling madly. Even with one paddler forced to bail water, they soon were at top speed and making up distance on the purple canoe. Jacob saw them coming. He had to give them credit; these guys weren't quitters. He turned back to the others.

"They're catching up. Give it all you got. Empty the tank boys!"

The boys upped the pace and kept pulling hard. They were just 20 yards from the red buoy. Jacob looked back, the white canoe was within striking distance.

"They're right behind us! All you've got now, this one's ours!"

Jacob felt the canoe jump ahead. He didn't know where the boys were getting their energy but they were pouring it on. He checked behind. The white canoe was closer but they were running out of water to make up distance. Jacob looked to the front, the buoy was dead ahead. Unless the white canoe had a propeller there was no way they'd win now.

The purple canoe sliced past the red buoy. Five seconds later the white canoe slid past, too late. There was silence on the water and on the shore. The A2 team hung their heads in shame. Toa, Moana and the others watched in stunned disbelief. Brigham was shaking his head, a huge smile on his face.

Jacob and his crew sat doubled over in exhaustion. The canoe drifted toward shore as their heads drooped down, gulping air. Torch threw up into the water. No one laughed.

Jacob finally arched his back and held up his paddle.

"Not bad for a bunch maggots!"

The others turned and looked at him. Torch thumped his paddle on the floor of the canoe. "Maggots . . . maggots . . . maggots."

The others joined in the chant.

"Maggots! Maggots!"

They raised their paddles and cheered. They dropped out of the canoe into the cool water and eased it to shore. Jacob and his crew walked over to Toa.

"Looks like we'll be racing after all," stated Jacob.

Toa scoffed at him, "You'll have to race again. That wasn't a fair race."

Jacob couldn't believe his ears, "Not fair? For who? They were ramming us and then they flipped over. That's their own fault, we won fair and square."

Toa glared at him, "It was luck."

"So what!" shouted a voice.

It was Moana. She limped over to them. "Luck is a part of racing," she continued. "It's a part of life . . . good and bad.

Toa looked away awkwardly, not wanting to be reminded of her bad luck. She pointed at the A2 squad. "They were so fiapoko, they deserved to lose. You said if the palagis won the race, they could race. Do you keep your word or not?"

Toa spun and stared at her, furious at her challenge. She didn't back down. The stare-down lasted a few more seconds; then he finally nodded.

"All right, they race!"

Jacob and his crew smiled.

"Yeah baby!" exclaimed Torch as he gave a high-five to Chico. The A2 team began murmuring angrily.

"But," interjected Toa and everyone went quiet again, "you only race in the 1500 meter race. My A2 are still racing the 500 meters."

Jacob mulled it over. One race was all he and Brigham needed. It might be smart to compromise, keeping Toa and his boys happy would make everything easier in the long run. He looked to his crew.

"Sounds fair. We're not greedy, are we guys?"

The others considered it and nodded in agreement to the compromise.

"We don't want to win all the gold medals," laughed Li.

Toa rolled his eyes. "You better not make us look like fools at Teuila.

You'll train as hard as the rest of my teams."

Jacob looked him straight in the eyes. "This isn't a joke to us either. You'll see."

"Yeah, we'll see," replied Toa, not exactly convinced.

Someone clapped.

Everyone turned toward the seawall. A tall young Samoan man, wearing dress shorts, an aloha shirt and sunglasses, stood clapping. Behind him along the roadside was a bright red jeep.

He smiled and nodded toward Toa. "Malo Toa! I see you got yourself some real professionals there. Are they the American national team?"

"What do you want, Markus?" replied Toa curtly.

Jacob instantly felt the tension between the two young men.

Markus flipped his sunglasses onto his head. "Just checking to see if your people need more tickets for the fundraiser. You know, I got Drew Vaai to DJ it. He's doing it for free, as a personal favor to me. "

Toa nodded, "Yeah, you told us at the meeting."

"About ten times," added Moana under her breath to Toa. He grinned.

"Well, if you need more tickets let me know. My guys have already sold over a hundred, hopefully your club can sell at least half that," noted Markus smugly. He hopped back into his jeep and accelerated away.

"Ufa," muttered Toa as he turned back to the canoes. He barked at his boys to jump in and they paddled off. Jacob looked at Moana. She was watching Toa - an almost sympathetic look on her face.

Jacob glanced to the road. "Who was the sharp dressed dork?"

She frowned. "Markus Williams. He's the captain of the Foelele Club. His dad is a Member of Parliament and his mom owns a travel agency. They bought Markus three new canoes to start his club two years ago. He's a bloody snob, and always trying to put Toa down. All the rich kids join his club, especially the afa-kasi party girls."

"Afa-what girls?" asked a puzzled Jacob.

"Afa-kasi, half caste. People who are part Samoan and part palagi."

"Pa-lang-ee, there's another word I don't understand. Toa calls us that and so does this big goon at camp. What does it mean?"

She smiled. "It means . . . well it's kind of hard to explain. Most people would say it refers just to white people, like you. But it could mean any outsider not from Samoa." "Is it an insult?"

She shook her head. "No, not really. Unless someone says 'You stupid palagi.' Then it is."

"So, if someone said 'You smart palagi', that's a compliment?"

"No," she replied quickly.

"Why not?"

"Because no one would say that, everyone knows there's no such thing as a smart palagi."

He shot her a surprised look, then saw her holding back a smile. She burst out laughing. "Gotcha!"

He grinned, "Okay, you got me."

"See, stupid palagi."

He playfully kicked sand onto her artificial leg. She jumped back. "Hey!"

Jacob admired her smile; it was beautiful. He looked out to the harbor. Toa and his crew were paddling hard towards the far end.

"So," he looked back to her with a mischievous grin. "Who's got the bigger ego . . . Toa or Markus?"

Her eyes widened, taken off guard by the question. She tapped her chin with her finger, deep in thought. "That's a tough question. They both have big heads."

Jacob wasn't going to let her get off that easily. "Then why do you paddle with Toa and not Markus?"

He could tell she wasn't sure if she wanted to reply to that question.

"Well?" he prodded.

She shrugged as she turned and walked back to the girls, "I guess I prefer a big, stubborn head rather than a big, empty head."

Jacob accepted her answer, but he also sensed there was a deeper reason than she was admitting to. Moana may act like she despised Toa, and vice versa, but underneath the gruffness there were still some raw emotions. Could they still be in love?

"Yo, good work partner!"

Jacob jolted from his thoughts by Brigham, was grinning ear to ear.

"I didn't think you guys had a chance. I figured our plan was shot, but you pulled it off, buddy. You guys are going to be the talk of the camp."

Jacob smiled. It did feel great to have beaten the odds. He looked at his team, sitting together on the beach. Torch was recounting the action at the turn and how the A2s had capsized. Tariq, an imaginary paddle in his hands, demonstrated his steering moves. They were no longer just a bunch of tourists playing around in canoes, they were racers!

"I wonder how they would have done in the real races?" mused Brigham.

"What do you mean, they'll . . . " Jacob stopped. He realized that once he and Brigham escaped, the others would be pulled from the Teuila regatta. A stab of guilt shot through him.

Brigham shrugged. "Oh well. They'll always have today."

Jacob looked again at the excitement in his team's faces. Then he turned away, ashamed.

CHAPTER 24

Now Jacob was in a real jam. Agreeing to be captain could hurt the escape plan. On the other hand, eight extra trainings in town would make the next few weeks a lot more bearable.

"I nominate Jacob for team captain," suggested Tariq from the back of the van. "I'll second that," agreed Torch.

The others quickly chimed in their approval. Sanele looked in his rear view mirror, amused to hear Jacob's name being promoted as a team leader.

Jacob held up a hand. "Thanks, guys, but I respectfully decline."

Li, sitting beside Jacob in the middle seat, elbowed him playfully.

"C'mon don't be modest. You deserve to be captain."

Jacob smiled and shook his head. "I'm not captain material, guys. Why don't you pick Tariq, he's the steerer."

Tariq threw his hands up in frustration. "Exactly! I have enough things to worry about just keeping the canoe in a straight line. I don't want to be captain."

"Maybe we don't need a captain," countered Jacob. "There's enough bosses on this island as it is."

Nobody could argue with that observation. Even Sanele grinned his agreement. Shaggy shrugged his lanky shoulders. "Well, like, maybe you can think about it and decide later."

"I guess," conceded Jacob.

The van made its way along the beachside road and pulled into camp. Sanele parked it and the boys started hopping out.

"Okay, boys," said Sanele, "Fifteen minutes to shower."

Torch raised his arm and sniffed his underarm. He wrinkled his nose.

"Sir, I think I may need more time than that."

Everyone laughed, including Sanele.

"I suppose you boys deserve a bit of a reward for your hard work today. Make it twenty minutes."

"Sweet!" exclaimed Torch as they made for the dorm to grab their shower kits. As Jacob passed beside Sanele, the teacher tapped him on the shoulder.

"Jacob, why didn't you accept their offer to be the team captain?"

Jacob was caught off guard by the question. How should he answer? He certainly couldn't confess that being a captain might complicate his escape plan, that being in the background was key to slipping away from the group unnoticed.

"Umm, I guess I just don't like being the center of attention."

Sanele shook his head. "I don't believe that. You've been the center of attention since you got here. I think you turned down the captaincy because you're afraid of the responsibility."

Jacob stood there silently, a little stunned by the remark.

Sanele noticed the awkward pause. "You can't avoid responsibility all your life, Jacob. You're becoming a man. You have the spirit of a chief inside you . . . a leader. I see it, so do the others. It is a gift from God, but when much is given to you, much is expected of you."

Jacob didn't know what to say, he had never been called a leader before.

Sanele began walking ahead. "Give it some thought, but right now you're missing out on your shower time."

Jacob followed him, glad to have something else to think about.

"You know," continued Sanele, "you only have four weeks until Teuila weekend. That gives you three Saturdays to train. Is that going to be enough?"

Jacob had to admit it didn't sound like it was nearly enough time to get their team into respectable competitive form. "It'll have to do, I guess."

Sanele picked up a piece of litter that had blown onto the path. He put it in his pocket.

"I was thinking that I might talk to Mr. Sefo and see if he would allow me to exempt the team from chores on Tuesdays and Thursdays. I could drive you boys to town for some afternoon trainings. It would mean you'd have to make up your chores by doing double on other days, but you'd gain eight more training days. What do you think?"

Jacob was shocked. Sanele must really think they had a chance to win the race, he thought.

"But," added Sanele, "it's on one condition. You must agree to be the team captain."

Now Jacob was in a real jam. Agreeing to be captain could hurt the escape plan. On the other hand, eight extra trainings in town would make the next few weeks a lot more bearable. It might even help him and Brigham to solidify their plans with the yachties. But he needed to discuss it with Brigham first.

"Can I sleep on it?" he asked.

Sanele nodded. "Sure. You can give me your answer tomorrow. But no later, I'll need to make the arrangements."

Jacob began jogging toward the dorm. Sanele called after him, Jacob turned. "I'm going out on a limb for you, Jacob. Don't forget that."

"Yes, I know. Thank you sir." Jacob continued on, the guilt thickening on his conscience.

"Guess what," he began. "Sanele is going to see if he can get permission to take our team to town on Tuesdays and Thursdays for extra paddling practice."

"Ohwww, I can't move."

Torch rolled over in his bed and moaned. The sun was just beginning to rise outside. Brigham got up and stretched.

"C'mon Torch, get up. I'm not preparing umu by myself," he yawned.

"I can't, my legs are so sore I can barely bend them. I'll be lucky to make it to service. Can't you ask someone else?"

Li looked up from his bed. "Torch, it's your turn this Sunday!"

Jacob sat up and stretched. His muscles were stiff and sore, reminding him of yesterday's brutal races. He could only imagine the pain the pudgy Torch must be in.

"I'll go with you," he said to Brigham. It will be a good chance to discuss Sanele's offer, he thought.

"God bless you," sighed Torch. "I owe you one."

Brigham and Jacob slipped on their dirty chore clothes and slipped out. The other boys went back to sleep, savoring every extra minute of shut-eye they got on Sundays.

Jacob arched his back and groaned. It felt like he'd slept on a rock. Brigham led him to a small open shack behind the kitchen. There was a mound of banana leaves, a stack of wood and a pile of black rocks. In the corner were two huge green banana bunches and a basket of husked coconuts.

"So what exactly is this umu thing we're making?" wondered Jacob.

Brigham started arranging the firewood on the stones. "It's an oven. We cook the rocks, then the rocks cook our food. Suka will be here soon to get the palusami ready. Our job is to stoke the fire, scrape the popo and peel the fai."

Jacob shrugged. "I understood half of what you said."

"You'll see. Let's get you started on the bananas."

Brigham dragged one of the banana bunches into the open. He grabbed a small wooden stool from inside the shed and put it beside Jacob. "Sit."

Jacob did so. Brigham brought out a metal bowl and small smooth stick with a rounded point that had been wedged in the shed's beams. He yanked off a banana from the bunch and held it in front of Jacob. He used the edge of the stick to slice the green skin on both sides of the banana. "Don't cut too deeply and try to work the edge of the stick under the skin," he instructed as he separated the skin from the banana. He dropped it into the bowl. He handed the stick to Jacob.

"One down, 99 to go."

"And what are you going to do?" asked Jacob.

Brigham dragged out the basket of coconuts and placed it beside another metal bowl and stool. This stool was different in that there was a protruding metal tongue on one end with a serrated edge. Brigham sat on it and grabbed a coconut. He pulled out a long knife from the basket and struck the coconut with the blunt edge. The coconut cracked. He hit it again and it split cleanly in two, some juice draining out.

Brigham then took one of the halves and placed it over the metal tongue. He set the metal bowl directly underneath. He began scraping the inside of the shell against the tongue. The white coconut meat inside began falling like thick snow into the bowl.

Jacob watched fascinated as Brigham quickly scraped the shell clean and chucked it to the side.

"You look like you've done this a few times," noted Jacob.

"More than I care to remember, that's for sure."

Jacob turned his attention to the bananas. He ripped another one from the bunch and did what Brigham had shown him. The green banana was gummy to the touch, especially once the skin was broken. He found it worked best if he used the stick to create a flap, then slipped his thumb underneath and slid the skin off slowly with it. The first few bananas broke, but he gradually was getting the hang of it. He looked over to Brigham, he'd finished another coconut. Jacob sensed it might be a good time to discuss Sanele's offer.

"Guess what," he began. "Sanele is going to see if he can get permission to take our team to town on Tuesdays and Thursdays for extra paddling practice."

Brigham stopped his scraping, surprised.

"Are you serious? He would really do that?"

"That's what he told me, as long as we make up our chores and Sefo agrees; he'll take us."

"Wow," exclaimed Brigham, "that would be sweet. And it would give us a chance to keep in closer contact with the Swedes."

"That's what I figured. But there's one slight hitch."

"What is it?"

"Sanele will only do this if I agree to be captain."

Brigham immediately frowned. "No way. It's too risky. I told you, we have to blend into the background. If you're captain you'll have to hang around Toa, going over rules and race times; all that stuff. You'll be right in the thick of things, which is exactly what we don't want."

"But with the extra trainings we actually might look like we belong in a race," countered Jacob.

Brigham stared at him, puzzled. "What are you talking about? It doesn't matter how we look on the water, because we won't be there, remember. We'll be gone and the others will get disqualified anyway."

Jacob shifted uneasily on his stool. He yanked another banana off the bunch. He wanted to do the training, if only for the sake of letting the others have a chance to get away from the camp over the next month. He figured they owed the guys that much. But he could tell that Brigham wasn't going to change his mind without a better reason than that. A thought popped into his head.

"You know, if we don't jump at the chance to do the training, it might look suspicious. I mean here we are given a golden chance to really do some serious paddling . . . and we fluff it off."

Brigham considered the observation then cracked another coconut open angrily. "Damn it, you're right. Why did Sanele have to insist on you being captain?"

Jacob shrugged, "I don't know. But it looks like we don't have much choice. I'll just have to try and be a very quiet captain I guess."

"An invisible one! And don't be chatting up that one-legged girl either."

"Moana?" Jacob laughed, "Why? What's wrong with her?"

"Because every time Toa sees you talking to her he puts a bulls-eye on your head. Invisible, remember?"

Jacob wanted to ask Brigham if he thought Toa was jealous, but before he could say anything there came the sound of someone clearing the phlegm from their throat and spitting. Suka came shuffling around the corner of the kitchen holding a stack of small green leaves.

"Ah, malo, boys. We make a good toonai today, eh?"

Sitting down on an old pandana mat, Suka began sorting his leaves as he watched them work, Jacob peeling and Brigham scraping. When Brigham finished all the coconuts, he handed the bowl to Suka along with a clump of wiry looking straw. Suka dipped the clump into the coconut scraping and began squeezing the clump tightly in his powerful, but grimy hands. White milk oozed through his fingers as the cream was expressed from the coconut meat. Suka then shook out the leftover pulp into another bowl. He repeated the action, again and again.

By the time Jacob had finished peeling his last banana, Suka had turned the bowl of scrapings into a bowl of thick rich cream. As Brigham stoked the fire on top of the rocks, Suka curled the leaves up into small bowls and poured the coconut cream into them. Then he tied the top end with a vine and wrapped the little package with more layers of leaves. Jacob watched him curiously.

"Are we going to eat that?" asked Jacob.

Suka chuckled, "Yes, we eat. Very nice palusami."

Jacob didn't like the idea of eating something that had been strained through Suka's filthy hands. He looked at his own sore fingers, covered in brown banana gum. His fingernails were black from being shoved under the sticky skins. He didn't think he wanted to eat anything that he had touched either!

As the fire died down, Brigham used a pair of wooden tongs to grab red-hot stones and place them in a circular fashion on an aluminum sheet. Jacob got closer and could feel the heat coming from the stones. Suka placed a few fresh green banana leaves over the rocks and placed his little packages on top of them. Brigham placed more hot stones around them. Then they took the peeled bananas and placed them onto the leaves. They added more rocks and then covered the lot with several armfuls of banana leaves. Jacob could see puffs of smoke and steam wafting from the bottom.

"And that cooks it?" he asked.

Brigham nodded, "Yup, in a few hours, it'll be ready after service."

He looked at Jacob and grinned. "I forgot that this is your first real

Sunday here. Last week at this time you were in a centipede induced coma."

Suka put a finger to his nostril and blew snot out. Jacob cringed. He suddenly felt very filthy and very tired. His muscles had stiffened again. Brigham must have read his mind.

"Let's grab a quick shower and get ready for service."

"And what exactly do we have to do at service?"

"Nothing. Just sit back and listen to Reverend Alapati read the Bible and give a sermon."

Jacob was relieved. For the first time in years, he was actually looking forward to church.

CHAPTER 26

"Is that so, Mr. Sleepyhead," growled Sefo. "It must be hard to get a good night's sleep in that noisy dorm. I know somewhere more quiet." Jacob knew what was coming. "Cooler!" ordered Sefo.

"And Judas greeted Jesus with a kiss on the cheek."

Reverend Alapati read from a large red Bible at the front of the room. The whole camp had gathered in the larger of the two classrooms. The desks had been placed along the walls and the boys sat tightly packed together on the chairs. Big Sefo and the other staff were seated in the back of the room. Sefo's eyes kept scanning the boys.

Jacob dug pieces of dirt from under his fingernails. The shower hadn't been able to clean all the grime from his hands. He listened to the reverend, but his mind kept wandering. He was imagining how his team would react when they discovered that he and Brigham had escaped. All that training for nothing -- they'd hate him for it.

"And thus Jesus was betrayed by one he had called his friend."

Jacob was startled back to Reverend Alapati's sermon. Jacob wished the good reverend had picked a different topic this week. Wasn't there something in the Bible about prisoners being set free? Why couldn't that be the reading?

He looked at Torch, sitting next to him. His eyelids were drooping. He looked like he was about to nod off to sleep. Jacob gave him a soft nudge with his elbow. It didn't help. Torch's head was dropping. Jacob slid his hand over and pinched Torch hard on the leg.

"Owww!" blurted out Torch groggily. He instantly became aware of his surroundings and froze. Everyone was looking toward Torch and Jacob. Reverend Alapati frowned, then concluded his sermon and invited everyone to stand. He gave the final blessing and exited solemnly.

Before the boys could file out, Big Sefo was looming at the door.

"Who was it? Who made that noise?"

The boys looked anxiously around, but said nothing. Sefo's eyes narrowed angrily. "Nobody leaves this room until I know who made that noise. You can stand here all day. No food, nothing. A whole free day wasted."

One of the boys pointed at Torch, "It was him. I heard him."

Several of the other boys nodded in agreement. Sefo glared at Torch.

"Was it you maggot?"

Torch's lower lip was trembling. Jacob felt terrible for him. Torch's body was already a wreck from the training. If the poor guy got the Cooler, he was going to be in agony.

"Well, pig-belly, answer me!"

Anger flashed through Jacob. Why did this goon have to call Torch that?

He looked at Torch, now as white as a sheet. Jacob stepped forward.

"Sir, I made that noise. I had fallen asleep. Torch pinched me, trying to wake me up. I'm sorry it disrupted the reverend's sermon." Jacob stared straight ahead, almost defiantly.

"Is that so, Mr. Sleepyhead," growled Sefo. "It must be hard to get a good night's sleep in that noisy dorm. I know somewhere more quiet."

Jacob knew what was coming.

"Cooler!" ordered Sefo.

Jacob nodded. He glanced quickly to Torch who had a baffled look on his face. Behind him was Brigham, who rolled his eyes. Jacob marched out the door, following Sefo. The big man sniffed the air and sneered.

"I think we might get some rain tonight. Be lots of atualoa out if it does."

Jacob wasn't sure why he took the rap for Torch, but he was already regretting it.

CHAPTER 27

"I don't appreciate name-calling. Toa deserves your respect."

Sefo made Jacob strip down to his underwear.

"No use getting those dirty, "he barked. He took the clothes from Jacob, shoved him into the Cooler and locked it.

"See you tomorrow morning. Sweet dreams, Sleepyhead."

Jacob sat cross-legged inside the hot box. He felt the cool earth under his legs and prayed it wouldn't rain. His stomach grumbled and his sore muscles ached. He rested his chin in his hands and tried to imagine he was sitting at his desk back home, playing computer games. He focused his mind on his Black Ninja game. He mentally recreated the first level, maneuvering his ninja through a base full of clumsy soldiers. He envisioned the bad guys all having Big Sefo's face. His ninja cut off their heads.

He was working his brain through the third level when there was a light knocking on the box.

"Jacob, you awake?" Brigham hissed through the hole. An ice freezie came sliding through the rear corner. Jacob wiped the sweat from his hands and grabbed it.

"Thanks, what time is it?"

"After two, everyone's having a siesta in the shade on the beach."

Jacob groaned. Oh to be lying on that beach, a soft cool breeze blowing over a full belly.

"Listen," said Brigham seriously. "What the hell were you thinking back there? Torch told us he was the one who yelled out, not you. Why did you cover for him?"

Jacob sighed, "I don't know. I felt sorry for the guy. He's walking around like a cripple today, he would have died in here. Besides, I was the one who pinched him, so it's half my fault anyway."

"So what, that's his tough luck," argued Brigham. "He has to take the fall, not you. You're supposed to be keeping a low profile. If you keep putting yourself in these situations you'll screw the whole plan. Then we'll never get off this rock."

Jacob nodded. "Okay, I already listened to one sermon today. I promise I'll be as quiet as a mouse from now on."

"Good! Now get some rest."

Jacob put his face closer to the hole. "Does it look like rain?"

Brigham laughed. "No, your good deed must have impressed the 'man upstairs.' It's a clear sky now. I'll see you tomorrow. Keep cool."

Jacob chewed on his ice freezie, relieved that rain was no longer a factor. He continued his mental exercise, having his ninja disembowel three samurai warriors who all looked like Big Sefo. He was on the fifth level of his cerebral game when heard someone approaching the Cooler. He still had the empty freezie plastic in his hand. He quickly stuffed it down his underwear.

"Jacob?" It was Sanele's voice.

Jacob looked through the hole. Sanele was holding a small green pouch. He winked and Jacob heard the lock on the door clank. The door opened a few inches. Fresh air flowed in, Jacob took a refreshing breath.

Sanele leaned down and handed him the green pouch made of leaves. It was warm and smelled like it had been charred. Jacob realized it was food from the umu they had made. Sanele smiled.

"I figured it's only fair you should be able to taste your first toonai. You can eat the whole thing, so there's no evidence."

"Thank you, sir. And I never did thank you for the chocolate bar you sent last week."

"You're welcome. I better lock the door in case Sefo comes sniffing."

"Sure, I understand."

The door closed and the lock was clicked shut again. Sanele came around to the hole.

"That was very noble of you to accept Torch's punishment."

"How did you . . . "

"I saw Torch jump a little when you pinched him. You're really acting like a leader, Jacob. Did you decide on my offer."

Jacob nodded, "Yes, we accept the offer."

"We?"

Jacob realized he'd slipped up.

"Uh, the team that it is. We all agreed it would be a good idea."

Sanele smiled, "I thought you would. It took some bargaining but I finally got Sefo to allow it. You boys will have to do triple chore duty on the off days though. And I talked with Toa, he said it was okay as long as you guys are serious about racing. I said you were."

Jacob frowned. "I already told him we're serious. Why does he have to be a hard ass?"

"Now listen, Jacob," retorted Sanele. "I don't appreciate name-calling. Toa deserves your respect. He didn't have to let you boys paddle with his team. But he loves the sport and wants to promote it to anyone who shows a genuine interest in it."

"I'm sorry," replied Jacob. "But he's just so grouchy all the time . . . especially toward Moana. You'd think he'd be extra nice to her considering what he did to her leg."

Sanele sighed. "You don't know what he's been through. He's had a lot of family issues to deal with. He was a different young man before the accident, believe me."

"If you say so," replied Jacob, unconvinced.

"Jacob, there's an old saying: 'don't judge someone until you've walked a day in their shoes.' If anyone can appreciate that it should be you."

Sanele stood up to go. "Give Toa a chance, the same way I'm giving you a chance."

He walked away, leaving Jacob to think about what he said. Why was Sanele being so supportive of a guy who ruined someone else's life through his own carelessness? Jacob just couldn't understand it. But in the end it didn't matter. He and Brigham were getting out of this madhouse soon enough.

He opened the green pouch. The rich smell of cooked greens and coconut wafted up. There were also two cooked bananas, broken in halves, inside. Jacob dipped the bananas in the grayish cream and was about to take a bite when he remembered Suka's dirty hands straining the cream. He held the banana near his mouth, still wide open. His stomach growled and the delicious smell overpowered him. He bit into the banana.

The gooey cream and roasted banana were heaven! He scooped more banana and cream, along with a chunk of the green leaf. It had a spinach taste, but not as bitter. This stuff was great. He savored each bite, letting the smoky flavors melt in his mouth. He popped the last chunk into his mouth and licked his fingers clean.

Samoan food may seem a little rough at first glance, he mused, but once you gave it a chance it wasn't half bad. He wondered if it wasn't the same with the people.

CHAPTER 28

Toa and the A2s dragged their canoe onto shore.
Behind them paddled in Jacob's crew. Brigham
looked like he was ready to faint from the
exertion. Toa immediately noticed Moana sitting
next to Jacob. His eyes blazed as we walked up the
shore toward them.

"C'mon guys, dig those paddles in," urged Jacob from his number five seat in the canoe.

"Hut!" called Li and they all switched sides. Jacob's switch wasn't perfect but it was getting there. This was their second Tuesday session and the extra training had made a big difference for the team. The timing of their paddle strokes was much more in synch and their speed was improving likewise. They certainly weren't looking out of place on the water.

Getting away from the camp on a regular basis had been as sweet as Jacob had imagined. Chico and Shaggy still couldn't believe they were allowed into town on a weekday. It felt weird at first, paddling during the after-work rush in Apia. It was so busy. But at the same time it was exciting to be in town with so much activity buzzing. The privilege wasn't without its sacrifices, most notably getting up an hour earlier every day in order to do their chores or homework.

Jacob was at least keeping Brigham happy. He hadn't seen the inside of the Cooler since Sunday and Big Sefo was leaving the team alone, so far.

"Hut!"

They all switched sides. The canoe was fifty yards from the red buoy.

"Finish hard!" yelled Jacob. The canoe surged ahead. Jacob was impressed; the boys were really listening to him.

The canoe shot past the buoy and they relaxed. They breathed heavily, but not as desperately as two weeks ago. With each practice their fitness level rose. Jacob even had them doing light exercises at the camp: push-ups, jogging in waist-deep water in the lagoon and lots of stretching for Torch so he didn't get all cramped up. When you added all the trainings on top of their regular chores, it provided quite the daily workout schedule. Jacob hadn't been in this good shape in months.

The boys wiped the sweat from their brows and eased into the shore. Toa was looking at his stopwatch.

"Too slow!" he noted. "The Foelele junior girls' team is faster."

The boys hung their heads. Jacob was frustrated. He had tried to be respectful to Toa, as Sanele had suggested, but the guy wouldn't cut them any slack. No matter how hard they tried, it was never good enough.

"Do it again," ordered Toa. Jacob motioned to Brigham who was sitting on the rocks. He trotted over to the canoe. Jacob handed him his paddle.

"You better take a turn," said Jacob softly, "even if you're the spare, you need to train."

Brigham frowned but nodded. "Yeah, better keep up appearances."

The boys turned the canoe around and headed back out into the harbor. Jacob went to sit on the rocks. Toa called to him.

"What's the matter? Not fit enough, Surfer Boy?"

Jacob wanted to tell him off, but he kept his mouth shut and sat down. He watched the A2 team race into shore. Toa checked his watch and shook his head. He barked something at them in Samoan. They hung their heads. The Foelele junior girls must be faster than them too, thought Jacob.

Toa ordered the number one paddler off the canoe and he jumped in. The canoe reversed and Toa demonstrated the proper technique. He called something out and the team got into position.

"Alo," he yelled and the team stabbed their paddles in and took off. With Toa as the lead stroker their pace was much faster.

Jacob heard footsteps. He turned and saw Moana and her girls had arrived. They were all sweating.

"I thought you girls were paddling tomorrow?" asked Jacob.

Moana nodded as she caught her breath."We were at Genesis Fitness doing weights. We just came here for the meeting."

"What meeting?"

Moana raised an eyebrow. "Didn't Toa tell you? He has some announcements about Teuila, so he told us all to meet here after practice."

"No, he didn't mention it. But he doesn't seem to tell us anything."

She sat down next to him. "Well, he should. You're the captain of your team. He's so thick sometimes."

Jacob grinned, "So why did you go around with him?"

She looked at him, surprised, "Who told you that?"

"A little bird," he laughed.

"Suka! Valea ia!"

Jacob laughed again. "So, it is true. You and Toa used to be an item."

She looked away, embarrassed. He stopped laughing.

"I'm sorry," he said. "But you're such a cool person; I can't picture you with Toa. What could you possibly like about him?"

She gave him a slightly annoyed look.

"There was lots to like about him . . . before."

"Before the accident?"

"Yeah. Toa was great fun to be around, always smiling and cracking jokes. We were best mates then. We still probably would be if . . . " She let the sentence trail.

"If the accident hadn't happened," finished Jacob.

"It wasn't just that. It was how he changed. I could have forgiven him. I think I could have forgiven him even if I had been completely paralyzed. But . . . "

Silence. Jacob was on the edge of his seat with curiosity.

"But what?"

She frowned, remembering the painful time.

"He never once said he was sorry."

Jacob was dumbfounded, "Why wouldn't he apologize?"

"I don't know. I saw him after the ifoga, alone. I thought we'd talk about how we felt and we would go on from there. But all he kept saying was that his family was really sorry and he didn't want to talk about it. Well, I was furious. His 'family' was sorry? 'What about you?' I yelled at him. He just looked at me, like I had no right to be angry at him at all. I told him that if he didn't personally apologize for what he did to me, we were through."

Jacob was fascinated by the story. "So what happened?"

"He just turned and walked away. Didn't utter a word."

Jacob couldn't believe it.

"So why do you paddle with his club?"

"I guess it's my way of trying to get on with my life," she sighed. "Plus paddling is one of the only sports I can still do. It was either Matagi or Foelele, and I'll take Toa's moodiness over Markus' ego any day."

Jacob was about to ask her if there wasn't more to it than that, if maybe she still had feelings for Toa. But the A2 team was streaking into shore. Their paddles flashed as they dipped in and out of the water. Jacob watched their smooth strokes and blistering pace. Toa had them cutting through the water like a knife.

He whistled. "He sure can paddle though!"

Moana nodded, also admiring Toa's prowess with the paddle. "He's a natural athlete," she noted. "His whole family is. His brother is in Australia on a rugby scholarship. He got it around the same time I got my netball one. They say he'll play for the Manu Samoa someday."

"The what-Samoa?"

"Manu Samoa. Our national rugby team. Toa might have been a rugby star too, but he chose outrigger instead."

"Do you have a national team for that?"

She laughed. "Not really. We send a team every two years to the World Sprints or South Pacific Games, but it's not the same. For us, winning Teuila is as big as it gets. It means bragging rights for a year. And when your rival is Markus Williams, it's a long year if you lose."

Jacob couldn't figure Toa out. He appeared to be a big-headed loser, who paddled because it was all he was good at. But everyone else was telling him that Toa was a super athlete and great guy.

Toa and the A2s dragged their canoe onto shore. Behind them paddled in Jacob's crew. Brigham looked like he was ready to faint from the exertion. Toa immediately noticed Moana sitting next to Jacob. His eyes blazed as we walked up the shore toward them.

"Everyone gather round!" he shouted. The paddlers and girls came and sat on the rocks facing Toa. Brigham eased himself on the rock next to Jacob. Toa grabbed a clipboard from a bag under the tree.

"Listen up. We had a Race Committee meeting yesterday and there are two rule changes for Teuila and one announcement."

Everyone listened carefully.

"The announcement is that it looks like we'll have a full house for the Association's fundraiser this Saturday night. We have the siva competition, Petelo will host that, and then the dance. Dress is semi-casual. And if anyone is planning to party hard. . . ."

Some of the boys nudged each other and giggled.

". . . you can forget it. If I catch anyone getting drunk I'll personally throw you into the pool at the Tusitala."

The Samoan boys nodded, getting the message loud and clear.

"Now for the rule changes. First, there will be no senior Women's heats, only finals, as there aren't enough entries."

Moana shrugged. "Everyone's pregnant this year."

Jacob thought she was being cheeky, but when he saw Toa and the others nod matter-of- factly, he realized it was no joke.

"And because we're adding the V-12 races," continued Toa, "there will be no repechage rounds this year. We have too many races as it is, so if you lose your race . . . you're out."

There were a few grumbles of complaint, but for the most part this didn't surprise anyone.

"Second," Toa continued, "all teams must wear their club uniforms. So if you've lost the one you used at the Independence regatta, you'll have to buy a new one from the Manumea shop . . . they have our print."

Brigham nudged Jacob, who raised his hand.

Toa grinned. "Yes?"

"Obviously none of my team has a uniform," Jacob said with all the politeness he could muster. "How much are they?"

"Sixty tala.'

"Sixty!" exclaimed Jacob and Brigham simultaneously.

Toa's grin widened. "That's right. But that includes the shorts, singlet, bandana and lavalava."

Jacob was frantic. "But none of us at camp has any money. Where are we going to come up with $420 tala for uniforms?!"

Toa laughed. "I don't know. That's your problem. I'm just telling you the rules. No uniforms . . . no race."

"This is total bull . . . " Jacob held his tongue.

Toa shrugged. "Maybe you can make some money picking bottles or selling leis at Aggies."

The Samoan boys laughed at the joke, as did some of the girls, but Moana shook her head in disgust.

"Okay," concluded Toa. "That's it. Girls, you and the junior boys have the canoes tomorrow. A1 and A2 boys will meet at Lino's place for a run up to Stevenson's. Faamalosi lau koleni!"

The Samoan boys carried the canoes to the storage racks. Jacob's crew huddled around him.

"It's not fair," moaned Tariq. "We've been training hard and now they throw this stupid rule at us."

"They know we don't have money," agreed Chico. "That's low, man."

The Blue Horizon van pulled up. Sanele waved at them.

"Like, there's our ride, we better shake a leg," said Shaggy.

The boys headed to the van. Jacob noticed Toa and his boys laughing. Jacob spit on the ground. He was sure this uniform rule must be Toa's idea.

Brigham stood beside him.

"Well, now what?"

Jacob shrugged; he had no answer. Moana limped over to them.

"Are you sure you can't get the money?"

Brigham looked at her and shook his head. "The only time they give you money at camp is at Christmas, so you can send some souvenirs home, or when you leave. Even if we pooled our bubblegum money and begged the staff for some, we'd never make more than a few tala. 420 tala might as well be a million."

Moana thought for a moment then snapped her finger.

"Can you boys dance?"

They both looked at her, baffled.

"What?"

"Can you dance? You could enter the siva competition on Saturday."

Jacob wasn't following her. "What's a see-va competition?"

She sighed. "Siva! It means dance'. It's part of our fundraiser. There's a cash prize donated by Markus' father."

"How much of a prize?" asked Brigham.

"500 tala," she smiled.

Jacob's hopes rose again. "We can dance all night if we have to."

"Oh, captain," interjected Brigham, "this isn't a dance marathon were talking about. It's a traditional Samoan dance contest. Not exactly something a bunch of white guys is very experienced at."

Jacob noticed Sanele waving at them to hurry up. He winked at Moana.

"Thanks. You may have just saved our hopes for racing."

He and Brigham headed for the van.

"Are you sure we can pull this off?" asked Brigham. "I know we have to do something or our plan is shot, but how are we going to learn to do Samoan traditional dance in five days?"

Jacob patted Brigham on the shoulder and nodded toward Sanele.

"We'll ask our Samoan culture teacher for some pointers. Really, how hard can it be?"

CHAPTER 29

Torch started singing, making up fake Samoan lyrics that sounded like gibberish. He spun around again and slapped his knees, then his thighs and as he crossed his arms he pretended to accidentally slap his groin.

"Do we have to wear our lavalavas? We look ridiculous."

Torch adjusted the sarong around his waist. The whole team stood outside behind the dorm, dressed only in their camp issued blue sarongs.

"Do I look like a girl in this thing or what?" worried Chico.

"Hey, I've been here a long time but I ain't that desperate," joked Li.

"All right, settle down," announced Sanele, as he inspected the group.

"This was your idea, remember. If you boys want to become Samoan dancers in order to win that prize money, you have to dress for it. Now, I'm going to teach you a simple slap dance. You should be able to learn it with just a few practices. Watch me as I run through it once."

He took off his t-shirt and put on a lavalava over his lean, muscular body. He focused himself and began singing in Samoan. As he sang, he began moving his hands and legs to the beat. Jacob watched carefully. So far the dance wasn't too complex . . . mostly some foot shuffling and kung fu arm moves.

Then the song got faster and so did the movements. Sanele began slapping his legs, arms and chest in a rapid-fire percussion. It not only looked cool; it sounded cool. The slaps became faster as the song reached its climax. With a sudden rush of frantic slapping and foot movements, Sanele finished the dance and bowed.

The boys clapped and whistled.

"That was like so cool," said Shaggy.

"Yeah, at least we won't be dancing like girls," added Chico.

Sanele caught his breath and smiled. "Thanks, I learned this one when I was a senior at Avele College."

"I'll do it again, slowly, and you boys try to follow along.

"He began the song again and moved in slow motion. The boys mimicked his movements. Jacob was amazed at how difficult it was to copy Sanele's moves. They seemed so easy, but his feet and hands didn't seem to want to work together. As the tempo increased, so did his lack of co-ordination. He glanced at the others who were all having similar problems. The exception was Torch, who despite his girth was keeping up with Sanele's pace.

"This ain't so bad," he said. The others grumbled at his observation. Sanele stopped. "You boys look like drunken monkeys. Concentrate on the beat; don't get side-tracked by the hand movements. Try it again."

Once again they followed his lead, trying to smooth their actions. It wasn't pretty, but at least they were moving in some sense of synchronicity - until Sanele started the more rapid slap movements. Jacob tried to keep up, but it seemed like his hands were two moves behind his brain. He slapped his foot, when he meant to slap his thigh and then slapped his chest when he should have slapped his shoulder. The others were little better, even Torch was off the mark. Sanele stopped and shook his head.

"And I thought I picked an easy one. I can tell this is going to take a lot of work. Let's try it once more at super slow speed. Try to feel the rhythm."

He led the boys through the dance again, going painfully slow for their sake. This time they were able to get it, especially Torch. Jacob had to admit that for a kid that was very unathletic, Torch was one heck of a dancer.

Sanele finished the dance and crossed his arms. The boys wiped the sweat from their foreheads.

"I think you need to practice at that speed for awhile then maybe we'll speed it up." He pointed to Torch. "You seem to have a good feel for it. Come here and lead the group. I've got other things to attend to . . . like convincing the camp Governors to allow you to go to the night-club for the competition. And I better check to see if the contest is still taking new entries. Keep practicing for now and I'll see if there is any improvement when I come back."

Sanele put his shirt back on and left. Torch stood in front of the others and started doing the dance. He concentrated hard, trying to remember the sequence correctly. It was difficult without the singing. For about fifteen minutes the others tried the routine again and again, but it was a half-hearted effort. Brigham stopped.

"This is stupid. There's no way we're going to win any competition no matter how long we practice."

The others also stopped, but Torch kept dancing, ignoring them.

"Brigham's right," agreed Chico," even if we get the moves down, we'll be competing against Samoan dance teams. These people have been doing this since they were kids. They're going to blow us off the stage."

"Maybe we just are meant to race," sighed Li.

Jacob could see the boys were giving up. He had to do something; the team had come so far. They couldn't fail now. Then he caught himself. He was doing all this so he and Brigham could escape, not for the sake of the team. Or was he? He felt very confused. He wasn't sure what his real motivation was anymore.

"What do you think, Jacob?" asked Tariq.

Jacob was speechless for a second. He looked at Brigham, who shrugged. What should they do? What should <u>he</u> do? His eyes fell on Torch, still off in his own little world, ad-libbing the dance. He was slapping himself wildly. He slapped his ears, his cheek and his buttocks. Jacob laughed at the goofy display. The others also turned to watch.

"Is that why they call it 'slap-stick'?" thought Brigham out loud.

Realizing he now had an audience; Torch started dancing with even more gusto. He slapped himself so fast and hard to the head that he acted like he was actually dazed by the blows. The boys laughed and cheered him on.

Torch growled, spun around and slapped his butt cheeks as if he was putting out a fire. Shaggy was bent over double, he was laughing so hard.

"Give us a song, Elvis!" yelled Jacob.

Torch started singing, making up fake Samoan lyrics that sounded like gibberish. He spun around again and slapped his knees, then his thighs and as he crossed his arms he pretended to accidentally slap his groin. He stopped - a mock look of shock and discomfort on his face. He fell to his knees and rolled over.

The hilarious finale sent the others into a fit of laughter. Shaggy wiped tears from his eyes.

"Oh man, like that's the sickest dance I've ever seen!"

Torch got back up and bowed, the others clapped their appreciation.

"Now that's my kind of dancing!" exclaimed Tariq.

"Yeah," agreed Li, "too bad they don't have a competition for that."

Jacob suddenly had a wide grin on his face. Brigham noticed it.

"What? What are you thinking?"

Jacob looked at the others, "Who says we couldn't do something like that at the competition? Just because it's funny doesn't mean it isn't a 'dance'?"

Brigham nodded. "That's true. I doubt there's any rule that says a

Samoan dance can't be humorous. In fact, from what I've seen, Samoans love slapstick."

Chico scratched his head. "You mean intentionally do some whacked-out dance number? Do we really want to make total fools of ourselves? We'd be the laughing stocks of Teuila?"

"So?" argued Jacob. "If we try and do a serious dance we're still going to get laughed at anyway."

"That's right," added Torch." I'd rather have people laughing with me, than at me."

"And we might just have a shot at that prize money," said Li.

"I say we do it," urged Brigham.

Jacob saw the others nod, except Chico, who still looked uncomfortable with the idea. "We do it," announced Jacob," but only if it's a unanimous decision. It will only work if we agree to it as a team. Right?"

Everyone looked at Chico. He chewed nervously on his lip.

"Oh, man, I hate being laughed at. But I guess you're right, better to go into it intending it. Let's do it."

The others patted him on the back.

"Don't worry, Chico," winked Torch. "Comedy is always a hit with the ladies. Take my word on it. It's something Brad Pitt and I have in common."

The others groaned and razzed Torch, not quite convinced of his expertise on the matter.

Sanele strolled around the corner. He smiled when he saw the boys in such good humour. "Well, you all look happy about something. Are you getting the moves down?"

"Uh, not exactly," replied Jacob,"but there's been some improvement."

"I hope so, because I just spoke with Mr. Edridge, one of our governors, and he has granted permission for the team to compete in the dance contest."

The boys high-fived each other.

"But," he continued, "we will only be at the club for the competition and we leave as soon as it's over. You're not getting a night out on the town."

The boys grumbled a bit, but certainly weren't about to complain.

"And you'll have to do extra clean up duties for a month, whether you win or lose."

The boys all groaned at the extra condition. Sanele raised an eyebrow.

"I think it was a very generous offer, but if you disagree I'll tell Mr. Edridge to forget it."

"No, no," blurted Jacob. "It's fair. We accept it."

Sanele nodded, "I thought you would. Now, I also spoke with Tasi Tamasese, who is on the Canoe Association's Fundraising Committee, to make sure you could still enter the contest. She told me they had already filled the contest's twenty slots."

Jacob's heart skipped a beat. Not again, he thought.

"However, as a special favor to me, she is going to squeeze you into the program. I told her it was part of your Samoan culture lessons."

Jacob breathed easily again. Sanele smiled.

"So, I've done my part. You are officially in the contest. Now you have to do your part and try to win it. Do you still think you can learn a traditional Samoan dance by Saturday night?"

They all grinned.

"That depends," replied Jacob, "on what you mean by traditional."

CHAPTER 30

"What you likely don't know," she continued, "is that these young men entered this contest hoping to win the 500 tala, which they urgently needed in order to compete in the Teuila canoe races. They've been learning outrigger canoeing as part of their ongoing study of our Samoan culture."

"Holy crap, there's a lot of people out there."

Chico came trotting back behind the Tusitala's large stage area. Jacob and the rest of the team stood anxiously beside a thick log column that stretched high above to the traditional-style timber and thatch roof.

It was pandemonium backstage. Dancers were coming and going off the stage. Jacob had never seen so many colorful costumes before. The male dancers were shirtless and wearing leis over their buff upper bodies. Some carried long, hollowed log drums, others rolls of pandana mats. The girls wore long patterned dresses and had their hair tied up along with a flower over the ear.

Jacob listened to the singing and dancing as the other teams went onstage ahead of them. It seemed like each group received a thunderous applause. As it got closer and closer to their turn, Jacob and his team grew more and more intimidated. It seemed like an eternity, but eventually they were the only ones left backstage.

Sanele talked with a woman holding a clipboard at the foot of the stage steps. She looked at her watch and pointed to something on the clipboard. Sanele nodded and walked quickly over to the boys.

"Okay, this is it. Tasi says the program is running about fifteen minutes late, so as soon as this last group finishes and exits the stage, you boys get out there and start dancing."

The boys removed their t-shirts and tied on their lavalavas. Sanele opened a bottle of coconut oil and each boy took a handful of the pungent liquid and rubbed it on his chest and arms. They had already slicked their hair back with it. Jacob opened a plastic bag.

"Put your leis on."

He handed each boy a lei. Tasi noticed this from the steps and her eyes popped. Instead of flowers, shells or seeds, the boys' leis were made from fresh bananas. She stifled a laugh. The singing and drumming on stage came to a crescendo and then stopped. The crowd cheered loudly. Tariq shuffled from foot to foot, nervously.

"I need to go to the bathroom."

Sanele shook his head. "No time. You can go when you're done."

"I hope I can hold it that long."

The last group began filing off the stage. They were smiling confidently. Jacob looked at his team, they didn't look at all confident. They looked as scared as he knew he did. He knew they had to turn that fear into positive energy. He slapped Tariq and Li on their shoulders.

"It's showtime, guys. Once again we're the underdogs but that hasn't stopped us so far. C'mon, let's show 'em how we do it . . . bad boy style!"

That got the boys blood pumping.

"Yeah," nodded Torch. "Let's rock n' roll!"

They tapped the top of each other's fists and charged toward the steps.

"Time to kick some butt," growled Chico.

Sanele rolled his eyes, but pretended he didn't hear the remark.

The boys marched onto the stage as the MC introduced them.

"And finally, ladies and gentlemen, a special group from America. Please welcome the Black and Blue Horizon Dancers."

There was polite applause, but most of the audience was giggling at the sight of the banana leis. The MC turned to exit and looked at the boys for the first time. His jaw dropped. He shook his head as he stepped out.

Jacob's heart was pounding. Despite a strong spotlight on them, he could see the crowd must be over a thousand in number. Because the hall was designed like a traditional, open Samoan meeting house, there were no walls, allowing the crowd to overflow to the outside edge of the concrete slab floor. At a short table on the left sat two women and two men. They looked very serious. They must be the judges, he realized.

All the other dance groups were standing at the rear near the bar, curious to see how the palagi boys would do. If this doesn't work, thought Jacob, they might be looking at a riot.

Torch stepped forward, rubbing his hands purposefully. The crowd quieted. Torch went perfectly still, allowing for a moment of dramatic tension.

"Talofa!" he called out energetically.

"Talofa!" answered the crowd.

Torch looked very serious. "This song and dance is dedicated to our teacher, Mr. Sanele." The crowd applauded politely.

"Malo palagi," someone heckled near the front row. Jacob saw from the corner of his eye that it was Markus Williams. A few people laughed, a few others hushed him.

Unfazed, Torch raised his hands and then brought them together hard.

This was the boys cue, and they all began stomping a right foot on the stage floor. Boom, boom, boom. Torch clapped again and the boys did the same in unison. They began singing with the beat.

"They say that in Samoa, the weather's always hot.

So wear a lavalava, or your underwear will rot."

As Torch sang the verse, Tariq took hold of the bottom of Torch's lavalava and lifted it. The others bent to look underneath, then wrinkled their faces and held their noses. Torch feigned embarrassment and slapped Tariq's hand away. The unexpected sequence shocked the crowd who hooted with laughter. Jacob noticed the judges were hiding a smile. As the boys kept stomping and clapping, Torch waited for the laughs to stop then continued his song.

"They say that in Samoa, the food is kinda bland. Nothing but bananas, and tuna from a can."

The boys each plucked a banana from each other's leis, bit the bottom off the banana skin and spit it to the floor with a disgusted look. The crowd laughed at the silliness. Torch swept both arms into the air and the boys joined in the chorus.

"Oh, I don't want no more of island life, please sir I wanna go

Back to Amelika, please sir I wanna go ho . . . o . . . ome."

As they sang the last line the boys made pleading faces and left their hands clasped as if in prayer. The audience again nodded their heads and laughed at the funny lyrics.

Torch made a cutting motion with his arms and the boys switched the stomping to the other leg and resumed clapping. Torch began the next verse.

"They say that in Samoa, the girls are born lovers. You could kiss them all night long, too bad they have big brothers."

Chico closed his eyes and made kissing motions with his lips as Torch sang, sending the crowd into a fit of whistling and catcalls. As the second line ended, Chico mistakenly kissed Jacob on the cheek. Jacob raised a fist and bopped Chico on the top of the head. Chico played up the blow, stumbling slightly and returning chastened to his spot. The crowd roared with laughter, even the judges were shaking as they chuckled.

Torch made an intense karate chop with his hand and the boys stopped stomping and began slapping their bodies in an up and down rhythm. Torch did the same as he sang.

"They say that in Samoa, the bugs are very big

Was that a cockroach I just killed, or someone's baby pig?"

For the first line the boys had acted as if a swarm of mosquitoes was around them as they slapped madly. Li let his own slap go astray and smacked Shaggy on his rear. He in turn gave an angry look and accidentally swatted a bug off the back of Li's head. As the second line was sung, they all raised their right foot and brought it down hard onto the stage. Again the crowd laughed heartily.

Torch raised his arms as he clapped and invited the crowd to clap along with chorus.

"Oh, I don't want no more of island life, please sir I wanna go

Back to Amelika, please sir I wanna go ho . . . o . . . ome."

The crowd was really getting into it. Jacob took a quick glance to his right and saw Toa sitting on the aisle. He was trying to hold back a grin, unsuccessfully.

Torch put his hands together as if in prayer. The group bent down onto one knee, while using the other to stomp loudly.

"They say that in Samoa, the churches are so strong.

They ask for all your money, and the sermons are too long."

The boys made sad faces and rubbed their fingers at the word "money", then stifled a yawn on "long". A big Samoan man near the stage stood up yelled his agreement.

"Sa'o lelei! Sa'o lelei!"

The crowd laughed even harder. Torch waited for calm, then continued.

"They say that in Samoa, that rugby is our game.

So if the Tongans beat us, we'll find a ref to blame."

The boys had jumped back up and huddled together as if in a scrum while stomping from foot to foot. Brigham acted as if he was a referee trying to separate them. As the second line was sung, the boys pounded on Brigham's head. He crossed his eyes, wobbled in a circle and held up his hand signaling a scored try.

The crowd loved it. They clapped and whistled. The boys lined up again and sang the chorus.

"Oh, I don't want no more of island life, please sir I wanna go.

Back to Amelika, please sir I wanna go ho . . . o . . . ome."

The crowd even joined in. Torch held up a finger, signaling a final verse.

"They say that in Samoa, you should always try your best.

So we've danced our best for you tonight, but now we need a rest."

The boys wiped sweat from their brows and pretended to be ought of breath. The crowd applauded enthusiastically, as the boys stomped and slapped once more to the chorus.

"Oh, we don't want no more of island life, please sir we wanna go

Back to Amelika, please sir we wanna go ho . . . o . . . ome."

Torch struck a fierce warrior pose as they finished, but Tariq grabbed his lavalava again and yanked. This time the lavalava came off completely, leaving Torch standing there in a pair of flower patterned underwear. Torch acted as if he was in a total panic and scrambled off the stage. The place shook with laughter, which quickly turned into a standing ovation from the crowd.

The boys stood there for a second, completely stunned by the response. Jacob scanned the smiling faces. Two of the judges were wiping tears from their eyes. He noticed Toa, grinning freely and clapping. A few rows back he caught sight of Moana who was still laughing. Their eyes met and she gave him a thumbs-up. He smiled back.

The boys made several overly dramatic bows. Torch came back out, a woven mat around his body. The crowd laughed and whistled their appreciation of his comedic talents. The group gave a final bow and exited. They gathered beside the big log column and high-fived each other.

"What a rush!" exclaimed Tariq.

"I'm so pumped. Wish we could race 1500 meters now!" gushed Li.

Jacob messed Torch's hair, "Buddy, you were a friggin' phenom out there. They loved you!"

Torch shrugged bashfully. "Go figure."

Jacob could see the sense of accomplishment in Torch's face. Jacob was proud of him. Torch had discovered talents he never knew he had. Win or lose tonight, no one could take that away from him.

"Do you think we won?" asked Li.

"You heard that crowd. We rocked 'em!" replied Chico.

"Those judges sure seemed to be enjoying themselves," added Shaggy.

Sanele rushed backstage. He motioned toward the boys.

"C'mon out front. They're going to announce the winners."

The boys followed him out along the far left end of the hall. The crowd was bustling with chatter. They took up a position behind a wing of chairs. People in the audience pointed at them and smiled.

Tasi Tamesese walked up onto the stage holding three envelopes. The crowd quieted.

"Ladies and gentlemen, our judges have selected our top three finishers. It certainly wasn't an easy task given the excellent talents we've seen demonstrated tonight. So . . . without further ado, I shall read out the winners."

She opened the first envelope, "In third place, and a 200 tala cash prize . . . the Saleimoa Methodist Youth!"

The crowd clapped, a section of it cheered wildly. Jacob looked nervously to Sanele, who gave him a hopeful smile. The Saleimoa group came up and accepted their prize. Tasi waited for them to finish waving and bowing to the audience, then she ripped open the second envelope.

"In second place and a 300 tala cash prize . . . "

Jacob held his breath; they needed the big prize, not second place.

" . . . the Avele College Boys!"

The crowd clapped and a loud cheer exploded from several rows near the back. The Avele boys hustled to the front, big grins on their faces, and accepted their prize. They all bowed gratefully toward the judges. Tasi waited for them to finish, but they were so giddy with their win, she finally had to usher them off the stage. She stepped back to the microphone stand and opened the last envelope.

"And now the moment we've all been waiting for, the first prize of 500 tala goes to . . .

" Blue Horizon . . . Blue Horizon . . . willed Jacob crossing his fingers.

" . . . the Leulumoega Catholic Youth!"

A huge roar went up from the right side of the hall as the Leulumoega supporters celebrated. Jacob stood there in total disbelief. They had gotten nothing! He turned and looked at Sanele, who shrugged sympathetically.

Jacob scanned the faces of his team; they all stared at their feet, completely heartbroken. Brigham shook his head.

"Kaput!" he muttered to Jacob.

"All that work for nothing," Torch said with a sullen face.

They watched the Leulumoega team accept their prize and sing out a victory cheer. Jacob felt sick to his stomach. Everything was lost now: the contest, the race, and the escape . . . all of it.

Tasi, still on the stage, held up her hand.

"If I could have your attention for just one more minute, please." The crowd hushed.

"We have one more item we'd like to bring to your attention. As you saw earlier, we had a special visiting group of dancers from America with us tonight."

Jacob snapped his attention back to the stage. The crowd looked in the boys' direction.

"I think you'll agree that while their performance did not exactly fall within the bounds of 'traditional' Samoan dance, it was one of the most entertaining acts we've seen tonight, and we Samoans always enjoy an item that makes us laugh!"

The crowd clapped in agreement.

"What you likely don't know," she continued, "is that these young men entered this contest hoping to win the 500 tala, which they urgently needed in order to compete in the Teuila canoe races. They've been learning outrigger canoeing as part of their ongoing study of our Samoan culture."

The crowd nodded approvingly as they looked at the boys. Jacob felt suddenly very shy.

"It would be a shame to see such good intentions go unfulfilled. So, I'd like to invite our young friends to come back up onto the stage and give us one more siva. I think there's one more Samoan custom we can show them."

The crowd nodded and clapped. Sanele pushed them forward.

"Go, go! This is your chance?"

"Chance for what?" exclaimed Jacob.

Sanele prodded them on toward the stage. "Just get up there and dance. You'll see."

Jacob led the others onto the stage. They lined up and began their dance again. This time as they danced the crowd didn't sit and watch politely. They began to get up and move about. Were they leaving, Jacob wondered.

The people started dancing toward the front of the hall. The first person to reach the stage was an older woman in a bright flowery dress. She twirled, as if dancing to music. She beckoned Torch to come to the edge of the stage. He inched over to her, wary of her intentions. The crowd laughed at his uncertainty.

The elderly woman raised a hand; in it was a clump of colored paper. Money, Jacob realized. She reached out and slipped the money into Torch's lavalava. He stood there embarrassed, which sent the crowd into howls of laughter. This spurred on another couple ladies. One was a very hefty woman, who motioned for Chico to come forward. He too had a wad of bills shoved into his lavalava. He winked at the lady, who giggled and danced at the front of the stage. The other woman asked for Shaggy, who advanced bashfully and received a rolled bill behind his ear. He gave her two thumbs-up as she also danced in front of the stage.

To Jacob's surprise, Moana had raced up the aisle and was waving money at him. He hopped closer to her and she crammed the money into his lavalava, right over his right butt cheek. She shook her head and laughed. "You're one crazy palagi!" Jacob just smiled, unable to quickly reply.

Suddenly it seemed like half the audience was making their way to the stage and tossing money onto it, or stuffing it into the boys' lavalavas. Torch actually had to run through the song twice, to allow everyone time to make it to the front. By the time the last bill was jammed down his lavalava, the stage was covered in money. Sanele grabbed a cardboard box and quickly put all the money into it. Jacob looked to the boys.

"Let's blow them a kiss and get the hell out of here before they change their minds!"

The boys all put their hands to their mouths then blew the kiss out to the audience. The crowd clapped at the acknowledgment. The boys headed backstage, giddy with excitement.

"How much is there?" asked Tariq, pulling money from his lavalava.

"Hurry, let's count it."

They sorted the bills on the table according to the colors, then Sanele counted them. "Four hundred and two!" he announced.

The boys cheered,

"We just need another eighteen bucks," noted Jacob.

"Not bucks, tala!" said a voice behind them.

It was Toa. Jacob's spirit's drooped. Now what was he going to come up with to try and block them from racing, he wondered.

Toa strutted over and looked at their financial windfall.

"So you're eighteen tala short."

Jacob crossed his arms defiantly. "We'll get it."

Toa smirked. "You already have."

Jacob looked at him confused.

Toa held out a fist and opened it over the table. A 20 tala bill dropped down. Toa smiled, "You palagis have got guts!"

He nodded and walked out.

The boys stared at each other. Sanele nudged Jacob.

"I told you there was more to Toa than meets the eye."

"I guess so," conceded Jacob. If even Toa was behind them, they must be destined to race. Torch wrapped an elastic around the money and pretended to hide it under his lavalava. Sanele smiled and motioned for him to hand it over.

"I'll hold onto that until Tuesday then I'll order your uniforms while you're at training." He pocketed the money.

"Now, get dressed. I'm going to get the van."

"Sir," began Jacob, "I think we should say thanks to Tasi."

Sanele nodded. "That's a very good idea. Go ahead, I'll pick you up at the front entrance. But don't linger, I told you this is not a night out. We're heading straight home."

"We'll be right there," replied Jacob

The boys began changing. Brigham got close to Jacob.

"Smart move, I saw them too," he whispered.

Jacob didn't understand. "What?"

"The Swedes. I saw them standing near the bar too. I'll make a quick contact while you pretend to thank that lady."

Brigham grabbed his stuff and winked at Jacob. "Good work, partner."

Jacob gave a curt nod. He hadn't even seen the Swedes. But Brigham had just reminded him that tonight's success would, in the end, only benefit two members of the Blue Horizon team. It was not a reminder that sat well in his gut.

CHAPTER 31

Jacob knew he should stay out of it, but he couldn't just stand there when it was three on one. He grabbed the closest boy and yanked him off Toa, ripping the boy's flashy aloha shirt . . .

The hall was bustling with activity. Half the crowd had headed for the bar, eager to replenish their cocktails. The Tusitala staff had then hurried to remove most of the plastic chairs, making room for a dance floor. A slick looking DJ was setting up his audio gear on the stage. The boys weaved their way through the sea of people. They found Tasi chatting with one of the other dance groups. As Jacob and the boys politely waited for their chance to thank her, Brigham slipped away to find the Swedes. The other dance group finally moved on and the boys each shook Tasi's hand and thanked her for her help.

"My pleasure, boys. Sanele told me how hard you've been training and I really wanted you to be able to experience the thrill of the Teuila races. Win or lose you'll have some great memories."

Jacob had to look away, racked with guilt. His eyes scanned the crowd, looking for Brigham. He spotted him on the far side of the bar, talking with the Swedes. He nudged Tariq.

"I'm just going to grab Brigham; you guys go ahead to the lobby."

Tariq nodded. Jacob made his way to the back. As he squeezed his way through a noisy pack of partiers, he noticed Moana standing by herself off to the side. He knew he didn't have time, but he just had to acknowledge the money she'd stuffed down his lavalava. He walked over to her. She smiled as she sipped from her drink.

"I thought Toa said there was to be no public drunkenness," he teased.

She stuck her tongue out. "It's just juice. I drink nothing stronger."

"Well, aren't you a perfect little angel."

She gave him a sly look. "Not always."

He nodded, "Not when you're jamming money down the back of some guy's lavalava, right?"

She laughed. "Manaia lou muli."

He gave her a quizzical look. "And what does that mean?"

She just shrugged coyly. He smiled at her playfulness.

"Well, thanks anyway. I mean that."

She raised her glass, as if toasting him. "You bad boys earned it."

He looked at her in the dim half-light and suddenly was aware of just how beautiful she was. With her long wavy hair flowing over one shoulder and her strong body showing under her beige dress, she looked like a supermodel. He was just about to tell her that, when a hand slapped down onto his shoulder.

"Malo palagi!"

It was Markus, and by the smell on his breath, Jacob could tell he'd been drinking heavily. Behind him stood two of his crew, dressed as sharp and cool as their leader. Markus grinned.

"You bad boys are a bunch of wankers. Real comedians."

Jacob forced a polite smile. "Thanks, I'm glad you enjoyed the act."

Markus took a gulp from his drink, "Yeah, it was a good laugh, almost as funny as watching you guys trying to paddle."

Markus' boys laughed arrogantly. Jacob kept smiling, coolly.

"I can see why you palagis paddle with Toa," Markus nodded. "One good joke deserves another."

Jacob kept his mouth shut, as Moana stepped forward angrily.

"You're a big talker when Toa's not around. Because you know damn well he can beat your ass on or off the water."

Markus glared at her. "You're nothing but a one-legged paumuku!"

Jacob wasn't sure what that meant, but he knew it must be bad because Moana threw her drink into Markus' face. Before Jacob could even move, Markus had lunged forward, pushing Moana hard on her chest. It caught her off guard, and she couldn't move her artificial leg in time to regain her balance. She tumbled backwards onto the floor. Jacob turned to help her up, but he was grabbed from behind and pulled back.

"Stay out of this palagi," growled Markus.

Markus loomed over Moana, about to dump his own drink on her, when a body came flying through and tackled him to the floor. It was Toa!

The two men rolled farther to the edge of the hall, as people shouted and leapt out of the way. Toa quickly overpowered the drunken Markus and had him pinned down. Seeing their leader in trouble, Markus' boys leapt onto Toa and began punching.

Jacob knew he should stay out of it, but he couldn't just stand there when it was three on one. He grabbed the closest boy and yanked him off Toa, ripping the boy's flashy aloha shirt in half. The boy took a vicious swing at Jacob, but he easily dodged it and replied with a hard jab to the jaw. The boy's knees buckled and he dropped to the floor. But the second boy, less intoxicated and much stronger, caught Jacob with a punch over the eye. Wham!

Jacob saw white stars in front of his eyes and felt blood trickling down his face. His attacker snapped another punch at him, but Jacob moved just in time and the blow glanced off his cheek. Burning rage overcame Jacob and he whipped his elbow out and drove it into the boy's nose. Blood gushed out. Jacob was about to give him another one, when the first boy suddenly launched himself up from his kneeling position and rammed a shoulder into Jacob's ribs. Jacob felt the air knocked from his lungs. He stumbled, his two attackers now ready to pounce again. He was in trouble.

Fortunately, Toa had cut loose from Markus' grip and smashed into the other two. He launched a flurry of punches that sent the boys reeling. He grabbed the larger boy and gave him a knee to the guts and a haymaker to the jaw. The boy sank to the floor and moaned.

Jacob had regained his wind and leapt up and wrestled the other boy to the ground, where he pinned him and rubbed his face into the cement floor as if it was an eraser.

Blood was dripping from Jacob's face onto his foe. A hand grabbed Jacob from behind and yanked him off the boy. He twisted to see who was attacking him now. He was ready to take on an army, he was so juiced.

"You want some too, come and . . . "

He froze. He was surrounded by blue uniforms. The police!

CHAPTER 32

"Because outrigger is more than just a sport. It's how our people came to this island. It's part of our heritage. Samoans used to sail across the Pacific in canoes, now most of them are afraid to go on the ferry to Savaii."

Jacob flew into the empty cell. Toa was thrown in behind him. The police officers locked the iron-bar door. One of them tapped a metal baton on the bars.

"No trouble, or I beat your heads!"

Jacob sat down on the one wooden bench in the cell and gingerly touched his eyebrow. Caked blood flaked off and fell the floor. He had a bad headache and his whole body was sore. Toa plumped down on the other end of the bench. Each boy sat alone in his thoughts. Jacob couldn't believe what had just happened. One minute he was celebrating their dancing success, the next minute he's sitting in a jail cell in the Apia police station. None of it was his fault; it was that idiot Markus that had started it all. He wondered why Markus hadn't been arrested. He looked at Toa.

"What's going on? Why are we in here? Didn't they realize Markus instigated the fight?"

Toa chuckled. "Markus' father is the Minister of Justice. Do you think the police are going to arrest him?"

"But that's not right!"

"Welcome to Samoa," sighed Toa. "Where family is more important than the truth."

Jacob could sense a deep sorrow in Toa's voice. It sounded like Toa had experienced this kind of injustice before. Jacob leaned back against the wall and thought about his own situation. It seemed like no matter what he did, he was always ending up on the wrong end of the truth.

"Thanks for jumping in," blurted Toa.

It took Jacob a second to realize that Toa was thanking him for joining the fight. He smiled.

"You're my club captain; teammates watch each other's backs, right?"

Toa smiled and nodded, "That's right."

The boys were silent again, suddenly aware they were on new ground with each other and both felt awkward about it.

Toa cleared his throat.

"I guess I was a hard on you guys, you in particular. Sorry about that."

Jacob shook his head. "Forget about it. I probably deserved it. I was kind of cocky in the beginning."

More awkward silence. Jacob shifted his position. "And thanks for the donation back at the hall, and what you said. It meant a lot to us."

Toa grinned. "You guys surprised me. I thought you'd all have given up weeks ago. But you're not quitters. I respect that."

"You take your sport pretty seriously."

"Yeah, I know I'm pretty hard on my crew," admitted Toa. "But I have to be. I've seen too many kids join my team and treat it like a social club. They don't train, they party too much . . . they show up on race day expecting to paddle. We're never going to win international regattas with that kind of attitude."

"And that's important to you, isn't it?"

"Shouldn't it be? I want to win a gold medal for this country, put it back on the outrigger map. It's been decades since Samoa won a gold medal at the World Sprints. The sport isn't going to be taken seriously here until we do."

Jacob listened to the competitive passion in Toa's voice.

"I heard you were a good rugby player. Why didn't you stick with that? It seems to be the only sport that matters here."

"Because outrigger is more than just a sport. It's how our people came to this island. It's part of our heritage. Samoans used to sail across the Pacific in canoes, now most of them are afraid to go on the ferry to Savaii."

Jacob considered the irony. Toa looked at him.

"Who told you I was good at rugby?"

Jacob grinned, "Moana. She said you could have been a star."

Toa turned away bashfully, "I'm too slow. My brother's the rugby star."

Jacob detected a hint of sarcasm in Toa's voice.

"He's the one on the scholarship?"

Toa eyed Jacob. "What other stories did she tell you?"

Jacob hesitated, not sure if he should answer. Toa huffed at him.

"Like she knows anything anyway."

Jacob threw his arms up in frustration, "What is it with you? She lost her leg thanks to your recklessness. Why do you treat her like crap?"

Toa glared at Jacob, "You should keep your nose out of my business."

Jacob didn't back off. "Why? What are you hiding?"

"Nothing!"

"There's something," pressed Jacob. "Was she cheating on you?"

Toa stood up. "What?"

Jacob knew he was pushing his luck, but he continued.

"Yeah, that must be it. You found out she was cheating on you and you deliberately drove the pick-up at her in a fit of jealous rage!"

Toa grabbed Jacob and shoved hard against the wall. He was furious.

"You fool. I loved her!"

Jacob's heart pumped with fear, but he kept digging.

"Then why did you drive your truck into her?"

"I didn't! I wasn't even driving, for God's sake!"

Jacob's eyes widened with surprise. Toa backed off, realizing he had said too much.

"What do you mean, you weren't driving? Someone else was in the vehicle with you?"

Toa sat down again, dejected.

"It's a long story."

Jacob looked around the cell, "I've got the time."

Toa leaned his head against the wall and sighed.

"My brother Tupu was driving that pick-up, not me."

"But you . . . then how . . . ?"

"I had gone to pick up my brother from his training at Vaimoso. It was his last training because he was heading overseas that week on his scholarship. The team threw him a farewell party after practice and everyone had way too much beer. Tupu insisted on driving home. I told him he was too drunk, but he was ready to fight over it. I didn't want to embarrass him in front of his team, so I let him drive. When we were passing by Apia Park, he spotted Moana biking home. He tried to speed up and drive right beside her, you know, as a joke to scare her. But he misjudged it. Before I could do anything he had hit her."

Jacob couldn't believe it. Toa winced as he recalled the accident.

"I rushed out of the vehicle. There was no one else around. Moana was unconscious. Her leg was bleeding and a total mess. I yelled at Tupu to come and help me. But he was gone."

"Gone?"

"He'd panicked and run off. He thought she was dead. She wasn't, but I knew she was going to bleed to death if I didn't get help. Thank God a taxi drove by and stopped. He raced to the fire station and they responded in minutes. They saved her life."

"But why didn't you tell them your brother was the driver?"

"I had jumped in the ambulance and went to the hospital with Moana. By the time the police arrived to question me, my family had already seen me first."

"So, why would that matter?"

Toa looked at him. "I told you; in Samoa family comes before the truth. My father told me that if Tupu was arrested, he'd lose the scholarship for sure. Tupu was a hero in my family, a rising star. My father said it would be a greater shame on the family if Tupu was arrested, than if I was. For the sake of my family's pride I was asked to lie, to confess that I had been the only one in the vehicle."

"How could they do that?"

Toa didn't answer. Jacob thought of Moana.

"So she never knew it wasn't you?"

Toa shook his head. "I couldn't tell anyone outside my family. We couldn't risk the secret being discovered, especially not now that Tupu is headed for the national team. You're the only person that knows this outside my family. I hope I can trust you."

Jacob nodded. "Of course. But you could have trusted Moana?"

"She would've told her family. I'm not sure it would have mattered."

"Why not?"

"Because she hated me after the accident. Even after my family did the ifoga, she insisted I personally apologize to her."

"Yes, she told me that," said Jacob. "So why didn't you just apologize?"

"It wasn't my fault! Why couldn't she just accept the ifoga? Why did she try and force me to further humiliate myself?"

"She wanted to forgive you! She needed to know you were sorry!"

"Of course I was sorry! I wish it had been my leg that was lost instead of hers. But it wasn't my fault!"

"She didn't know that!"

Toa went silent again, filled with confusion and frustration. Jacob leaned toward him.

"Do you still love her?"

Toa was surprised by the question.

"No, it's over between us."

"Is that why you jumped on Markus and tried to tear him apart?"

"I was protecting my teammate, that's all."

"That's bull! You weren't just sticking up for a teammate; you were sticking up for your girl!"

Toa turned away. "Even if I did have feelings for her, she hates my guts. She always will."

"No, she doesn't. She just doesn't understand what happened to you after the accident. And how can she, if you won't tell her?"

"If she had really loved me, she would have accepted the ifoga and not pushed me."

"And if you had really loved her, you would have told her the truth and trusted her."

Toa made an annoyed grunt and went silent. Jacob shook his head.

"The two of you are the most stubborn, hard-heads I've ever met."

Toa turned with an angry face, about to say something when two policemen stepped up to the doors and opened them. One pointed at Jacob.

"You . . . palagi. Let's go."

Jacob looked at Toa, but he turned away. Jacob exited with the officers. They led him to the front desk where Sanele was filling out a form. He thanked the officers and motioned for Jacob to follow him. As they exited the station and headed for the van, Jacob wondered what would happen to Toa.

"What about Toa?" he asked.

"His family is coming to pick him up."

"Are we in trouble?"

Sanele shook his head, "No, fortunately Moana and a few other witnesses confirmed you two didn't start the fight."

"Are they going to arrest Markus?" asked Jacob.

Sanele laughed, "I rather doubt that. Just consider yourself lucky."

They approached the van. The others were inside waiting for them. Jacob was worried by Sanele's general silence.

"Am I in any trouble with you?" asked Jacob.

Sanele stopped and looked at him. "No, I think you should have stayed out of it, but I don't think it warrants disciplinary action. But it's not my call."

Jacob rolled his eyes. "You're not going to tell Sefo, are you?"

"He's going to hear about it anyway. This is Samoa, remember? Better he hear it from me than through the coconut wireless. Hopefully that cut on your head will buy you some sympathy with him."

Jacob highly doubted that.

Somehow, in the dream, Jacob knew the two paddlers were searching for each other, but the harder they paddled, the farther they drifted apart. Jacob tried to yell out to them, but the waves swallowed his voice.

"But I'm telling you it wasn't his fault!"

Outside the dorm, Sanele stood angrily in front of Big Sefo, who was gripping Jacob by the shirt. Sefo glared menacingly at Sanele.

"This one's been trouble since he got here. You admit you didn't even see the fight?"

"No, but I talked to others who did."

"Then they're probably lying, just like this maggot. Well, I'm not buying it. He's doing a day in the Cooler . . . and I'm disbanding the whole team!"

Jacob looked to the night sky in silent desperation. Maybe a comet could drop from the heavens onto Sefo's head.

"You don't have the authority to disband the team," argued Sanele.

"That's my call. I was there, not you."

Sefo didn't like the challenge. "It was your stupid idea to let them go to that nightclub. I told you they'd make a fool out of you. And I bloody well have the authority to clean up your incompetence."

Sanele's eyes blazed with anger. "You're not putting him in the Cooler and you're not disbanding the team."

"Just watch me," growled Sefo as he hauled Jacob away.

Sanele grabbed Sefo's arm. "I told you he's innoce . . . "

Sefo spun around and with his free arm shoved Sanele to the ground.

From the dorm window the boys gasped in shock. Sanele was also stunned and didn't move. Sefo continued on with Jacob in tow.

"I've had enough of your spoiling these maggots, Sanele. You want this one back, you show me real evidence he didn't start that fight. I won't hold my breath waiting!"

Jacob knew the routine by now. He was tossed into the Cooler, the door locked shut. Sefo predicted rain for the night. The only difference this time was that no one snuck around afterwards with food. Jacob knew it was because of Sefo's violent outburst. If he was berserk enough to knock Sanele down, there's no telling what he might do if he caught them outside the dorm at this hour.

Jacob lay on his back and relived the entire evening in his head. What a rollercoaster it had been. Too bad it ended with a big crash, he thought. It certainly looked like this time the escape attempt was dead for sure. He felt sorry for Brigham, who was obsessed with the plan. But Jacob had mixed feelings now about it. On one hand he was disappointed that the team was disbanded and wouldn't be able to race, on the other he was relieved because it meant he no longer would have to betray his friends in order to escape.

He rolled onto his side. He laughed as he remembered Torch's antics on the stage. This was a good bunch of guys. Even Sanele was cool. If it wasn't for rockhead Sefo, Blue Horizons wouldn't be a half bad place.

He closed his eyes and drifted off to sleep. He was soon dreaming that he was paddling a canoe. Behind him, another canoe full of policeman was giving chase. Then the dream shifted and he saw two canoes crossing in front of him. But because of the rolling waves, the canoes could not see each other, only him. In the one canoe Toa paddled furiously, as if looking for something. The paddler in the other canoe was doing the same. It was Moana.

Somehow, in the dream, Jacob knew the two paddlers were searching for each other, but the harder they paddled, the farther they drifted apart. Jacob tried to yell out to them, but the waves swallowed his voice. He tried to get their attention waving his paddle, but they each thought it was a greeting and merely waved back. He dug his paddle into the sea and tried to catch Toa's canoe. He paddled and paddled, but his canoe barely moved. The current was dragging him back. Soon the two canoes would be too far away, he doubled his efforts, to no avail. The moment had been lost. He slumped down in the canoe and pounded the sides in frustration.

"Get up!" shouted a voice.

Jacob thought it was the police. He tried to act like he was dead, maybe they'd leave him alone.

"C'mon, wake up!"

He felt someone shaking his arm. His mind was pulled away from the dream and back into consciousness. He opened his eyes. Sanele was crouched in the open Cooler doorway. It was morning. The sun was well up in the sky. Jacob sat up, his body ached.

"I thought you were in a coma! That fight must have drained your batteries pretty good."

Jacob nodded. He must have been exhausted alright. He suddenly realized he was being allowed out.

"Where's Sefo?" he asked.

"He's gone to services in the village. He couldn't stand being around me, after he was proved wrong."

"What do you mean?"

Sanele smiled. "Two star witnesses showed up first thing this morning."

"Who?"

"Toa and Markus."

"What? Why?"

"I called Toa and told him what happened here. He tracked down Markus and convinced him to give Sefo the facts as to what really happened."

Jacob just sat there, absorbing the news.

"So the team is still a go?"

"Yes, you boys are still in the race."

"Wow, thanks for your help, sir!"

"Don't thank me, thank Toa. Whatever he did to convince Markus to drive out here on a Sunday morning, well, it made the difference. If there's one thing Sefo respects it's people higher up on the ladder than he is . . . and Markus' father is near the top. But he sure didn't like having to admit I was right."

Jacob finally crawled out of the Cooler and stretched. Sanele tapped him on the shoulder.

"Go grab a quick shower and get ready for service. The rest of the team will be happy to see you."

Jacob nodded and headed for the dorm. It was great to be off the hook and out of the Cooler. Thanks to Sanele and Toa that problem was resolved. But his spirits dipped again when he realized that he was still left with the old dilemma. After all they'd been through, how could he stab his team in the back?

Then again, Sefo would be back in an even nastier mood, just waiting for Jacob to make the slightest mistake. This was still a question for survival, wasn't it? Surely the others would understand his predicament.

He rubbed his sore neck. Why did things have to get so complicated? Maybe if he prayed hard at service, God would show him a way out of this mess.

The two canoes slid into the shore. Toa's boys leapt out and greeted Torch and the crew. They laughed as they recalled the Saturday night dance routine, as well as the fight.

"Let's kick some butt out there!"

Torch pumped his fist enthusiastically as he jumped from the van onto the seawall. Tariq followed him.

"We've only got three trainings left, let's make them count!'

The rest of the team hopped out of the van and made their way to the shore. In the harbor the two Matagi canoes were racing each other toward the familiar red buoy. Jacob hung back from the others. Brigham walked over to him.

"What's with you?" he asked quietly, "You haven't been yourself since you got out of the Cooler on Sunday. You sick or something?"

Jacob shook his head, "No, I've just been thinking."

"About what?"

"Is there anyway we could cut the guys in on the escape plan?"

Brigham's eyes popped. "Are you crazy?" he hissed. "There's no room on the yacht for seven of us, not that we'd make it that far anyway. A crowd like that and we'd be caught before we hit the water."

Jacob knew it was useless to push it further. "Could we at least tell them our plan. I think they'll understand."

"No, we can't risk it. One of them might rat us out, just to spite us."

Jacob sighed. "I wouldn't blame him."

Brigham edged closer and looked at Jacob.

"You're not getting cold feet on me, are you buddy? C'mon we've only got ten days to go and we're out of here. Don't lose your focus. We've come too far to blow it now."

The two canoes slid into the shore. Toa's boys leapt out and greeted Torch and the crew. They laughed as they recalled the Saturday night dance routine, as well as the fight. Jacob was glad to see that his team had finally earned the respect of the A1 and A2 teams and was accepted as part of the Matagi club. Toa walked over to Jacob, smiling.

"Are you just going to stand there, or did you come to train?"

Jacob smiled and nodded, "Train! Thanks to you."

Toa shrugged, "Well, if you guys didn't paddle, my twenty tala investment would have been wasted. I figured if Markus set the record straight, you boys would get your chance to paddle."

"But how did you convince Markus to confess that he started the fight? I wouldn't think he'd be real anxious to do you any favors?"

"Not unless I did one for him," replied Toa.

"Like what?"

"Markus has paddle problems, half his foe have broken blades and he broke a steer foe last week. He knows I'm the only one who can fix paddles on short notice. Naturally I wasn't going to repair them until after the regatta. But in exchange for his confession, I agreed to fix them in time for Teuila."

Jacob was stunned by the gesture.

"I didn't know you fixed paddles."

Toa laughed and pointed at the canoes. "Who do you think made all our foe, or fixes the canoes every time someone wrecks them on the rocks?"

Jacob was impressed. "You're a man of many talents."

"Of course. You're wasting training time. Get your crew on the water."

Jacob offered him his hand. The two young men shook hands.

"Thanks," Jacob said, "Faafetai tele lava."

Toa smiled. "Who taught you that?"

Jacob made for the canoe. "Sanele. He said you deserved to hear 'thank you' in your own language."

The crew sat in the white canoe, limbering up with their paddles. Tariq waited for Jacob to jump into the canoe then he pushed them into deeper water and pulled himself up and in. Jacob turned and looked back at the shore. Brigham sat on a rock, staring out toward the Swedes' yacht.

Toa was busy leading his crew in a stretching exercise. Jacob wondered which of the two he would ultimately betray.

CHAPTER 35

Sanele patted him on the shoulder, "That's the spirit. Never quit! You know, I took a big chance on this racing project. If it had failed I might have lost my job. But you didn't let me down."

Scrape, scrape, scrape. In the heavy air of the hot, humid kitchen, Jacob scrubbed the burnt rice from the bottom of a big blackened pot. Beside him, Suka drained the last bit of mutton-flap gravy into a plastic container. He smiled at Jacob.

"We gonna get one more meal outta dis batch."

Jacob's forced a smile onto his face, but his stomach buckled as he contemplated yet another meal of burnt rice and greasy gravy. Suka tossed the gunk filled gravy pot into the sink. Jacob groaned, he'd be here another hour at this rate. He still had homework to do before lights out.

This was his third straight night on pots and pans. He'd already done triple shifts on toilet patrol and laundry this week. With the races beginning tomorrow, Sefo was obviously desperate to break him, hoping Jacob would get so frustrated with all the chores that he'd flip out. That would give Sefo the excuse he needed to toss Jacob into the Cooler and cut him from the team.

Well, it wasn't going to work, vowed Jacob. He wasn't going to crack on the eve of the regatta. By this time tomorrow night, he thought, they'd be camping in Apia with the rest of the Matagi paddlers. And that meant . . .

"Put some more elbow grease into it, Captain!"

Jacob turned to find Brigham entering the kitchen from the back door. Suka made a 'tsk, tsk' sound.

"Don't you be stealing any more ice pops," he muttered.

"Don't worry Suka. I just want to talk to my canoe captain."

Suka nodded. "Oh ioe, you boys paddle in Teuila on Saturday. You gonna beat Foelele."

"That's right," grinned Brigham, "we'll be coming back Saturday evening as champions."

"Manaia!" Suka cackled happily as he picked up a basket of scraps and went outside.

"I go feed da dogs," he said.

As he left, Brigham sidled up to the sink. Jacob tossed him a scrub brush.

"Here, make yourself useful."

Brigham reluctantly took the scrubber and started on the gravy pot.

"So are you ready?" Brigham asked.

Jacob nodded. "Yeah, Sanele's going to hand out the uniforms tomorrow morning, and the guys have really got their timing down. You saw us on that last sprint in this afternoon; we gave Toa's boys a run for their money."

Brigham gave him an annoyed look. "That's not what I meant."

Jacob sighed. "Yes, I'm ready."

"Good. Because we're only going to get one shot at this. The Swedes will be watching for us on their deck. As soon as everyone is asleep, we slip out of the church hall and follow the path to the unlit side of the church. We make sure there's no one on the road, then sprint across and down over the rocks. It's going to be almost high tide, so we can slip right into the water and swim to the yacht in less than a couple of minutes."

"What about the moon?"

"Only a half moon and we might have cloud cover, if we're lucky."

"And what about the dogs in town?"

"I have a little distraction planned for them," Brigham smiled craftily as he checked the door, then headed to the freezer. He opened it, reached in deep and pulled out a brown paper package. Jacob's eyes widened.

"Those are the sausages for the teachers' Sunday toonai!" he hissed.

"I know," chuckled Brigham, "so we won't even be around when they notice the meat's gone."

He dropped the package into a plastic shopping bag and stuffed it into his pocket. He returned to the sink.

"So what time is Sanele driving us in?" he asked.

Jacob scrubbed the pot angrily. "After three. We have to be there for the rules meeting for all the clubs. Then we watch the juniors' heats before heading to camp."

"Good, that will help keep the attention off of us."

Jacob rinsed the big pot and placed it on a drying rack. He took the half-cleaned gravy pot from Brigham.

"I'll finish up. You better go and hide those sausages."

"Okay," he winked at Jacob. "Just think; this is our last night in this hell hole. The end is near, buddy."

"Yeah, right."

Brigham left and Jacob finished cleaning the last pot. He set it on the rack and tidied the sink area. He wiped his hands dry and headed for the dorm, nearly exhausted. As he walked across the dark courtyard, he noticed someone approaching from the staff block. He quickly prayed it wasn't Sefo coming with another bogus chore to do. As the figure got closer he could see it was Sanele. Jacob breathed easier.

"Good evening, Jacob."

"Evening, sir."

"I see Sefo has you on slave duty again."

"Yeah, but I can handle it."

Sanele patted him on the shoulder, "That's the spirit. Never quit! You know, I took a big chance on this racing project. If it had failed I might have lost my job. But you didn't let me down. You boys have come along way in the last month and I just want you to know that win or lose, I'm proud of you all . . . but especially you."

Jacob couldn't find a single word to reply. He merely smiled gamely and nodded. Sanele gave him another pat on the shoulder.

"Sorry, I didn't mean to put you on the spot. We'll have time for a good chat after the races. I better let you get some much needed sleep. Good night . . . Captain Michaels."

"Uhh, okay, thanks sir. Good night."

Sanele smiled and headed back to his office. Jacob continued on toward the dorm. He wondered if this was how Judas felt, the night before he sold out Jesus.

CHAPTER 36

The boys headed across the compound to the van. All the other boys in camp stopped their chores and came to look at the team. Some guys whistled teasingly, but everyone secretly wished they had signed up for paddling too.

"Here's your uniforms."

Sanele tossed a bag onto Jacob's bed. The boys gathered round as Jacob handed out each of their uniforms.

"Should we put it on now?" asked Li.

"Of course. Or were you planning on dressing in the van?"

The boys took off their camp shirts and slipped on their new Matagi t-shirts. The shirts were light purple, with bold black lettering. Polynesian tattoo designs circled both sleeves. On the front of the shirt over the chest, was written "Matagi Canoe Club" in stylized letters. On the back of the shirt was the club's large logo: a silhouette of a canoe cresting a wave in a fierce storm of black clouds and lightening bolts.

"Cool!" exclaimed Torch as he admired the logo on Tariq's back.

"Notice anything special on the arm bands?" hinted Sanele. The boys checked the designs on their sleeves and found the letters "BH" stenciled prominently on top of the bands.

"Just a little extra, to remind you that this Blue Horizons team is special," smiled Sanele.

Next they put on their purple and gray lavalavas, which also had the intricate Polynesian patterns striped across them. Sanele showed them how to double up the lavalavas, so they were the proper length for racing.

Lastly they tied the bandanas onto their heads. These were off-white, with tie-dyed purple streaks running through them. On the front of the bandana, in black, were two crossed paddles with "Matagi" centered between the handles.

Jacob had to admit they really looked like a racing team now. He reached into the bag and brought out one of the singlets. It was also light purple and looked similar to the t-shirts, only with a smaller logo and lettering. He started tossing the singlets to the boys.

"Here, we wear these when we race. Don't lose them."

Sanele looked at his watch. "C'mon, grab your overnight bags and load up the van. We don't want to be late for the rules meeting."

The boys went to their bunks and stuffed their singlets into their overnight bags. These were recycled plastic rice sacks, sewn together with a zipper. Sanele had picked up them up cheap at the market. They looked tacky but they did the job, holding the boys' spare clothes, toiletries and towels.

The boys headed across the compound to the van. All the other boys in camp stopped their chores and came to look at the team. Some guys whistled teasingly, but everyone secretly wished they had signed up for paddling too. Jacob and his crew strutted proudly past the envious audience.

Suka called out from the dining room door, "Malo le alo, boys! You go come back with trophy!"

Jacob and the boys laughed and saluted Suka. As the team reached the van and began loading their bags into it, Jacob noticed a large figure approaching, reflected in the van window. Big Sefo!

"I want a word with this maggot," he growled, as he pointed at Jacob.

Sanele gave the big man a stern look. "Be quick, we're in a hurry."

Jacob followed Sefo warily off to the side. He could see the fire in those bloodshot eyes. Sefo turned and put his hand onto Jacob's shoulder.

"Enjoy your two days in town, maggot. Sanele's pulled a lot of strings for this little joyride. But after Saturday, things get back to normal around here . . . "

He leaned closer. Jacob could smell his oily breath. ". . . and that means your ass is mine again, white boy. If you thought I was hard on you before, you ain't seen nothing yet. I may even put your name on the Cooler, because you'll be spending plenty of time in there."

Sefo flashed an evil grin and patted him on the shoulder. "Have fun."

The big man walked away, chuckling to himself. Jacob trudged to the van. The others were already inside. Sanele looked at Jacob. "What did he say?"

Jacob jumped into the van. "He wished me good luck."

As he pulled the door shut, he glanced at Brigham, who nodded discreetly at him. Jacob took a final look at the camp as they drove off. There would be no turning back.

CHAPTER 37

Jacob didn't know what was being said, but he was impressed with the respectfulness of all the paddlers. Folasaitu finished his prayer. "Amen," replied the throng of paddlers in one voice.

"It looks like a rainbow puked!"

Chico shook his head in disbelief as the boys approached the seawall in front of Aggie Grey's hotel. It was a sea of colors as all the canoe clubs gathered together on three sets of concrete steps that descended to the sloshing waters of the harbor. At each set of steps, different clubs had set up base. On the far steps, was a large group of younger paddlers in yellow and red uniforms. On the same steps, in front of them, were a dozen or so huge, muscular men in dark blue uniforms. On the middle steps was a club in blue and white aloha shirts and neoprene shorts. Jacob spotted Markus among them and realized this was the Foelele club. Lower on their steps was another group wearing green and black uniforms.

As they approached the closest steps, the boys saw familiar purple and black colors. Matagi only had half their steps to sit on, as there was a small tent at the bottom, with a table and several older people flipping through piles of forms. Jacob assumed these must be the officials.

Sanele tapped Jacob on the shoulder. "I'm going to watch from the shade of those trees farther down the wall. When you need your things from the van, just come and get me."

Jacob nodded and along with his crew found a spot to sit among the Matagi. Despite all the hustle and bustle, many paddlers stared at the newcomers. The boys tried to act cool, but Jacob knew they were all feeling way out of place.

Jacob scanned the crowd of teams. He noticed the yellow and red club had a banner tied to the step railing. It read, "SamCo Aufaigalu – Wavemakers." The Foelele also had a banner, raised on two long sticks. It had their name: "The Foelele Outrigger Canoe Racing Club of Samoa" with a picture of an eagle with two paddles in its talons. The green and black team also had a small sign; it had a logo of an orca whale, leaping out of the ocean.

Jacob looked among the Matagi. He recognized most of the teams, especially the A2 crew who nodded politely at him. There were some much younger paddlers, which he deduced were the junior teams. They rarely trained on the same days so most of the faces were new to him. He saw Toa talking with one of the younger boys. By the animated hand gestures Toa was using, Jacob guessed they were discussing last minute racing strategy.

"Hey palagi, lookin' good!" said a female voice behind Jacob.

Moana sat down beside him. Her hair was tied back with her bandana, the long mane flowing down her shoulder blades. Jacob admired how her t-shirt was a size too small and highlighted her powerful, curvaceous upper body. She placed her lavalava over her artificial leg.

"Man, it's hot. I hope my leg doesn't melt."

"You're making it even hotter," winked Jacob.

It took her a second to realize he was giving her a flirty compliment. She punched him lightly on the shoulder.

"Cheeky!" she chided, but Jacob was sure she blushed somewhere under that dark tanned skin. He looked over at Toa. How could the guy let a gorgeous, amazing girl like Moana slip away? Why didn't Toa just tell her the truth?

"I haven't seen you since the big fight," noted Moana, "I've been working with my junior girls' squad, so our training times were always opposite."

Jacob nodded, "Yeah, I only saw you girls jogging on the seawall a couple of times."

"Well," she continued, "I just wanted to thank you . . . for jumping into the fight to help me."

"Just sticking up for my teammates," he grinned, "Besides I couldn't let Toa have all the fun."

She shook her head, "I've never seen him go so crazy."

Jacob looked at her, "You've never seen him that jealous before?"

"Jealous?"

Jacob nodded. "A guy like Toa only goes ballistic like that for two reason; someone disrespected his mother . . . or his girl. And I didn't see his mom in the building."

Confusion, maybe even hope, flashed across Moana's eyes.

"Why are you saying that?" she blurted out quietly. "Did Toa say something to you at the police station?"

Jacob felt the urge to tell her everything. But deep down he knew it was Toa who had to be the one that made that decision. He looked away.

"Not really. It's just a hunch I have."

Moana wasn't letting him dodge the question so easily. She nudged him.

"Please, tell me what he . . . "

BEEOOOUUU! A high pitched siren sounded. A tall man at the official's tent held up a bullhorn.

"Attention everyone. We will now begin with our Samoa Outrigger Canoe Association Teuila program."

The crowd went silent. Moana bit her lip, frustrated with having to cut the conversation short.

The official looked at his clipboard.

"We have a big turnout this year. It's great to see such a good mix of teams. We have the up and coming Samoa College Aufaigalu . . . "

The red and yellow team cheered enthusiastically.

" . . . the very fit Fire and Rescue Department's Nomads . . ."

The big men in blue let out a quick cheer.

" . . . the always competitive Tafola Canoe Club . . ."

The green and black team let out a yell.

" . . . the soaring Foelele Outrigger Canoe Racing Club . . ."

Markus and his crews chanted their name three times.

" . . . and the defending Teuila champions, the Matagi Canoe Club."

Toa raised a paddle and they all cheered. Jacob and his boys were caught up in the energy and joined in the cheer.

The official flipped a page over on his clipboard. "Your captains have all gone over the rules with you, so we'll just go over a few reminders. As you know we've been experiencing some large tidal swells in the harbor recently. This will be affecting the far end of the course, especially on starts. Our boat officials will be giving only two warnings during the lines up. If you start over your mark, you will be disqualified. So keep that in mind."

He pointed to a chart board that another official was holding.

"We'll set this up in front of the middle steps. This board will have the schedule of races, as well as the lane assignments and point standings. Teams will receive three points for a first place finish, 2 points for second and 1 point for third place. The club with the most points at the end of racing tomorrow will be our champions."

He checked his clipboard. "All team lists have been entered and no changes may now be made. The only exception is the V12 races, where teams can be formed from all available paddlers, as long as they are on an existing team list."

He made one more quick check of his list.

"That's all for now, so we'll begin with our junior heats, after our Association Patron Folasaitu Joe Annandale has led us in a prayer."

All the paddlers stood up silently as a tall man stepped forward. He spoke loudly and clearly in Samoan. Jacob didn't know what was being said, but he was impressed with the respectfulness of all the paddlers. Folasaitu finished his prayer. "Amen," replied the throng of paddlers in one voice.

The other official picked up his bullhorn again. "Junior girls, to your canoes please, for the 500 meters heat."

Moana turned to Jacob. "I've got to coach my girls. Can we talk later?"

Jacob shrugged, "Sure."

She moved off with the Matagi junior girl's squad. Jacob turned his attention back to his crew. The boys were taking in all the activity around them. Chico and Li ogled some of the Tafola girls, who giggled at them. Torch and Tariq were talking with the A2 boys about the swells the official had mentioned.

Shaggy was leaning against the railing, calmly catching some sunshine and eating a banana someone had given him. Brigham slipped over next to Jacob.

"Damn, that's going to be a long swim now."

Jacob didn't understand. "Swim? Where?"

"Are you blind? Look at the harbor!"

Jacob scanned the harbor. He noticed several yellow buoys, which marked the lanes for the canoes. There were several on the distant end of the harbor too. What was Brigham going on about? Then he looked to the right side of the harbor and realized the problem. The yachts had all moved. In order to run the races, the yachts had to re-anchor closer to the wharf. The Swedes yacht was now 500 meters farther from its original position. Jacob and Brigham were either going to have to swim much farther; or swing around on land and try to swim from the wharf side. But that would mean more risk of being spotted under the streetlights along the seawall, as well as crossing over, or under, the bridge that crossed the river mouth adjacent to Aggie's.

"This is not good," mumbled Brigham.

CHAPTER 38

The canoes lined up and someone raised a white flag on the officials' boat. There were a few moments of calm, then the white flag dropped and a green flag shot up. The wet paddle blades of the competitors reflected flashes of sunlight as they charged ahead. The race was on.

"I'm going to do a little recon."

Brigham moved down the seawall, trying to get a better idea of the distance to the Swedes' yacht. Jacob was also considering their escape options when he noticed several canoes being paddled out from the river mouth. It was the junior girl's squads making for the far end of the harbor and the start line.

A canopied fishing boat roared to life farther down the shoreline and pulled up to the steps in front of the officials' tent. Two men and a woman hopped onto its bow and it too headed for the start line.

Moana returned and joined her women's team, who had binoculars and were watching the junior girls paddle out. Jacob looked across to the other clubs, who likewise watched their junior squads through binoculars.

Jacob and the others contented themselves with squinting and trying to figure out which club was in what lane. There were five canoes. Jacob could tell that the red and yellow Aufaigalu had two squads, making up for the lack of a crew from the all-male Nomads.

The canoes lined up and someone raised a white flag on the officials' boat. There were a few moments of calm, then the white flag dropped and a green flag shot up. The wet paddle blades of the competitors reflected flashes of sunlight as they charged ahead. The race was on.

The canoes clawed their way toward shore. The official's boat motored ahead of them and took up a position at the end line. As the canoes reached the halfway point, the clubs began yelling and urging them on. Moana and her girls led the Matagi cheering section. Jacob and his boys found themselves screaming along with others. The hysteria was infectious.

On the water it looked like the Aufaigalu had established a clear lead, followed by Tafola, Matagi and Foelele. The second Aufaigalu team was a canoe length behind Foelele. As the canoes hit the last 50 meters to the finish line, everyone on the steps shouted even louder.

"Alo!"

"Faamalosi!"

"Powa!"

"Faster," screamed Torch.

The Aufaigalu girls crossed the line first, letting out excited squeals of excitement. Their supporters on the steps let out a whoop. The Tafola girls slid past the buoy, a half canoe length ahead of the Matagi girls. Foelele just edged out the second Aufaigalu for fourth place. Jacob looked over at Markus, who was breathing a sigh of relief that his squad hadn't come last.

Jacob stepped over beside Moana.

"They did good, coach!"

She shook her head angrily. "They waited too long to pick up the pace!"

Jacob was surprised at her intensity.

"It's just a heat, right?" asked Jacob. "They qualified for the final."

"Yeah, the top four are in. But they can do much better."

Jacob suddenly realized how serious these races must be. If Moana was this intense over a junior girls heat, he could only imagine what the men's finals would be like.

The official appeared with the bullhorn, "Junior boys, 500 meters, to your canoes please."

Toa barked some encouragement to his young crew and they hustled down the rocks and into the chest-high water. The junior girls hopped into the water, allowing the boys to jump into the canoe and paddle out.

As the Foelele junior girls climbed out of the water and onto their steps, the boys from all the clubs stared at them. The Foelele girls wore tight, tight spandex style shorts, with a similar type of sports bra. The water glistened off their uniforms, highlighting every curve, every bump. The girls strutted sexily up the steps and adjusted their long blonde-streaked hair teasingly, knowing they had an audience.

Moana had a disgusted look on her face.

"Did they come here to paddle, or model?"

Jacob had to admit, the girls were dressed more for show than sport. But he wasn't sure why that bothered Moana.

"What's the big deal?" he asked her.

"It shows they're only here to flirt and party. They'd rather lose looking good, than win. No wonder our sport isn't taken seriously."

Jacob smiled at her. "You sound a lot like Toa."

"Ha ha, very funny," she replied sarcastically.

The Matagi junior girls, dripping wet, sat down on the steps. Moana limped over and launched into an impromptu coaching session. Unlike the image conscious Foelele girls, the Matagi girls were more interested in improving their performance and listened intently to Moana.

Jacob stepped down to where Toa was observing through the binoculars.

"Markus' junior boys are going to be tough to beat," Toa grunted.

"They're all seventeen." Jacob nodded then realized something.

"Seventeen? I'm seventeen! I think all my guys are. How come my team can't paddle as juniors?"

Toa continued scanning the race course. "You can't, you turn eighteen this year. I already checked that with Sanele. Two of your boys, the tall kid and your spare, turn eighteen in December. Too bad, you would have had a better chance."

"Thanks for the vote of confidence," huffed Jacob.

"Don't worry; we won't need the points anyway. Markus can't beat my A1 team, and his women's team can't beat Moana. Even if they scoop some early points in the junior races, we've got him beat."

"What about the other clubs?" asked Jacob. "They looked good in that first race."

Toa nodded, "Yeah those SamCo kids aren't bad. And Tafola has improved since the last regatta. But SamCo only has junior teams and Tafola has a weak men's team. The Nomads are good, but they're only two men's teams. So for overall points it's really just between Foelele and us. Which is why I could afford to let you boys paddle in the 1500."

"Hey, we earned that spot in the 1500, remember?"

Toa grinned, "Yeah, but in the weeks after I agreed to it. Or are you going to say luck had nothing to do with your beating my A2's that first time?"

"No comment."

In the harbor the green flag went up on the officials' boat.

"Here we go," said Toa.

The pace of this race was noticeably faster than the girls'. The officials' boat had to zip ahead, as the five canoes slashed toward the shore. At the halfway point Foelele's juniors were in the lead, followed by Matagi, Tafola and the two Aufaigalu squads. The clubs cheered on their paddlers.

Suddenly, with 100 meters to go, the Foelele boys surged ahead. The Matagi boys found themselves being challenged for second by Tafola and one of the Aufaigalu canoes. At the finish line it wasn't even close, the Foelele canoe sped in, sending Markus and the others into a victory chant.

It was hard to be sure who crossed next, Tafola or Aufaigalu, but Matagi was clearly half a length behind both . The other SamCo canoe finished last.

Toa made a 'tsk,tsk' sound. The Matagi crews looked disappointed.

"They didn't pace themselves," exclaimed Toa. "They choked up. I keep telling them to breathe, save it for the last 50 meters. If they paddle like that in the 1500, they'll run out gas after the first turn."

The official came out again.

"Junior girls, 1500 meters, make your way out to the starting line."

Moana huddled close with her junior squad and gave them a last minute Samoan pep talk.

Then they chanted "Matagi" and headed for the water.

Jacob noticed heads turning toward the middle steps. The Foelele junior girls were slinking their way down to the water. They bent over provocatively at the bottom step, showing off their smooth race shorts, and dove in.

Jacob looked at Toa. "What do you think of that?"

Toa shrugged. "Good looking girls, too bad they can't paddle."

As the junior boys returned to the steps, Toa gathered them together and berated them for not listening to him. Jacob decided to stand beside Moana again for the girls' race. He found her leaning against the railing, taking the weight off her artificial leg.

"You okay?" he asked her.

"Just a little sore. I suppose you and Toa were discussing the Foelele girls' butts?"

Jacob feigned a shocked look. "Who? Us?"

She rolled her eyes. "Yeah right. Well, they're going to get those butts kicked in this race."

"You think so?" teased Jacob.

She just smiled and looked through her binoculars.

The green flag was up and the canoe hurdled forward. The pace was much slower, the teams needing to pace themselves for a much longer haul. As they reached the end line, the canoes began their turns around the yellow buoys. Jacob could see the young steerers heaving with all their might, trying to swing the back ends of the canoes around. The clubs cheered their squads on. This time Matagi and Aufaigalu seemed to be the leaders, with the other canoes just a length or two behind.

The canoes headed back toward the far end, the officials' boat following them on the side. After a minute, Moana handed Jacob the binoculars.

"See, I told ya."

As the canoes turned around the far ends' buoys, it was obvious the Foelele girls were in trouble. They were still a good 50 meters from their buoy, but the other canoes had already made their turns and were charging back on the last leg.

The clubs screamed their girls on down the stretch. The officials' boat chugged ahead and set up on the line. The distances between the canoes were greater in this race. Aufaigalu came in first, followed by Matagi and Tafola. The other Aufaigalu team took fourth. Nearly 100 meters behind them lagged the Foelele girls. The canoe finally crossed the line, the girls hunched over and gasping for air.

"Wow!" Jacob handed the binoculars back to Moana, "How did you know they'd be so wiped?"

Moana smirked. "They're party girls remember, I've even seen them smoking after their trainings. As athletes, they're total fakes."

Jacob had to agree. The Foelele girls might be hot out of the water, but on it they just looked foolish. He vowed his crew wouldn't end up like that. Then he remembered, he was supposed to be escaping tonight!

"Junior boys, 1500 meters, this is the last race today."

The official's bullhorn barely registered with Jacob. He sat down along the opposite railing and thought about his situation. He'd really been hooked by the racing bug. The excitement of watching the first three heats had him eager to get out on the water and race too. He wanted to show everyone that his crew could paddle.

The racing wasn't just an excuse to camp anymore. Jacob realized he was actually enjoying the experience. This was the biggest sporting event he'd ever been involved with, certainly the most intense. He knew by looking at the faces of his BH crew that they felt the same. Except for Brigham, who was as focused as always on their escape.

Jacob heard the clubs cheering as the canoes made their first turns. He felt the raw energy of the race. Even Shaggy was jumping up and down, yelling, "Like, paddle harder."

Jacob looked at Moana and Toa. This regatta meant so much to them. How could Jacob disrespect them by walking away from it? But Toa did admit that he didn't need them in the long run. Yet what about his boys . . . they were itching to paddle.

The cheering became louder and louder. Jacob snapped back to the moment. He stood up and saw the junior squads were all very close. What a finish this would be! The juniors made their last push for the line.

The Foelele boys edged out Aufaigalu, who in turn inched in ahead of

Matagi. Tafola just squeaked in ahead of the Aufaigalu's second canoe.

Torch ran over to Jacob.

"Great race! Think we'll be in a close one like that?"

"Uh, maybe."

With the races done for the day, and the sun beginning to set, the clubs paddled their canoes back to their racks and everyone packed up their stuff. Toa called for his paddlers' attention.

"Okay, everybody can head for the hall. Bring everything you need, because curfew is 6:30 tonight. No exceptions. Let's go."

The Matagi began walking down the street. Jacob and his crew found Sanele and grabbed their bags from the van. Sanele closed the van's side door.

"I'm going to be staying at the house just next to the Pastor's. So if you need anything; that's where you can find me. Other than that, I hope you boys enjoy the experience of camping with Samoans. Remember your manners and make sure you pitch in. I'll see you in the morning."

The boys hustled to catch up with the other Matagi paddlers as they turned down a dirt road beside the church. Brigham grabbed Jacob and motioned for him to hang back a bit so they could talk alone.

"I think we can make it to the bridge and then slip under and swim along the rocks towards the wharf side. When we get more or less even with the yacht, we can swim directly out. It's still a good 200 yards or so, but that's as close as we can get without being exposed by those streetlights along the seawall. What do you think?"

Jacob nodded. "Whatever you say."

Brigham nudged him. "C'mon man, show a little enthusiasm. We're a few hours away from freedom. Just imagine the look on Big Sefo when he hears you're gone."

Jacob thought back to Sefo's threats before they had left the camp. It reminded him of why he had no choice; he had to escape with Brigham. If they missed this chance, Jacob would be spending plenty of nights in the Cooler regretting it. Maybe someday the others would understand that.

CHAPTER 39

Jacob sat against the wall, listening to Toa's racing tales. He caught a flash of something in the corner of his eye. In the back of the kitchen, Moana waved to him to come in. He nonchalantly got up, stretched and wandered into the kitchen. She leaned against the wall.

Camping with the whole club wasn't as chaotic as Jacob thought it would be. It was actually pretty well organized. Everyone chipped in with the cooking -the boys peeling bananas and taro, the girls frying up cans of herring with onions and greens. Jacob and his crew helped out by cutting chunks of papaya and pineapple for dessert.

When the food was almost ready, Toa gathered the teams in the big open hall. They sat in a circle and did their evening prayers. They sang a hymn then Moana read a few verses from the Bible. Toa finished with a long prayer in Samoan.

As soon as everyone had said "Amen", Toa motioned toward the kitchen.

"Let's eat."

The hungry paddlers lined up to grab their high rimmed plates and spoons. One of the girls dished out the herring, while one of the boys used his hands to toss hot boiled banana and taro onto the plates. The helpings were huge, almost overloading the plates.

Everyone went back into the hall and sat down to eat. Jacob listened to the Samoan kids slurping and smacking as they ate. Even Moana, who sat on a chair because of her leg, shoveled the food eagerly into her mouth. At one time Jacob might have found the very audible eating noises disgusting, but not now. He just smiled as he stuffed a handful of herring and banana into his mouth, grease dribbling down his chin. He wished someone had given this recipe to Suka.

When everyone had finished supper, there was another burst of activity as dishes were washed and more mats were carried into the hall, along with blankets. The mats and blankets were spread out along the walls. Mosquito coils were set up on empty pop bottles and lit.

With the kitchen duties complete, everyone went into the hall to pick a sleeping spot. The girls all went to the right side, the boys to the left. Everyone placed their bags onto a mat and made themselves comfortable. Several people gathered around and began playing cards. One of the boys brought out a guitar and softly strummed out a tune.

One of the A2 boys invited Jacob's crew to join them in a card game. It was a game they called "kaisu", which the BH boys soon discovered meant "hit the nose". It was a game that involved the losing players being struck on the nose with their remaining cards by the winners. Naturally the newcomers were easy victims and the game soon had the Samoans laughing hysterically as the bad boys were one by one soundly whacked on their noses.

Jacob had been smart enough to stay out of it, but Moana finally forced him to play a few hands. It wasn't long before Jacob's nose felt the sting of a quarter of the deck. Moana almost fell over, she was laughing so hard.

As the evening wore on the energy level dropped. It had been a long day, especially for the junior teams. They were soon readying themselves for bed:

brushing their teeth, making a final trip to the outside toilet, settling in under their sheets. The guitar player yawned and put his instrument away.

In the corner Toa was recounting stories of past regattas to his boys, along with Torch, Tariq and Li. Chico and Shaggy were zonked out on their mats. Brigham, looking bored, laid on his side and read a week old newspaper.

Jacob sat against the wall, listening to Toa's racing tales. He caught a flash of something in the corner of his eye. In the back of the kitchen, Moana waved to him to come in. He nonchalantly got up, stretched and wandered into the kitchen. She leaned against the wall.

"What's up?" asked Jacob.

"You know what's up. I've been waiting all evening for a chance to talk to you alone. I want to know what Toa told you."

"About what?"

"You made it sound like he still has feelings for me. Is that true?"

"Look Moana, ask him yourself? Why can't you two just talk?"

She stared at the floor.

"He has to make the first step. He owes it to me."

Jacob clenched his fist in frustration.

"Don't you think this stubbornness has gone on long enough?"

She nodded, "But it won't for much longer."

Jacob detected something in her voice.

"What do you mean by that?"

She shifted her position and looked at him. "If I tell you, do swear you won't tell anyone, especially any of the team?"

Not again, he thought. These people are full of secrets.

"Yes, I swear," he agreed.

She double-checked to see if anyone was around.

"I'm leaving for New Zealand this Wednesday," she said softly.

It took a second for this to register with Jacob. "For a holiday?"

"No. My uncle's wife has family there. They want me to come and help baby-sit the kids because the parents both work. They're paying for my airfare and everything."

"But you said you wanted to study commerce. Why move now?"

She shrugged. "I could use a fresh start. I mean New Zealand might be just what I need. What's keeping me here, anyway?"

He could tell by her voice that there was one person that could keep her here. But that person was as bullheaded as she was, and by the time Toa realized he was going to lose Moana, she'd be gone. Jacob wondered if he should tell her Toa's secret. But what if he did and she went to Toa and confronted him? Knowing these two, it might just lead to a bigger fight and disrupt the whole camp. That in turn could jeopardize the escape.

But he liked Toa and Moana and he knew in his heart that they still loved each other. He was the only one who had been trusted with both their secrets. If he bailed on them, they probably would never get back together.

Moana limped back toward the hall. He wanted to scream at her, "Wait, there's something you need to know", but he just stood there frozen with indecision. Before he could do anything else, the main lights were being shut off.

"Lights out," he heard Toa say quietly. He slipped back into the hall. Everyone had gone to their mats. The sound of snoring was already beginning.

Jacob lay down on the mat that was next to Brigham. Brigham leaned towards him.

"We'll wait an hour or two," he whispered, "to make sure everyone's asleep. Then it's go time."

Jacob nodded. No turning back now.

CHAPTER 40

They spun around to find a pack of dogs quickly creeping up behind them. Brigham reached into his shorts' pocket and pulled out the brown paper package and opened it. Jacob winced as the smell of the exposed sausages wafted into the air. The dogs stopped in their tracks, saliva dripped from their mouths.

The two hours seemed like twelve to Jacob. He listened to the other paddlers snoring, to the dogs barking outside; he even listened to the sound of a drunk singing somewhere on the main road. His mind wouldn't settle. He imagined what would happen to Sanele when it was discovered that two of his students had escaped. He pictured Toa finding out that Moana had left for New Zealand. He visualized her crying on a plane, heading for her new life in New Zealand. He saw the faces of his teammates, shocked and betrayed by their captain's disappearance. He even thought about his parents and how they would freak out when they heard he was missing.

Then the face of Big Sefo flashed before his mind's eye. Hatred boiled up in Jacob, obliterating the images of all the others. His one and only consolation was knowing that he would have the last laugh on the maniacal thug.

Finally, he felt Brigham tapping him on the shoulder. The two of them rose silently and tiptoed toward the kitchen. Jacob didn't see the foot sticking out from the mat closest to the kitchen door. Jacob bumped the foot and the owner snorted. It was Torch.

"Where you going?" he mumbled groggily.

Jacob dipped down instantly and hushed him.

"Just have to pee. Go back to sleep."

Torch, still half-asleep, smiled and closed his eyes.

Brigham scanned the room, but no one else had awoken. Both he and Jacob breathed easier and continued into the kitchen. They kept walking carefully and opened the back door and slipped outside. They placed their sandals on the ground and slid their feet into them. They walked slowly along the hedge line, ducking under a clothesline and onto a path. They soon were several meters from the hall, but they still kept a calm pace . . . though their hearts were racing.

They followed the path and were soon in the shadows of the church walls. The road was just ahead. They were almost there.

GRRRRRRRR.

They spun around to find a pack of dogs quickly creeping up behind them. Brigham reached into his shorts' pocket and pulled out the brown paper package and opened it. Jacob winced as the smell of the exposed sausages wafted into the air. The dogs stopped in their tracks, saliva dripped from their mouths.

Brigham chucked the package over the hedge to the right. The dogs chased after it, crashing through the hedge. The boys ran quickly to the road, hearing the sound of the dogs growling over the meat.

Jacob checked the road. There was no one around. There were cars, but farther in town. They had plenty of time. They trotted across the road and walked quickly toward the bridge. They hopped over the railing and onto the rocks that lead to the riverbank under the bridge. They were about to jump down further when they heard voices under the bridge. A man laughed, a woman giggled.

Brigham cursed silently. He pointed toward the concrete steps back to their left. They picked their way carefully over the rocks to the steps and hunched down on the step closest to the water. The moon was nestled behind the clouds, as they had hoped.

"Well, thanks to Romeo and Juliet we can't go by the bridge," whispered Brigham.

Jacob wrinkled his nose. "Wash your hands. Those sausages stink."

Brigham grinned. "They should, they've been on the bottom of my bag all day. Good thing I brought them, though."

Jacob looked out over the harbor. The sea was calm, but very dark. He shivered as he wondered what might be swimming in those inky depths. "So, what's the plan?" he asked.

"We have no choice. We swim it from here."

"It's a long way . . . in the dark."

Brigham scanned the water and nodded.

"We can make it."

They took off their t-shirts and sandals. Jacob stared at the water then turned to Brigham. "I can't do it."

Brigham slapped him on the back. "Sure you can. We'll stick together. Just don't think about it."

"That's not it. This isn't right."

Brigham gave him a confused look.

"What are you talking about? We're here! You can't turn back now!"

"As long as I'm not on that yacht, I can still turn around."

Brigham couldn't believe his ears. "Have you lost your mind? For a month this is what we've been working for. All those trainings, everything. How can you just throw that away?"

"Exactly! How can I throw that all away? Don't you see, we wanted to escape because we hated this place. But I don't hate it anymore, because of everything we went through. These races, these people, mean something now. Didn't you feel that at the dance competition? We were a team."

"Okay, so we did some decent male bonding. That doesn't change the fact that Blue Horizons is run by a 300 pound psycho, who can't wait to make our lives miserable. Did you forget about that?"

"I know, but it's also a place with a guy like Sanele . . . a guy who took a chance on us and now we're stabbing him in the back. Sanele, the team, Toa, all of them. I'd rather suffer Big Sefo's rage than let those guys down."

Brigham sat down on the step and rubbed his forehead. Jacob crouched beside him. "Let's go back."

"No," growled Brigham angrily. "I've been here nine months. I can't take it anymore."

Jacob thought for a second. "Toa told me your birthday is in December. Is that true?"

"Yeah, so?"

"Well, don't they have to send you home when you're eighteen . . . you'll be an adult then, right?"

"Yeah, me and Shaggy both go home at New Year's."

"So, if you only have three more months, why so desperate to escape?"

"I don't want them to think they won."

"Who?"

"My folks. Back home, whenever they got on my case, I used to run away. They always found me, eventually. Utah's a tough place to hide. They told me when they sent me here that this was one place I'd never run away from."

"But when you go back in January you can go wherever you want, do whatever you want."

Brigham held up his hand. "That's not the point. They've controlled me my entire life. When I wanted to go skateboarding or hang at the mall, they wouldn't let me. When I dated a girl that wasn't Mormon, they forced me to break up with her. When I told them I didn't want to do my two year missionary stint, they started to sending me to a Mormon shrink. They tried to brainwash me."

Jacob had never seen Brigham open up like this.

"I started doing drugs, shoplifting, running away, anything to fight back. I wanted them to hurt, like they hurt me."

Jacob patted him on the back. "I know how you feel. My parents acted like my life was theirs to live, not mine. They never trusted me about anything. Maybe that's why I don't want to leave here. I've accomplished something that isn't theirs to mess with. It's mine." He tossed a pebble into the water.

"Sanele trusted me with this team. I don't want to let down the one person who ever had that kind of faith in me. I just can't."

Brigham sighed. "I had a feeling you were going to do this. Well, you can stay, but I'm going."

"Please don't."

"Look, I'm sorry if this screws up your races. Maybe Sanele will let you guys paddle anyway. You only need six paddlers."

"I don't care about that. You and I have been a team since the first day I got here. If you leave, it won't be the same. Don't you see, you're just running away from your parents again. Only this time you're really only hurting yourself."

Brigham was silent for a long moment, then turned and offered Jacob his hand. "You're a good man, but we're different people. I have to do this."

Jacob shook his hand. "Good luck. Send me a postcard from Oz."

Brigham slipped into the water. Jacob watched for a minute as his friend swam out into the deep water, then he turned and snuck back toward the hall. He was lucky, the street was empty and the dogs were nowhere to be seen. He tiptoed into the kitchen and back to his mat.

He looked over at Brigham's empty mat and wondered how he was going to explain it to the others. He had to buy Brigham time, but Sanele would know Jacob was lying. What if he pulled them out of the regatta? He'd have to be honest with Sanele, he'd understand. But what would Sefo do when he found out? Jacob just knew he'd be taking the fall for this, one way or another.

He rolled over on his side. It was beginning to look like a no-win situation as far as he was concerned. Maybe he should have gone with Brigham, after all. He reflected on that for a minute then closed his eyes. No, he had made the right decision. Even if he had to spend a week in the Cooler, at least his conscience was clean. He said a quick prayer, asking God to help Brigham find his way in the dark, deep waters.

CHAPTER 41

Jacob went rigid with anger. To hell with promises, he fumed. He had sacrificed everything coming back last night. He was staring at a month in the Cooler and it wasn't going to go to waste, in spite of this lunkhead's stubbornness.

"Everybody up!"

Jacob opened his eyes sleepily. In the dull half-light of the hall he could see the others sitting up and stretching groggily. Jacob sat up and looked behind him to the louver windows. Outside there was barely a hint of daybreak in the sky. He noticed Torch was also up, stretching his neck and back. Torch looked at Chico in the mat next to him, still sound asleep. He gave him a good shake.

"Wake up, Sleeping Beauty, we've got races to win!"

The hall was soon bustling with activity as campers began folding blankets, rolling up mats and trekking back and forth to the toilet. In the commotion, no one noticed Jacob cleaning up Brigham's mat and rolling it up.

Several of the Samoan boys got busy in the kitchen preparing large kettles of hot cocoa. Moana and some of the girls put on their sandals, opened the big front doors and went outside. They walked up the path to the road. Toa went and stood in the door's frame and stretched. Jacob seized the opportunity. He walked over to Toa, determined to talk some sense into him.

"Where are they going?" he asked nonchalantly.

Toa acted as if he hadn't even noticed Moana and the girls.

"What? Oh, the girls. They're going to get fresh bread for breakfast."

Toa continued stretching. Jacob leaned against the frame. The sky was beginning to turn blue with a tinge of orange. It looked like it was going to be a beautiful day.

"You know if you don't do something soon, you're going to lose her," Jacob blurted out, surprising both Toa and himself with the blunt remark.

Toa hesitated for a moment then returned to his stretching.

"Do I look worried?" he said defiantly.

Jacob tapped his head against the frame in frustration. What would it take to wake this mule up? He wanted to tell Toa about Moana's leaving, but he had promised her he wouldn't.

"Toa, if you don't tell her the truth now, you may never get the chance again until it's too late."

Toa shot him an annoyed look. "Look, I've got races to worry about. Quit bothering me with your woman's talk. Why don't you mind your own business for a change!"

Jacob went rigid with anger. To hell with promises, he fumed. He had sacrificed everything coming back last night. He was staring at a month in the Cooler and it wasn't going to go to waste, in spite of this lunkhead's stubbornness. He leaned close to Toa.

"All right, I'll mind my own business, tough guy, but let me just tell you one more thing. That girl, who you pretend not to love anymore, is moving to New Zealand on Wednesday."

Jacob glared at him for dramatic effect then stormed back into the hall. When he looked back, Toa was gone. Jacob had a hunch the news would have one of two effects on Toa. He'd either come to his senses and talk to Moana, or he'd bury it angrily and further harden his heart. Either way, the final outcome was in Toa's hands now.

Jacob didn't have time to worry about it anymore, as he had spotted Li and Tariq rooting inside Brigham's bag. He quickly strode over to them.

"Hey, guys, what are you doing in Brigham's bag?" he asked.

They both frowned. "Something stinks in there," griped Li.

"Yeah, he should throw it out. Where he is he anyway?"

Jacob responded. "Must be outside somewhere. I'll take care of it."

He reached to the bottom of the bag and found a smaller plastic grocery bag. It had blood caked inside it. Brigham must have had the sausages wrapped in it. It reeked.

"Get me another bag," gagged Jacob.

Tariq quickly handed him another small bag and Jacob stuffed the soiled one inside it and tied it tight.

"Toss that into the big can in the back," he said as he handed it to Li. "I gotta wash my hands."

Jacob went into the kitchen and washed his hands in the sink. As he dried them, Moana and the girls returned with several large bags of hot, fresh bread, tubs of margarine and jam. They cut the loaves in half, lengthways, slapped on the margarine and jam then placed the halves together again. Each loaf was then cut once in half, widthwise. One by one everyone was given their half loaf, along with a steaming cup of sweet cocoa and two ripe bananas.

Jacob and his crew sat down to eat. Torch tore into his bread hungrily and washed the piece down with his hot cocoa.

"Breakfast of champions."

"Like, if only I had some peanut butter and hot peppers to go with it," said Shaggy. The others looked at him as if he was nuts.

"Loading up for a busy day, boys?"

Sanele strolled into the hall from the kitchen. The boys nodded as they chewed on their food. Jacob's heart beat faster. He'd hoped this confrontation would have happened later in the morning. He quickly downed his cocoa and got up to get more. Maybe with more movement, Sanele wouldn't notice Brigham's absence yet.

"Where's Brigham?" asked Sanele curiously. Jacob almost tripped.

"I think he must be in the bathroom," blurted Jacob a little too quickly.

He saw Sanele give him a look. Jacob cursed himself as he poured another cup of cocoa. Stay cool, he thought. He went back and sat down.

"Everyone get a good sleep last night?" asked Sanele.

"Not bad," replied Tariq. "My back's stiff from the floor, though."

The other boys nodded in agreement.

"How about you, Jacob?"

Jacob's heart beat wildly again. Why was he singling him out, wondered Jacob. Does he suspect something?

"Slept like a baby, sir."

Sanele smiled. "Good. So the dogs weren't a problem?"

Jacob almost choked on his cocoa. How did he know about the dogs? Wait, maybe he didn't. "You mean the constant barking?"

"Yes, the dogs here in town are terrible at night. They didn't keep you up with their yapping?"

The boys shook their heads.

"You're lucky; they must have been roaming elsewhere last night."

Jacob wasn't sure if Sanele was baiting him, or maybe paranoia was setting in. Sanele looked around the room, then back to the boys.

"How long has Brigham been in the bathroom? Is he all right?"

The boys looked at each other and shrugged.

"Actually I haven't seen him all morning," noted Torch.

"Yeah, me either," added Chico.

Jacob's heart was pounding like a drum.

"Maybe he's in the shower, trying to get that smell off?" laughed Tariq.

"What smell?" asked Sanele.

"He had raw meat in his bag and it must have gone bad," explained Li. "Jacob found it and we threw it out."

Sanele was beginning to look concerned. He looked at Jacob.

"Why would he have raw meat in his bag?"

Jacob shrugged. "Beats me."

Sanele's suspicion was growing, Jacob could feel it.

"Have any of you seen Brigham this morning?" he asked them, though he looked directly at Jacob.

Sweat began to form on Jacob's hands. He knew he couldn't lie to Sanele, but technically he had seen Brigham this morning, albeit it around 1:00 am in the harbor. "Yeah, I saw him."

"Well, where is he then?" pressed Sanele.

Jacob took a long sip from his cup, trying to stall long enough to think of how to reply. "He's outside," he responded truthfully. "Maybe in the shower."

He could be in the shower on the yacht, Jacob reasoned to himself. Or maybe in a rain shower at sea. He knew he was running out of half-truths to tell. Sanele continued to watch Jacob suspiciously.

"Jacob," Sanele said with a very serious tone, "where is Brigham?"

Jacob stared at the floor; he couldn't face Sanele. He was about to spill the truth, when someone walked through the kitchen door.

"Looking for me sir?"

Jacob's head snapped up. There, in a lavalava and drying his hair with a towel, was Brigham!

CHAPTER 42

"I actually made it. I swam the whole damn way. I haven't been so friggin' scared in all my life. I was expecting a shark to take a bite out of me with every stroke . . ."

It took all the self-control Jacob could muster to not jump up and lift his friend into the air with a bear hug. Instead he acted like he knew Brigham had been in the shower all along. Sanele seemed appeased, if still a little confused.

"Kind of early for a shower, isn't it?"

Brigham nodded, "Yeah, I know but I was up half the night with terrible diarrhea and the sweats. I felt pretty scummy this morning, Needed a shower."

Sanele looked concerned. "How do you feel now?"

Brigham patted his stomach. "Much better. I think it was food poisoning. While we were watching the races one of the Samoan guys offered me a piece of barbecued chicken. I guess it wasn't fully cooked."

Jacob picked up on the cue.

"That explains the smell in your bag."

Brigham slapped his forehead dramatically. "That's right, I left the wrapper in my bag. Man, I don't think I'll be able to eat chicken for a month!"

Sanele considered the explanation and shrugged.

"Well, be careful what you eat from now on. Contaminated meat can put you in the hospital."

The boys finished off their breakfast and followed the lead of the others and changed into their paddling uniforms. Jacob was bursting with curiosity . . . he was dying to know what had happened to Brigham between the time that they'd said goodbye until the moment he'd stepped through the kitchen door.

"Let's go!" came the command from the front doors. It was Toa. He was in his uniform and had a grim look on his face. Jacob had completely forgotten about Toa. Had he confronted Moana about her leaving? Whatever had transpired, Toa looked like a man with a crushing weight around his neck.

The Matagi teams hustled out the hall doors and up the path to road. Sanele walked along with the Blue Horizon squad. Brigham and Jacob hung back, trying to get a chance to talk privately. As the others pulled ahead a few yards, they got their chance.

"Surprised to see me?" grinned Brigham.

"Hell, yes! What happened?"

"You won't believe it."

"Try me."

"I actually made it. I swam the whole damn way. I haven't been so friggin' scared in all my life. I was expecting a shark to take a bite out of me with every stroke. It took forever to reach the yacht. The Swedes had a rope ladder on the side waiting for me and I climbed up. I found them below deck, getting ready to sail. I'm pretty sure they were stoned."

They crossed the road to the seawall. Jacob glanced out into the harbor. The Swedes yacht was nowhere to be seen. "So they did go?"

"Oh yeah, they were ready to move on all right."

"But you weren't?"

Brigham laughed softly. "I thought I was. But when I climbed out of that water, I felt . . . free. Not just free from the camp, free from them."

"Your folks?"

"Yeah. I left all that stuff behind, in that black water. It was an amazing feeling. I must have been laughing out loud or something, because the Swedes came up and gave me a weird look. I realized that I didn't need to go with them anymore. So I thanked them and . . . dove in and swam back."

Jacob stopped walking and grabbed his arm, "You're full of . . . "

"I'm serious!" Brigham insisted. "I just dove in and swam back."

"But you just said it scared the hell out of you!"

"It did, the first time. On the way back I wasn't scared at all. Just excited. I knew that everything was going to be okay. No matter what happened here or back home, I was in control of my own life."

"Then where were you the rest of the night?"

"When I got to the steps, the moon had just come out from behind the clouds. It was so cool. I lay down on the steps and watched the moon for awhile. The next thing I knew the sun was coming up. I went back up to the road and then snuck to the hall. I saw Sanele going in, just as I came around the back way. I heard him ask about me and knew he'd smell the salt water on me. I grabbed a towel off the line and jumped in the shower. I was coming in and I heard you telling him I was in the shower. I figured you'd seen me and set that up, but when I saw the look on your face . . . I realized we'd just gotten lucky. But I had to make that bar-b-que chicken story up pretty quick."

Jacob shook his head in amazement.

"I still can't believe you're here," he said.

"Neither can I!" laughed Brigham.

Jacob patted him on the back. "Well, I'm damn glad you are. I guess I owe you one."

"Are you kidding? I'm the one who owes you."

"Me? What did I do?"

"You led the way, buddy, you led the way."

They reached the main steps in front of Aggies. The other clubs were also arriving. Jacob looked at Brigham.

"I'll try to sub you in if we make it past our heat."

Brigham smiled and shook his head. "I'm more than happy to be the team cheerleader. This is their day. I got my exercise last night. I'm looking forward to just kicking back and chillin' out. Besides, somebody has to keep the girls company when you studs are busy racing."

Jacob laughed and playfully punched him on the shoulder. "Good to have you back bro."

"Good to be back. Now let's kick some tires and light some fires!"

Torch overheard Brigham. "That's how I got here, remember!"

The team laughed as they grabbed a spot on the steps. Jacob saw Toa stretching with his crew. He still had a pained look on his face and kept glancing over at Moana. She was busy going over race plans with her girls. She looked focused and ready to race, unlike Toa who was obviously distracted.

He still hasn't talked to her, thought Jacob. The stubborn ox was going to let her slip away. Jacob was ready to give up; Toa was hopeless. But then he looked at Brigham, joking around with the guys. Jacob had completely given up hope in ever seeing Brigham again, and yet here he was, sitting right in front of him. If Brigham could have a change of heart, maybe there was still hope for Toa.

The green flag shot up! The canoes began their charge. Right from the first dip of the blades, this race had the fastest pace Jacob had seen yet. It seemed like only seconds and the canoes were nearly halfway home. The paddle blades glinted in the sunlight as they churned through the sea.

"I wish we raced first, instead of sixth!"

Torch looked at the race schedule that had just been posted on the big board. The rest of the crew gathered around. Jacob looked over their shoulders. There would be two Men's 500 meters heats, two Junior 1500 finals and the first Men's 1500 meters heat before the Blue Horizon crew got their chance to paddle. He turned to Brigham.

"Looks like we'll be spectators for most of the morning."

The boys sat on the steps. The official appeared with his bullhorn.

"Men's 500 meters, Heat 1. Please make your way to the start line."

The Matagi A2s finished their stretching, grabbed their paddles and headed for the river to get the canoes. The Foelele A1s, led by Markus, strutted by in the same direction. A team from the Nomads, and another from Tafola, followed suit.

Jacob looked out at the sea. It was a sunny day, with a light breeze. But he also noticed that at the entrance of the harbor the yellow buoys had disappeared. He strained his eyes, but still couldn't see them. Then suddenly they appeared again. He kept his eyes focused on the buoys. A minute or two passed and they vanished again. A few more moments passed and the buoys became visible again. He realized what was happening. He watched the far end of the harbor, where the seawall snaked around a large government building. Waves splashed into the rocks at the wall's base and sprayed into the air.

A tidal swell! It was only lightly affecting the mouth of the harbor, but Jacob would have to keep an eye on it. It could get worse as the day worn on.

Tariq came and sat down next to them.

"Is the 500 meters set up the same as the 1500 meters, as far as advancing to the final?

Jacob nodded. "Yeah, first place in each heat advances, plus the next two fastest times overall."

"So it could happen that a team that finished third could actually have a faster time than the first place team from the other heat, but wouldn't make the final?"

"Exactly, so we'll just have to make sure we win our heat."

Tariq took a deep breath. "Looks like."

The canoes had reached the start line along with the officials' boat. Toa and Moana, on opposite sides of the steps, watched through their binoculars. Jacob didn't need binoculars to tell that the sea was rougher than yesterday. The canoes seemed to dip in and out of the water.

The green flag shot up! The canoes began their charge. Right from the first dip of the blades, this race had the fastest pace Jacob had seen yet. It seemed like only seconds and the canoes were nearly halfway home. The paddle blades glinted in the sunlight as they churned through the sea.

As the four canoes rapidly approached the finish line, the clubs yelled louder and louder. Foelele had the highest decibel cheer going, as their A1 team had a clear lead over the other canoes. The Matagi A2s were in a dogfight with the Nomads for second.

With 50 meters to go, the canoes kicked into final power pace. The crowd screamed encouragement to their crews. Markus, stroking in the front of his canoe, raised his paddle boldly as his canoe streaked across the yellow buoys. The Foelele roared their approval.

Second place came down to a last final push, and the Matagi crew surged forward and crossed a half-length ahead of the Nomads. Two seconds later the Tafola team slid past.

Toa clapped his hands satisfied, if not happy, with the result. He handed his binoculars to one of the junior boys and barked at his A1 crew. They hopped down the rocks to the water and dove in.

"Men's 500 meters, Heat 2," announced the official.

The A2s switched off with their A1 teammates and made their way up the steps to watch. The girls and juniors congratulated the A2s. Jacob and his boys made a point of high-fiving their Matagi brothers. It was hard to believe that this was the same team that they'd been ready to go to war against a month ago. Nothing like a common enemy . . . the Foelele . . . to bring a team together.

Jacob scanned the canoes as they paddled out: Toa's team, another Nomad squad, a younger team from the Aufaigalu and Markus' A2 crew.

Brigham nudged him.

"What'd you think? Toa will kill them in this one?"

"His guys won't even break a sweat."

The canoes lined up in the distance. There seemed to be some confusion as two canoes looked to be in the same lane, then one slid across a few meters.

The green flag flashed up. Again the pace was blistering. The official's boat had to gun ahead to get to the finish and set up on the line. At the 100 meter mark, it was clear it was no contest. Toa and his boys were comfortably in front. The real race was between the Nomad and Foelele canoes, running tip to tip.

The Matagi canoe glided across to a loud cheer. It was almost four seconds before the Nomad crew nosed in ahead of the Foelele. It was another ten seconds before the outclassed Aufaigalu chugged in.

Toa steered his canoe over to the official's boat. He pulled alongside and began talking to the officials onboard. Jacob could see he was arguing with them. Suddenly he pushed the canoe angrily away from the boat and slapped his paddle violently on the water. The A1s hung their heads. The entire Matagi club went silent.

Jacob and his boys looked around in bewilderment. Jacob noticed Markus quietly laughing with his boys.

"Junior Girls 1500 meters final. Please head to the starting line," called out the official.

The junior girls made their way into the water, passing the A1s as they waded in. There was no congratulating going on. The mood of the returning paddlers was so sour, that neither Jacob nor his boys dared asked what had happened.

Finally, after Toa seemed preoccupied with observing the next race through his binoculars, one of the A1 boys come over with the news.

"Disqualified," he said softly. "Toa lined us up in the wrong lane." He looked toward Toa and shook his head. Jacob understood the body language. Toa had messed up, badly.

Brigham leaned over. "Ouch, what a way be knocked out of the final."

Jacob nodded. "The only silver lining is that the A2s must now be in, they definitely had a faster time than that SamCo team."

"I don't think that's much consolation to Toa right now."

Jacob couldn't argue with that observation. Toa must be fuming. To have made such a rookie mistake, in a race they dominated, must be eating him up.

But there wasn't time to sulk right now. The junior girls were about to begin their 1500 meters. This would be the first of the ten finals, and the first race to count toward the overall points standings. Jacob turned his eyes to Moana. She was watching her girls through binoculars; occasionally she glanced over at Toa.

Jacob squinted to see the start line. The two Aufaigalu crews were on the ends, the Matagi girls and Tafola in the middle lanes. The flag went up. After the high speed of the previous two races, this race seemed much, much slower. It was also due to the fact the girls had to pace themselves for the longer distance. It took awhile, but the canoes rounded the first turn. Seeing that it was a very tight race, the clubs yelled enthusiastically to their crews. The four canoes were almost even after the turn.

Chico elbowed Li, "Hey, where are those babes in the spandex?"

"They didn't make the final, remember."

"All I remember are those legs!"

Torch reached over and slapped Chico on the back of the head.

"Oww, what's that for?" moaned Chico.

"Fraternizing with the enemy!"

Jacob smiled at Torch's team spirit. At the far end of the harbor the girls were making their second turns. Suddenly there was a flash of white. Several people stood up.

"Fuli!" Moana exclaimed.

"What happened?" wondered Brigham.

Jacob knew. "Someone capsized."

"Was it ours?" asked Tariq.

The officials' boat rushed over to the overturned canoe and could be seen helping right it.

Jacob saw red and yellow uniforms bailing the canoe. It was one of the Aufaigalu teams. The officials stayed with the canoe until it was slowly moving again. The boat then sped up and just managed to reach the end line ahead of the remaining three canoes.

It was another tight finish, but the Aufaigalu would have something to offset their capsized team as their other squad reached the line first. A huge cheer went up for the victors. Even Moana clapped her appreciation of the hard won race. Just meters behind, the Tafola girls took second place. Breathing down their necks came the Matagi girls with a well-fought third.

The clubs applauded the girls as they drifted toward shore.

Brigham shrugged. "It's only a point for third, but at least Foelele didn't get anything."

Jacob watched Moana congratulate her girls as they came up from the water. She patted them on the back proudly. Toa barely acknowledged them as he gave some last minute instructions to his junior boys.

"Junior boy's 1500 meters final, to the start," announced the official.

The boys headed into the water. Jacob saw the Foelele boys do the same. This race would be the first head to head battle for points between the rivals.

"Should be a good one," noted Brigham.

"I hope the boys don't choke. Toa sure puts a lot of pressure on them."

The junior teams climbed into their canoes and paddled out to the start line. Jacob noticed the canoes were bobbing more, the swell was increasing.

The green flag shot up. The paddles flashed. The canoes zipped forward.

"Nice pace," observed Brigham.

The canoes made their way rapidly to the first turn. Like the girls' race, the canoes almost made the turn simultaneously. As the clubs screamed encouragement, the canoes tore back toward the start buoys. Jacob looked at Toa, who rubbed his chin nervously. Jacob glanced over at Markus, who likewise was pacing anxiously. Though it was only the second final of the day, there was obviously a lot of pride on the line. Toa and Markus each saw himself as the best coach on the island. The junior boys were settling the matter for them on the water.

The four canoes made their second turn. It looked like Matagi and Foelele were still even, but Tafola and Aufaigalu had dropped off a length. Toa breathed easier seeing no one had capsized.

The crews hit the homestretch, kicking in their last reserves of strength. The crowd was going wild. Jacob and the others stood up, caught up in the excitement. The Matagi and Foelele were still neck and neck. It was going to be a nail-biter of a finish.

With 50 meters left the paddlers bore down with all they had left. Foelele pulled ahead slightly, then the Matagi shot ahead. Ten meters from the line the Foelele crew gave a final all- out heave and poked ahead of the Matagi right at the line. Both teams raised their paddles in victory, but the officials were already pointing toward Foelele as the victors. A deafening roar went up from Markus' club. Toa slammed his hand hard onto the railing.

The Aufaigalu crew crossed a half-length ahead of the Tafola boys to complete the race. Jacob realized he was still clapping. He felt it had been a great race and the Matagi boys had given a gutsy showing of themselves. But clearly Toa didn't see it that way. Markus had won, and he had come in second.

As the junior boys drifted up to the shore, utterly exhausted, Toa ignored them. He merely called together his A1 squad and leapt into the water. The junior boys hung their heads in shame as they switched off with Toa's crew. Jacob shook his head and looked at Brigham.

"Can you believe this? Those guys just raced their hearts out and he's treating them like they came in dead last."

"Not the best way to build team morale."

The official appeared again with his bullhorn. "Men's 1500 meters Heat 1. To the line please."

The Matagi canoe made for the harbour mouth, followed by the Nomad's top squad, the Foelele A2s and the Aufaigalu rookies. The canoes quickly reached the start and lined up. Jacob didn't observe much bobbing this time. They must be between swells, he thought. The Matagi were in the third lane. He hoped for Toa's sake, it was the correct lane.

The flag went up. Two dozen paddles stabbed into the sea and the canoes exploded forward. Again the increase in the race speed was impressive. The canoes chewed up the distance to the first turn. Toa's team was clearly in the lead, sure to reach the turn first. But as they approached the buoys, the canoe began to angle sharply inward. Everyone was confused, why was Toa steering the canoe on a diagonal course. Then Jacob realized what had happened. Toa was confused as to which buoy represented his turning lane.

The Matagi canoe almost cut in front of the Aufaigalu, a sure DQ. Toa could be seen jabbing his paddle into water on the canoe's starboard side, swinging them back just in time to the proper lane. The Matagi crew had completely lost their rhythm and Toa was screaming at them to keep paddling. He directed the canoe back against the grain and swung it around the correct buoy. They were back on course, but the mistake had cost them dearly.

Foelele and the Nomads had completed their turn and the Aufaigalu canoe was almost around the buoy. Toa's canoe was now bringing up the rear and would have to make up several lengths, just to get even again with the front two canoes.

Jacob looked over at the Foelele crowd. Markus was laughing and high-fiving his boys. It looked like Toa had blown it again. Jacob noticed Moana shaking her head as she looked through the binoculars. At the second turn the Nomad canoe and Foelele were running even. Matagi had gained back some of the distance and were now pulling ahead of the Aufaigalu.

"Does he have enough distance left to catch them," wondered Brigham.

Jacob shrugged, he wasn't sure. At the 400 meter mark, Toa's boys had closed in some more. By the halfway point, they were only a length behind the leaders. With 100 meters they were almost even again, by 50 meters they were tip to tip with both the Nomads and Foelele. But Toa's boys had used up all their reserves of energy just to catch up. While the other two canoes were able to kick in a final burst of power over the last ten meters, Toa's crew simply had no gas left in their tanks.

The Nomad team streaked across the finish, a quarter length ahead of the Foelele A2s. A few feet behind them arrived the Matagi in third place. The Aufaigalu slid in a slow fourth.

As the Nomads and Foelele clubs celebrated, the Matagi stared at their feet. Their best team, their club captain, was in danger of not making it to another final. Tariq crouched beside Jacob.

"He still has a chance, right?"

"Only if his time is better than the second place canoe in our heat."

Our heat, he thought. He had been so caught up in the other races he'd forgotten they were next. But this was it, the moment they'd all sweated and suffered for. He raised his eyes skyward and said a quick prayer, that win or lose the boys from Blue Horizon would make a good showing of themselves. They had earned that much.

"Let's go boys," he called out. The boys jumped up. Brigham gave Jacob a pat on the shoulder.

"This is what you stuck around for. Enjoy the moment!"

Jacob smiled. "Damn straight!"

The familiar face of the official stepped out of the tent. "Last race before the break, Men's 1500 meters, Heat 2."

Torch was the first into the water; the others close behind. They waited for Toa's crew to drift in closer and hop out. The tension was obvious. The Blue Horizon boys wanted to encourage the A1s, but they knew it was best to leave them alone. Jacob avoided looking at Toa. He knew the Matagi captain was an angry bomb ready to explode.

As they began paddling out, Jacob felt a sense of relief. Anything would be better than sitting on the steps next to Toa in his foul mood. To their right, the Foelele canoe zipped ahead. Markus waved from his position at the front.

"Malo palagis," he called out mockingly, "you should have raced against the junior girls!"

The Foelele quickened their pace effortlessly and sped ahead. Chico, Torch and Li stabbed their paddles in deep and pulled hard.

"Easy boys," Jacob yelled, "save it for the race."

They all settled into an easier pace and made for their lane. Jacob turned toward Tariq in the steerer's seat.

"We're in lane four, right?"

"Yup."

"You're sure?"

"I checked the board ten times. We're lane four."

Jacob looked ahead to the start line. The buoys were dipping in and out of view. The swell was getting stronger. He counted the ripples in the swell. As the four canoes reached the start, the swell calmed down again. Jacob scanned the sea further out past the wharf. He spotted a few small crests approaching in the distance.

Tariq guided the canoe to the far lane and straightened the canoe beside the buoys. The boys all looked toward the shoreline. It looked a million miles away. This far out they couldn't hear the crowds or the traffic on the road. The only sounds were the other crews and the officials' boat.

"Canoes to the line," announced an official with a bullhorn.

The Foelele canoe eased into position in lane three. Markus called over.

"I hope you boys have better luck than Toa staying in your lane."

Jacob was tempted to yell out a reply, but he was preoccupied with the crests of water rolling in just behind them. They seemed to be folding in upon themselves, forming deep depressions.

"Lane two, move back," warned the official.

The Nomads back-paddled to reset their position behind the buoys. Jacob could see each canoe was trying to sit as close to the start line as possible. Tariq edged them a few feet closer to their buoys.

Jacob took another look at the sea behind them. A large ripple of water was heading right for them. Jacob's eyes widened. He'd seen this kind of wave before, on the north coast of California. It was a rogue wave, building underneath the surface.

He gauged the distance to the rocks on the right of the racecourse. The rogue wave would be hitting the under flow, forcing it to surge right about . . .

"Back-paddle, everybody!" he grunted to the others.

"Back?" exclaimed Tariq, "But we're right on . . ."

"Just do it!"

The intensity in his voice overrode their concerns. They back-paddled. Markus and the A1s looked at them and laughed.

"Paddles up!" the official announced. All eyes turned to the flagman, as the paddlers readied themselves for the first big stroke. The Blue Horizon canoe was almost two lengths behind the other three. Then the rogue wave rose up like the back of a giant whale. The back ends of the four canoes tipped upward as the wave rolled up under them and carried them forward . . . just as the green flag was being raised.

The Blue Horizon canoe surfed forward, the boys barely having to paddle. They shot across the line and were carried a good twenty yards by the wave's momentum. By the time the surge died, they had a full head of steam behind them.

"What a start!" yelled out Tariq.

"Shut up and breathe, "commanded Jacob. The wave had given them a nice push, but it had helped the other teams as well. He looked at the other canoes. They were a few meters ahead of them.

Li called out the switch and they whipped their paddles out and over to the other side. Jacob smiled, their timing had really improved. They had a good pace going too; they were almost even with the other crews.

As they approached the first turn, they could now hear the roar of the crowd on the steps. Jacob's adrenaline was firing in his blood. He knew the others were feeling the same. Their strokes became stronger as they angled in for the turn.

The Foelele were already halfway around their buoy, the other two canoes were just behind them. Tariq groaned as he dug in his paddle and ruddered the canoe around the buoy. The boys churned the water up as they paddled hard to regain their forward speed. It was a perfectly executed turn.

Now came the grueling leg back to the start line and the second turn. The cheers of the crowd faded and soon all that remained was the sound of six paddlers straining against the sea. Jacob concentrated on his breathing, trying his best to ignore the pain in his arms. As they finally approached the buoys, they could see the Foelele had completed their turn already and were heading for home.

"Paddle hard!" Jacob urged.

The boys gave it their best, paddling strong as Tariq u-turned them around the buoy. Jacob noticed the water was now smooth as glass. He almost laughed, but his aching body wouldn't allow it.

The Blue Horizon canoe was about four lengths behind Foelele, two behind the Nomads and one length behind the Tafola squad. Jacob was surprised they were still so close. They had a serious shot at overtaking some canoes.

"Let's do it! All we've got . . . the rest of the way!"

He barely got the words out. He had to suck wind to regain his oxygen. The boys picked up the pace and drove their paddles in. The canoe sliced forward. Within seconds they caught and passed the Tafola. Jacob could sense the confidence rippling through the team. They pulled even harder and clawed their way even with the Nomad team. The boys fed off their success and found themselves gaining on the Foelele. Could they actually catch and beat Markus' best, wondered Jacob?

With about 100 meters to go, Markus yelled out, "Power!"

It was like the canoe had a motor hidden under it. The canoe took off like a torpedo. "Power!" gasped Jacob, but he knew they were already at top speed. There wasn't a drop more in their tanks. Seeing the Foelele leaving them in their wake, the boys' exuberance turned back to exhaustion. Their paced deadened and the Nomad canoe shot past them. With twenty yards remaining, the Tafola canoe also surged past. Jacob wanted to yell for one more push, but he knew it was useless.

The Foelele crossed the line the clear winner, followed by the Nomads and Tafola. The Blue Horizon crew crawled in last, a full two lengths late. The boys slumped over the sides, physically wiped out.

Torch shook his head.

"We had them, we could have won!"

Chico splashed water over his face. "I doubt it, they're too fit."

"We shouldn't have back-paddled," griped Li.

Shaggy leaned back and arched his back. "Like, at least we gave them a run for their money."

Jacob had been keeping an eye on the officials' boat. The other canoes, as he expected, had headed over to it as soon as they finished the race. He watched Markus and the other two captains listen to the officials. The once cheering crowds had gone silent.

Shouting broke out at the officials' boat. Markus and the other captains were yelling angrily in Samoan to officials, who were shouting back. Jacob smiled.

"What the hell's the problem?" wondered Li.

"Boys," grinned Jacob," we might just be in that final after all."

They all looked at him confused, saying "What?" in unison.

"Remember the start?" he explained. "The wave that surged under us?"

"So what?" said Torch, "It helped them as much as it helped us."

Jacob sighed. "Where were we when it hit?"

"Two lengths behind everyone else," said Li.

"Exactly, and where were we when the green flag went up?"

"Right on the line," replied Chico.

"So where do you think the other canoes were?"

"Across the line . . . "Li finally understood. A second later the others also pieced it together.

"Like, we were the only ones who started fairly!" exclaimed Shaggy.

"They're all disqualified?" hoped Torch.

The boys looked over at the officials' boat. The Nomads and Tafola were paddling away angrily. Markus was still shouting at the officials. Finally he sat down in his canoe, slapped his paddle against the water. The paddle blade shattered in two.

"Let's see if we're right," Jacob said. They paddled over to the officials' boat. A chubby man in a baseball cap and holding a clipboard motioned for them to come in closer.

"Malo boys. You won the heat. The other teams are DQ'ed."

The boys let out a whoop.

The officials laughed. One of them shook his head. "Either you palagis know the sea better than us Samoans, or you are just damn lucky."

"Both," replied Jacob.

The boys headed for the steps, smiling from ear to ear.

Torch turned back toward Jacob. "Wait a minute! If you knew the others had blown the start, why did you let us kill ourselves out there?"

Jacob shrugged. "I didn't know for sure if they all were DQ'ed. Besides, you guys looked like you needed a good sweat."

The others moaned. Jacob laughed. Maybe it had been luck, or maybe God had answered his prayer and sent that wave Himself. One thing was certain: the boys from Blue Horizon were in the final!

CHAPTER 44

She glanced over at Toa. "What's wrong with him? I've never seen him mess up two races in a row. It's not like him to be so unfocused during a regatta."

"If I hadn't seen it with my own eyes, I wouldn't have believed it!"

Brigham high-fived his teammates enthusiastically as they made their way up the steps. The other Matagi paddlers likewise congratulated Jacob and his team. Jacob sensed that the mood was less tense than before. The disqualification of Markus' squad had clearly lifted the spirits of the Matagi. The only exception was Toa, still dour faced. He waved to three young kids at the top of the stairs, who quickly carried in several large cardboard boxes and a basket of fresh drinking coconuts.

"It's only a thirty minute break for lunch," Toa reminded them sternly.

"We've got eleni sandwiches, fruit and niu. Don't overeat or you'll cramp in the races. And keep hydrated!"

The paddlers crowded around the boxes and grabbed their food. The Blue Horizon boys jumped into the frenzy, each coming out of it with a big sandwich in one hand and ripe bananas in the other. They sat down to eat. Chico was first to bite into his sandwich. He chewed on the piece and nodded.

"Not bad, tastes a bit like tuna salad."

"It's herring, Sherlock" corrected Li.

Shaggy shrugged. "Like, whatever it is, it sure tastes good."

As they ate, Jacob kept an eye on Toa. The club captain wasn't eating; he sat by himself and sipped from a coconut. Jacob noticed Moana, three steps down, sitting by herself. He shimmied down beside her. She smacked her lips as she finished her sandwich. She looked at Jacob.

"So you made the final. Well done."

"Thanks, but I'll admit we had some help from the sea."

He took another look at Toa, then swung back to Moana.

"So, you and your girls race after the break."

She nodded. "Yeah, finally! Hopefully we'll put some points on the board for us. It's tied 3-3, so we need them. Especially with . . ." She lowered her voice," . . . with the A1s getting knocked from the 500 meter final."

Jacob nodded, "Toa's had a rough morning."

She glanced over at Toa. "What's wrong with him? I've never seen him mess up two races in a row. It's not like him to be so unfocused during a regatta."

"Something's on his mind, or someone," hinted Jacob.

She looked at him. "Who? What do you mean?"

Jacob didn't know if he was doing the right thing but he decided to chance it. "I told Toa you were leaving."

"You!" She stifled her voice and looked to see if anyone had heard her outburst. Seeing that everyone was more concerned with their lunch, she leaned closer to Jacob. "You promised you wouldn't say anything!" she hissed.

"I only told him. And I did it for both your sakes. You see, that's why he's so upset and out of it. It's bugging the hell out of him. He doesn't want to lose you."

"Then why doesn't he say something. Why are you the one who's always telling me how he feels? He's got a tongue!"

Jacob sighed. "You know how proud he is."

"Then let him have his pride, if it means so much to him. I don't care."

Jacob felt like he was back on the treadmill with these two. No matter how hard he ran, he never seemed to get anywhere. He decided to give it one last shot.

"Look, Toa is acting like a man without hope. If you'd give him even a sliver of it, I know that thick ego of his would crack. Then you'd see the real Toa. But you have to give him something to work with."

Moana didn't reply. She stared at her knee as she massaged it. Jacob sensed he'd planted a seed. He decided to back off and let it grow its own roots. He got up and left her. He set himself down again beside Brigham, who gave him a confused look.

"You sure spend a lot of time talking with that girl. Have you got the hots for her or what?"

"Could you blame me if I did?"

Brigham smiled. "She's a babe alright, one-leg or two."

"And she's got a good head on her shoulders," added Jacob, "but to answer your question . . . no, I'm not chasing her."

Li and Tariq came over with armfuls of coconuts.

"Grab a fresh niu, the Samoan Snickers bar."

The boys all grabbed a nut and broke off the soft top. They sucked out the cool sweet water inside. Jacob loved the taste of it. He wondered why anyone would choose to drink Coke or Pepsi when they had an island full of these babies. After they downed the refreshing juice, they cracked the nuts on the cement and ate the white flesh inside the nut's shell. It was rich and creamy.

"Like, that was just what the doctor ordered," smacked Shaggy.

"I wish we were paddling next," said Torch.

Li stretched his legs and leaned back. "Well, you better save that energy, because we've got five races ahead of us again."

"That's right, man," said Chico. "And from now on, they all count for points. Things are going to be intense!"

Tariq nodded his agreement. "It'll be a war. I wouldn't want to be betting on this one."

Jacob looked at Toa and Moana, ignoring each other across the steps.

"Amen to that," he said.

CHAPTER 45

She held his gaze for a second longer and then jumped into the water. Toa went back and leaned against the rail. Jacob was blinking his eyes. Had he just seen what he thought he'd seen? The ice between Toa and Moana was thawing!

"Women's 500 meter Final. To your canoes please."

The official's call sent everyone back into action. The short respite was over. Moana and her girls finished their last minute stretching and grabbed their paddles. Moana unhooked her artificial leg and set it against the rail post. She hopped down to the water behind the others.

"She's got spunk, you gotta give her that," remarked Brigham.

"I hope she wins," replied Jacob. "She deserves it."

The four women's teams paddled out to the start line: Matagi, Foelele, Tafola and Aufaigalu. The men of all the clubs were disappointed with the Foelele women. Unlike the junior squad, the Foelele ladies wore more conservative uniforms. They were still the trendiest of the bunch, but nowhere as provocative as the juniors. Jacob knew this meant that the Foelele women were a serious threat on the water, if not on a catwalk.

The canoes lined up at the far end. Jacob could see all the buoys. There hadn't been any swells for awhile now. It would be a clean start.

Green flag! Paddles flashed. Everyone on shore stood up. This would be a good one. "Go, girls, go!" called out Torch.

The pace of the race was almost as quick as the men's heats. The first half of the distance was covered in no time. The four canoes looked to be dead even across the lanes. Tariq tore at his hair and turned around.

"I can't watch, it's too close!"

Chico and Li grabbed him and turned him back around.

The canoes were approaching the 100 meter point. It was still impossible to tell if any one canoe was in the lead. The clubs began yelling, "Power!" Jacob knew the same call was being screamed in each canoe.

"C'mon, Moana, you can do it."

With 50 meters to go he could see Moana digging hard with her paddle. The stroker in the Matagi canoe suddenly picked up the pace. The canoe lurched ahead, almost violently. The girls had kicked in their last reserves of strength. The other canoes must have already been at full speed, because they didn't challenge the Matagi.

With ten meters to go, the Matagi had opened a half-length on their opponents. The only question now was who would come in second. A deafening celebratory roar went up around Jacob as Moana's crew crossed the finish line. Two seconds later the Tafola canoe squeaked in a paddle length ahead of Foelele. The young Aufaigalu paddlers settled for fourth.

Jacob high-fived Brigham. "Three points!"

Moana steered her canoe over to the steps. The Matagi chanted for the victors. Jacob looked for Toa. He was gathering his A2 squad. He was the only person on the steps who wasn't smiling.

The official popped out of the tent. "Next up, Men's 500 meter Final."

Toa growled at his A2s and they scrambled to the water. Jacob didn't envy them. They not only carried the pressure of being the only Matagi squad in the race, they also had the burden of Toa's expectations on their backs.

The women's team climbed the steps, dripping wet and smiling brightly. Toa just gave them a polite nod. Moana didn't even look at him. Toa turned his icy stare back to the water. The A2s were on their way out, along with Markus' A1 and A2 crews and the powerful Nomad squad.

Jacob looked at Moana, she glanced over at him. He pointed at her and then signaled that she was #1. She grinned and nodded her thanks. Then Jacob pointed discreetly in Toa's direction. Her grin turned to a frown. She shrugged. Jacob hoped she was softening a bit.

"They're ready," Brigham noted. "This is going to be fast!"

Jacob threw his attention back to the race just as the green flag shot up. Brigham was right, the pace was unbelievable. Every crew was going flat out from the start. It looked like the Matagi might be a bit behind, but by the 250 meter point they had evened out again. Then the Foelele A2s opened a lead on the others, but the Matagi and Nomads charged ahead and overtook them.

Toa banged his hand on his thigh. Foelele A2s had come even with the Nomads and Matagi. Everyone was kicking into power pace. Markus' canoe, surprisingly hanging back a length from the others, seemed to be a stroke or two slower. With 50 meters to go, it was still anyone's race to win. Then Markus' pace almost doubled. The Foelele canoe shot forward like a dart and was even with the others in seconds.

Like a rocket afterburner the Foelele A1's zoomed past the other canoes and headed for the finish line. What had been a close race between the other three canoes wasn't by the end.

Markus' canoe crossed the line a full length ahead of the others. The Nomads held on for a clean second place. Third was within the Matagi canoe's grasp, but the Foelele boys' pace was a stroke faster and they lunged ahead at the last second and stole third.

On the Foelele steps, there was the joy of victory. On the Matagi steps, there was silent disappointment.

"Damn, that's four more points for them," noted Li. "That gives them eight, and we stick on six."

Jacob watched Markus showoff for his club, twirling his paddle and pretending to shoot it like a gun at the other canoes.

"There's still a lot of racing to go," spat Jacob.

The official announced. "Junior girls 500 meter Final, to the start."

Moana gave her girls some last-minute instructions and sent them on their way. The A2 squad quietly wished them luck as they exchanged places in the canoe with them.

As expected, many heads turned to watch the Foelele juniors girls slink down the steps to their canoe; their now infamous uniforms showing off every inch of their nubile bodies.

"Babe-alicious!" remarked Chico.

The Foelele princesses climbed into their canoe and paddled for the start line. Jacob turned his attention back to Toa.
He was chastising the A2s loudly. "I told you they'd use their A2s as bait! They got you to burn out too early. All Markus had to do was sit back and save his power for the end. You fell right into his trap!"

The A2s hung their heads with embarrassment. They looked like they wanted to crawl under the rocks and hide. Jacob felt sorry for them. They'd fought a good battle out there. Maybe they had made a tactical mistake, but who was Toa to complain after his two gaffes?

The junior girls lined up in their lanes: Tafola, Aufaigalu, Matagi and Foelele. The water was calm. The flag whipped into the air. Young muscles dug their paddles into the sea. Compared to the men's race, the girls seemed to be going in slow motion.

It was a close race for the first 100 meters, then the canoes began to show some distance between them. True to form, the Foelele girls had dropped off the pace. Tafola had jumped into a lead over Matagi and Aufaigalu.

At the half, Matagi had pulled even again with Tafola. But suddenly Aufaigalu put on a quick spurt and passed them both.

Moana pumped her fist anxiously, willing her juniors more speed. It wasn't working, instead the Tafola made a move and pulled ahead of Aufaigalu.

With 100 meters to go the girls pushed themselves to their limits. Matagi inched closer to the Aufaigalu. Together they both were gaining slightly on Tafola.

Fifty meters! The teams hit their power strokes. Tafola leapt ahead of the others. There would be no catching them now. The clubs cheered frantically for their teams. Aufaigalu was ahead by a nose as they approached the finish. Jacob could see the Matagi girls paddling desperately, trying to steal second place. They almost did it, but they simply ran out of time. Aufaigalu sailed in two feet ahead of them. Matagi would have to settle for third.

Moana nodded, accepting the outcome stoically. Toa was poker-faced. The only consolation for Matagi was that the Foelele junior girls finished a distant fourth.

"Well, at least we got a point," said Brigham. "That brings us within one point of Foelele."

Jacob nodded, but was preoccupied with Toa's behaviour. His negative attitude was bringing down the whole club. Rather than spurring them on, Toa was demoralizing everyone with his frustration. It suddenly struck Jacob how selfish Toa was being. People were paddling their guts out for him and he wasn't even acknowledging them. The more he thought of it, the more he became fed up with Toa. He hopped down the steps toward Toa.

Everyone was giving Toa a wide space. His foul mood wasn't something anyone wanted to be too close to, especially if it were to lash out. Jacob didn't care. He hadn't sacrificed his escape plan just to sit around and watch Toa and the Matagi implode. He stood next to Toa, but kept his gaze toward the sea.

Toa looked at him. "You want something?"

Jacob took a deep breath, "I want you to start acting like a club captain instead of a child."

Without even looking, Jacob could feel Toa's eyes burning into his head.

"What did you say?" growled Toa. Jacob didn't flinch.

"You heard me. You're taking your frustration out on your teams and it's affecting their paddling. You've got them so tight they can't even breathe."

"Listen, palagi, this is your first regatta so don't . . ."

"This has nothing to do with racing," shot back Jacob. "It's about her."

Toa clenched his teeth. "You better quit pushing me, boy. I told you to stay out of my business."

Jacob knew he was taking a chance, but he had to spell it out for Toa. He risked one more push. "Toa, this is the last thing I'm going to say to you. Life's too friggin' short to wait for it to be perfect. You either seize your chance, or you drown in the past. That stubborn pride you're wearing around your neck is an anchor. Cut it loose before it drags you to the bottom."

Jacob turned and stormed off. He half expected to be punched in the back of the head, but Toa didn't so much as curse at him. As he passed by Moana, he watched her congratulate her junior girls coming up the steps. He could tell the girls were disappointed with third, but Moana's encouragement had them smiling and feeling good about their effort. That was the kind of positive energy the club needed right now. Jacob just knew that if Toa and Moana could get on the same page, the whole Matagi would do a 180 in their morale. But he was done with interfering. He'd laid it out for the two of them. It was up to them from here on. He was going to concentrate on his team.

"Junior Boys 500 meter Final to the line," announced the official.

This time Toa didn't bark at the juniors. He calmly watched them jump in the water and hop into the canoe. In a way, his silence was more unnerving than his yelling. Was the bomb about to go off?

Brigham nudged Jacob. "What were you and Toa talking about?"

"I just wanted to ask him if it's a DQ if the ama crosses over the buoy on the turns."

"Of course it is, you knew that."

"Yeah. I guess I just forgot. I must be nervous."

"Relax, there's still this race and women's 1500 meters before you guys. Save some adrenaline for the race."

Tariq came up behind them. "Think our boys can win this one?"

Jacob shrugged. "There's some good crews out there. They need to have a great race."

The junior canoes lined up, Matagi and Foelele beside each other in the middle, Aufaigalu and Tafola on the outside lanes. Jacob could imagine the trash talk going on between the canoes. This would be a grudge match.

Flag up! The teams took their first deep strokes and launched down the course. As usual, the canoes were nose to nose for the first 100 meters. Then there started to be a bit of separation between them. Foelele was in front, Tafola not far behind, then Aufaigalu and Matagi.

Jacob was surprised to see the Matagi hanging back. Their pace was several strokes slower than the others. As they crossed the halfway point the canoes' positions was unchanged. Matagi was still in the rear. Jacob could see them better now. They were definitely well off the pace of the others. He wondered if they were burnt out, or even demoralized by Toa's attitude. Something was wrong.

At the 100 meters Foelele were holding their lead, Tafola was one length behind them. Aufaigalu was on their tails. Matagi was still lagging the pack. At the 50 meter mark the clubs' cheering became thunderous. The paddlers kicked in their final power pace. Jacob and the others watched in surprise as the Matagi canoe suddenly doubled their pace and surged ahead. In seconds they had passed Aufaigalu and were gaining on Tafola. This forced Tafola to increase their pace. Both they and the Matagi began to overtake the Foelele. Matagi's momentum looked like it would propel them past the others.

Jacob grabbed Brigham's arm. "They're trying to do what Markus did, steal it in the last ten meters!"

As the canoes hit the finish line it was impossible to tell from shore which had crossed first. The clubs cheered hopefully for their squads. The canoes slid over to the officials' boat. There was busy commotion on board the boat as officials conferred and double-checked a stopwatch.

They looked up at the three crews waiting anxiously for the results. From shore everyone watched as the head official pointed to the canoes in the order of their finish: Foelele, Tafola and Matagi.

Markus let out a victory whoop. The Matagi's spirits drooped, a light applause their only response.

"Damn!" cursed Brigham, "They almost did it."

Jacob nodded. "They waited a few seconds too long to power up. Another five meters and they'd have been in front for sure."

The juniors slid into shore, completely dejected. Someone began clapping. Everyone looked and saw Toa applauding his junior boys.

"Malo le alo boys! It was a good gamble. A few more feet and you'd have beat 'em."

The junior boys nodded and smiled. Everyone was a little baffled by

Toa's sudden change of attitude, but Jacob could immediately sense the tension ease among the crews. Had his little rant gotten through to Toa?

"The good news," began Brigham, "is that we got a point for coming third. So we've got eight points. The bad news is that Foelele got three and now have eleven points."

"True," conceded Jacob. "But Moana and her girls are next. And don't forget, we've got two canoes in the men's 1500 meters. Things are just getting interesting."

As if on cue, the official appeared with his bullhorn. "Women's 1500 meters final is next."

Moana's team headed to the water. Jacob watched her as she hopped on her good leg after them. As she hit the bottom step, she landed on a patch of wet concrete and slipped to the right. She dropped her paddle, but was able to regain her balance. She leaned over to grab the paddle, but someone else had already picked it up for her.

Toa handed her the paddle. There was an awkward silence.

He smiled. "Good luck. Kick some butt out there."

Moana took her paddle and smiled back. "Thanks."

She held his gaze for a second longer and then jumped into the water. Toa went back and leaned against the rail. Jacob was blinking his eyes. Had he just seen what he thought he'd seen? The ice between Toa and Moana was thawing! He replayed the scene back in his mind. His hope surged. There was still a chance. But niceties wouldn't be enough. One of them had to take that big risk and open up to the other. He tried to imagine scenarios where either Toa or Moana might make the first move. It wasn't easy. These were two headstrong people. He couldn't really envision either of them giving in.

"Go!" yelled Torch, startling Jacob out of his daydream. The race had begun. He watched the paddles churn water and sunlight. It was a good pace out of the start, but it soon became clear there was not going to be a close race for first. The Matagi canoe was steadily opening a lead on the others. Moana and her girls were first to the buoys for their turn, three lengths ahead of Foelele and Tafola. The Aufaigalu were totally outclassed.

Tariq whistled. "What the heck did our girls eat at lunch?! Steroid sandwiches?!"

"Like, you could water ski behind them," joked Shaggy.

The Matagi canoe had made its second turn and was 50 meters down the home stretch before the other canoes had even reached their buoys. Moana and her girls could have coasted the rest of the way, but they maintained their furious pace. They powered their way through the last 50 meters and zoomed across the finish line. The Matagi club chanted deliriously. It had been the most dominating performance of the day. Jacob could feel the morale of the Matagi bursting. His own boys were as pumped as he'd seen them all day.

The only drama left in the race was for second place. Foelele and Tafola were neck and neck up to the last ten meters, but the Tafola women were out of gas. Foelele finished a half- length ahead of them.

Brigham tapped his chin, figuring out the points. "That gives us eleven now, and they have thirteen. We gained a point on them."

Jacob grinned confidently. "We'll gain more than that in our race."

Moana and her crew paddled up to the steps to a hero's welcome. Toa was leading everyone in a cheer for the victors.
The official had to turn up the volume on his bullhorn to be heard. "Men's 1500 meter final, to the start. This will be the last final before the afternoon break."

Jacob huddled his boys together. "This is it, you crazy maggots. Let's show them we deserve to be in this final. Stay loose and focus on the timing. And if I catch anyone slogging off, he's doing a week in the Cooler."

The boys laughed. They tapped each other's fists and headed to the water. Jacob jumped into the water. In front of him Toa was switching off with Moana. Jacob waded closer towards them, straining to hear above the commotion. Toa waited for her to slip out of the steerer's seat. He hopped in. Jacob could tell that they wanted to say something, but neither knew what to say. Jacob wanted to scream at them "Talk you fools!"

"Great race," said Toa finally.

Moana smiled, "Thanks. Good luck out there."

Toa nodded. Jacob ground his teeth. That was it?

Moana turned to head to the steps, but suddenly turned back to Toa. "I could change my mind, if other things around here change."

As quickly as she had blurted out the cryptic remark, she was hopping back to the steps. While Toa was left scratching his head, Jacob was beaming. Moana had just made the first move. Jacob slid past the A1 canoe, wading out to the Blue Horizon canoe. Toa looked at Jacob, a confused look still on his face.

Jacob tapped his temple. "Think about it. She just threw you a rope."

Toa thought for a second and then nodded. The two captains paddled with their crews to the start line. Jacob looked across the water at Toa. The big lug had a determined smile. Jacob's spirit was soaring now. This race could be the biggest moment in their lives.

CHAPTER 46

There was nothing they could do but watch as the Nomads canoe crossed the line a paddle length ahead of them. The boys from Blue Horizon slumped over in their seats, completely drained.

"Ease it right up to the line this time, Tariq."

Jacob had checked the sea. Apart from the odd small crest near the harbor entrance, the tidal swells had subsided. There would be no magic waves to help them this time.

The Blue Horizon crew was in the second lane, to their left were the Nomad A1s and to the right was the Foelele's A2s. Toa's A1s were in the fourth lane. There was no banter between the canoes this time around. Everyone knew this was a big race and every eye was fixed on the flagman.

Li was bent over in the front seat, his paddle poised to strike.

Torch shifted in his seat. "I wish he'd raise that flag; waiting is murder."

"I need to pee," mumbled Chico.

"Then pee," replied Jacob. "We've got a bailer."

The boys chuckled at the joke. It helped them relax and breathe easier. Jacob noticed the flagman twitch.

"Get ready . . ."

The green flag whipped up. The boys dug their paddles in and pulled the

canoe forward. The other crews likewise lurched forward. Jacob reminded himself to breathe properly. It was so easy to hyperventilate in the excitement of the first 100 meters.

It looked like all the canoes were checking their pace. No one wanted to burn out on the first 500 meter leg.

"Hut!" Li called out the change again and the boys switched sides flawlessly. Jacob smiled, the boys were in a groove.

At the 250 meter mark Jacob noticed Toa's crew had taken a slight lead, with the Foelele A2s endeavoring to stay close. The Nomads were roughly even with Blue Horizon. This remained the case right up to the first turn. Toa's canoe was first around the buoys, much to the delight of the Matagi cheering section.

The Foelele made their turn next, followed by the Nomads and Blue Horizon. Tariq oversteered slightly on the inward turn and put them a half-length behind the Nomads.

"Sorry," muttered Tariq, annoyed with himself.

"It's okay. Stay sharp," yelled Jacob.

Half way back to the far end Jacob's shoulders began to burn with fatigue. He was finding it hard to breathe. He could tell by their weakened pace that they all were hitting the wall. The Nomads were putting more distance between them.

"C'mon guys, we gotta pick it up," he gasped.

They all doubled their effort. Slowly they crept back up on the Nomads. By the time they reached the second turn they had almost drawn even again. This time Tariq made a perfect turn and they lost no distance on the Nomads. Jacob glanced to the sides. The Foelele and Matagi A1 were several lengths ahead. He realized they would be battling it out for first. For him and his crew it was going to be a fight for third.

"Keep it pumping boys, we're in this!" he yelled. He gulped in some air.

He wouldn't be able to shout too much . . . he needed every breath just to keep from passing out.

The Nomads were picking up the pace a little. Jacob wondered if they should follow suit. Or should they hold back their reserves for the final push? He waited, watching how far ahead the Nomads were getting. They passed the halfway mark. They weren't far from home now. The Nomads had gained another canoe length on them. Jacob knew they couldn't wait any longer.

"Power! We gotta make our move!"

The boys kicked in their last reserves of strength. The canoe torpedoed ahead. The Nomads didn't see them coming until they were even with their stern.

Then their steerer looked over and called out to his team. "Powa!" The Nomads canoe shot forward. There was 100 meters to go. Jacob's body was screaming at him to stop. He tried to ignore his pains. They were so close now.

"All you got! It's now or never!" He sucked in air. He knew if he yelled out again he'd probably pass out.

Where his boys found the energy, he couldn't guess, but the Blue Horizon canoe drew even with the Nomads. The two canoes ran nose to nose past the 50 meter mark. The crowd was cheering madly.

Ten meters left and the Nomads steerer cried out to his crew for one last charge. Jacob wanted to do the same but he couldn't spare the oxygen. He knew his crew could give no more anyway. They were paddling on vapor at this point.

There was nothing they could do but watch as the Nomads canoe crossed the line a paddle length ahead of them. The boys from Blue Horizon slumped over in their seats, completely drained. Torch leaned over the left side and threw up. Jacob put his hand in the water and splashed himself. He spat white phlegm from his mouth, he felt sick to his stomach and his muscles burned.

He finally looked up and saw the Matagi celebrating on the steps. Toa was doing a victory pass, waving his paddle in the air. Jacob cleared his throat.

"Hey, guys, at least Toa won."

But most of them were watching the Foelele A2 and Nomads squads.

"We were so close!" sighed Torch.

"I thought, like we had them for sure," added Shaggy.

Jacob understood their pain. He had wanted to steal that one point so bad. This was a huge disappointment. As they drifted closer to shore, the Nomads crew pulled up beside them.

Their steerer called out, "Malo boys, you gave us a good race. You palagis got guts."

Jacob and his crew sat up proudly and nodded their appreciation.

"Thanks," replied Jacob. "Congratulations on getting third."

The two teams paddled back to their respective steps. Jacob felt better about things now. Yes, they may have come in last, but they had done so respectably. After the fluky way they won their heat, Jacob had to admit that they hadn't exactly earned anyone's respect, until now.

"We did good, guys! We gave it our best shot and we've got nothing to hang our heads about."

As if to punctuate what he'd just said, the Matagi crews on the steps cheered as the canoe drifted in. Toa and his crew had just hopped into the water. Toa gave them a thumbs-up.

"That's the best you guys have paddled. I know you won those uniforms at the fundraiser, but after a race like that . . . you really deserve to wear them."

Jacob and his boys nodded their thanks and hopped out of the canoe. They headed up the steps proudly. Brigham met them and high-fived each one.

"You guys rocked!" he exclaimed. "To be honest, I didn't think you'd be in it at all. But man, you guys almost stole third."

Torch sat down. "If I had to race that again I'd drop dead after 50 meters. That's the most grueling thing I've ever survived. I'd do a week in the

Cooler before I do that again."

Jacob laughed. "Once you've had a bit of rest, you'll be the first one back in the canoe!"

Torch layed back, using a bag as a pillow. He put his towel over his face. "Wake me up when the break's over."

Jacob turned back to Brigham. "What's the scoop on the points?"

Brigham frowned. "Toa's crew scored three to give us 14, but the Foelele A2s picked up two more, giving them 15."

"Damn! If we could have taken third we'd have tied it up."

"There's still the two V12 finals," Torch mumbled from under his towel.

"Yeah, but from what I've heard, those twelve-man races are always close," said Jacob. "I think our combined women's and junior girls' team can beat anyone. But I'm not sure about the men's team. Toa needs his best twelve, and while his A1s are all good, the A2s aren't as strong as the Foelele A2s."

Brigham nodded. "I overheard some of the girls talking. They said Foelele has never been ahead going into the last races. Maybe they're finally due for a win."

Jacob shrugged. "I suppose. I just wish they weren't so smug about. You can be sure Markus will be rubbing Toa's nose in it for the next year."

What Jacob didn't add was that the Matagi bad start was likely his fault. If he hadn't interfered with Toa and Moana's situation, a focused Matagi club would already have clinched the regatta on points. But he wasn't going to second guess himself. He'd see this thing through to the end. Win, lose or draw.

CHAPTER 47

Jacob laughed as he went to give Toa the names. He found Toa going over a list with Moana. Jacob kept back, not wanting to interrupt, but also wanting to hear the tone of their voices.

"Lash that lapa on good and tight!"

Toa and the boys were busy converting the two Matagi canoes into a single double hull vessel. They removed the long curved amas and outriggers then connected the two hulls with thick crossbeams. They used strips of inner tube rubber to lash the beams to the hulls. The resulting canoe was impossible to tip, but unwieldy in the water.

Jacob and Tariq watched them ease the canoe back into the water off the riverbank. Four of the boys paddled it back out to the harbour. Toa and the rest hiked back to the bridge. Toa walked next to Jacob and Tariq.

"You tired?" asked Toa.

Jacob was a little surprised by the question, "Not too bad."

"I'm trying to decide who to pick for the V12 race. I'm thinking of taking three paddlers from each of our teams. Three from my squad, three juniors, three of the A2s and three of your crew."

Jacob looked at him with surprise. He'd assumed, as did all the Blue Horizon boys, that Toa would have selected only from his A1 and A2 teams.

Opening it up to potentially weaker paddlers was a bold risk. It would be a huge team spirit exercise, but what if they lost?

"You're sure?"

"Yeah, just make sure you pick your best three. Give me the names when you've decided."

Toa moved ahead. Tariq pulled on Jacob's t-shirt. "Let me race!" he said excitedly. "I'm not as burnt out as you guys. Steering lets you save a little energy. I could sit in number three or four and really give 'er."

Jacob nodded. "Okay, I'm convinced . We'll see who else is keen on it."

They made their way back to the steps. The others were lounging around, waiting for the action to restart. Torch looked out from under his towel.

"So, was it a big job?"

Tariq shook his head. "Nah, they just took off the outriggers and put some beams across. Toa practically did it himself."

"But we did get some interesting news," hinted Jacob.

The boys sat up, curious.

"What's up?" asked Brigham.

"Toa wants three of us to paddle in the race."

The boys looked at each other in shock.

"Are you serious?" inquired Li.

"Very. Tariq has already asked to paddle and I think it's a good idea since he should have some power left over, being a lazy steerer and all."

Tariq rolled his eyes at the slight. Jacob grinned and continued.

"So who else wants to have a one more go at being a hero?"

No one responded at first. Then Torch spoke up.

"Not me. I'm toast. I'd just be a liability in that canoe."

Li nodded, "Yeah, me too. It wears you out when you're the stroker."

"Fair enough," replied Jacob. "What about you, Shaggy?"

"Like only two problems with that. My back is killing me and I just ate four sandwiches. I wouldn't want to puke on the guy ahead of me."

The others laughed. Jacob looked at Chico.

"And you?"

Chico rubbed his head. "I don't know. I gave it all I had in the last race. What about Brigham?"

They all looked at the Utah rebel. His eyes widened.

"Me? But I'm just the spare, remember."

"Exactly," said Chico. "You're the only one of us who hasn't raced. Your arms are totally fresh."

Jacob had to admit it made some sense. Brigham was a decent enough paddler, thanks to all those trainings. He was fit enough . . . the midnight swim proved that. But most of all he had those fresh arms. Jacob looked at his buddy.

"Well, partner, feel like earning your uniform?"

Brigham considered the offer then smiled. "What the hell, why not?"

"Good, we just need one more."

The boys all stared at Jacob. He got the message.

"You realize I'm as tired as you dorks," he said.

"Then all things being equal," argued Li, "we might as well have our captain out there, right?"

They all voiced their agreement. Jacob held up a hand.

"Okay, thanks for the vote of confidence, I think. We'll do our best."

"You better," teased Torch. "Or you'll do a week in the Cooler!"

Jacob laughed as he went to give Toa the names. He found Toa going over a list with Moana. Jacob kept back, not wanting to interrupt, but also wanting to hear the tone of their voices.

". . . and Tina, Elena and Akenesi from my juniors."

Toa nodded. "You've got a strong team, you'll win."

Moana smiled. "We'll make you proud, don't worry."

"I'm already proud of you," replied Toa calmly.

Jacob almost tripped on a paddle, stunned by the big guy's newfound spirit. Moana was also surprised, but pleasantly so.

"When the races are done, maybe we could talk," she said; a hint of uncertainty in the asking. Jacob held his breath.

Toa nodded. "Sure. That would be good."

Jacob breathed again. It wasn't the most emotional exchange he'd ever seen, but given the iron wills of the two people involved, it was a promising start.

Toa noticed Jacob standing there and turned. Both he and Moana looked a little embarrassed and she quickly headed back to where her girls were sitting. Jacob acted like he hadn't seen or heard anything.

"Just came to give you my paddlers' names. Me, Brigham and Tariq."

Toa nodded. "Gambling on the fresher arms, not a bad idea. You'll be number five on the left side. Your boys will be four and five on the right. So far it looks like we should have a lighter crew than Foelele or the Nomads, but more power than Tafola or Aufaigalu."

BEEONNNKK. The bullhorn siren squealed.

"Please prepare for the Women's 500 meter V12 Final. Thank you," announced the official.

"Showtime," remarked Jacob.

Toa cracked his knuckles. "More like showdown."

CHAPTER 48

As they waded over to the twin-hulled canoe, Jacob watched Toa as he moved toward the stern where Moana was sitting. He held up his hand and she high-fived him.

"Imagine trying to race those in a 1500 meter race!"

The boys watched the four double-hulled canoes as they chugged their way out to the start line.

"Hey boys, great race," called a voice behind them. They turned around to find Sanele walking over to them. He was sweating.

"Sorry I didn't come by to congratulate you earlier. I've been meeting with some people today, so I've been running back and forth trying to catch as many of the races as possible. I saw your final. You guys did pretty well for a bunch of bad boys who hadn't even seen an outrigger a few months ago."

"Thanks, sir," replied Jacob. "We're not done yet. Tariq, Brigham and I are paddling in the V12."

"Wow, that's excellent. When does it start?"

"The girls are racing now then we're up."

Sanele looked at his watch. "Sole! I have to make an overseas call. Maybe if I hurry I can get back in time for your race."

He gave them two thumbs-up. "Good luck and have fun."

He turned to leave but stopped. He looked like he was thinking something over. He looked at the boys.

"I might have a nice bonus for you when we get back to camp."

He rushed off before the boys could ask him for more details.

"Maybe he bought us some of that New Zealand ice cream," Torch licked his lips.

"Or maybe a hot pepper pizza!" drooled Shaggy.

"No chores for a week!" wished Chico.

Brigham suddenly pointed to the racecourse.

"They started!"

They looked to see the green flag up and the four canoes driving forward.

With the extra width of the canoes it was easier to see the race unfolding. The red and yellow of the Aufaigalu was showing an early lead. Foelele and Matagi were tied for second, with Tafola slightly behind them.

"Those SamCo girls are all juniors, but they're in front!" observed Tariq with surprise.

"They're lighter, that's why," explained Brigham.

At the halfway point the Aufaigalu had slowed significantly, allowing all three of the other canoes to overtake them.

"See, light but running out of power already," commented Jacob.

It was a three canoe race now. Tafola was trying to establish a lead but the Matagi and Foelele kept up the pace. At the 100 meter mark the Tafola canoe began to drop off. The exertion of trying to maintain the fast pace had wore them down. The Foelele and Matagi canoes charged ahead.

"It's going to be close!" shouted Torch.

The clubs began screaming encouragement to their crews. Jacob could see the Foelele steerers yelling at their paddlers. By the uniforms he could tell that nine of the Foelele paddlers were from the women's team, only three were from the sexy, but weak, junior team. The Matagi, however, was an even split of Moana's crew and the junior girls. Now Jacob understood why the race was so close. The two clubs were almost an even match.

With the last 50 meters to go, both teams cranked up their power pace. The Foelele pulled ahead slightly. The Matagi kept their pace. At 20 meters the Foelele were just holding on to their lead by a canoe length. Moana gave a final yell to her girls and they found an extra gear. The Matagi canoe soared ahead. At five meters the two canoes were even, then right before the line, the Matagi passed their rivals for the victory.

The Matagi on the steps went nuts. Torch and Chico hugged each other, jumping up and down. Everyone was chanting and cheering. Jacob high-fived Brigham.

"It's all tied up, buddy, seventeen to seventeen. One race left . . . winner take all!"

The official came out of the tent, waited for the noise to subside then he held up his bullhorn.

"This is it. Last race of the regatta. Men's 500 meter V12. Let's go."

The men's teams headed for the water. Jacob, Tariq and Brigham fell in with their Matagi teammates. Brigham loosened up his wrists and arms.

"My heart's racing like a rabbit."

As they waded over to the twin-hulled canoe, Jacob watched Toa as he moved toward the stern where Moana was sitting. He held up his hand and she high-fived him. Their hands stayed clasped together for a moment. Then Moana put her hand on his shoulder and used him as a brace as she hopped over the side into the water. Toa put a hand under her arm to help steady her. She looked at him with a soft expression then punched him playfully on the arm.

"Faamalosi!"

"Pole fua," he answered.

Toa climbed into the canoe. Jacob jumped into the seat in front of Toa. He watched Tariq and Brigham settle into their seats on the other side.

"Let's go," commanded Toa. The boys back-paddled the big craft, then got it turned around and headed for the start line. Toa called out the strategy.

"Timing is critical with this kind of race. Our power is wasted if both canoes aren't paddling together. Watch the strokers. We're going to use a three-quarter pace until half, then full pace to the 50 meters. Then it's power to the line. Don't worry about the other canoes. This is a longer race than it looks."

Jacob and the others practiced their timing, focusing on the strokers. It was a little sloppy at first, but by the time they arced into their lane, they were in near perfect synch. The other canoes had already arrived and were adjusting their positions. The Nomads and Tafola had the outer lanes. The young Aufaigalu crew was on Matagi's right. The Foelele were in the lane to their left. Markus looked over and smiled. He said something to his crew and they laughed.

"What's so funny?" Jacob wondered out loud to himself.

Toa leaned forward. "Look at his crew. It's his A1s and A2s. No juniors. He thinks he's got us beat already."

Markus called over to them. "Toa, are you sure you're in the right lane?"

"He's trying to rattle you," said Jacob.

"I know."

"Why don't you say something back?"

"Talk is cheap. We'll settle it with our paddles."

Spoken like a true warrior thought Jacob. Toa might be a stiff-necked, ego-driven pitbull . . . but at least he led by example. Jacob glanced over at Brigham, who looked nervous. Jacob winked at him and gave him a thumbs-up. Brigham nodded, forced a smile and tried to calm his breathing.

"Paddles up," called out Toa.

Jacob snapped his focus back to the official's boat. It seemed like the paddlers sat there in their first lunge position for a minute, before the green flag finally shot up.

"Alo!" yelled Toa.

The team stabbed their paddles in and pulled. Jacob could feel the canoe heave forward. It was much more sluggish than the regular six-seater mode. The first ten strokes were needed just to build a good opening momentum.

"Three-quarter pace!" Toa reminded them.

The boys concentrated on their strokers. They could see out of the corner of their eyes that the Aufaigalu and Nomads had pushed ahead. Foelele was even with them and the Tafola had dropped back a bit.

Jacob tried to ignore the other canoes and focused on his breathing and timing. His shoulders had already begun to burn.

"Hut!" called the strokers and they all switched.

They had covered at least 100 meters. The canoes seemed to be holding their positions. The Nomads might even have increased their lead on the pack.

"Timing Lino," warned Toa, as the number two paddler on the left had gotten off the pace.

As the canoes approached the halfway mark, the Aufaigalu had dropped back even with the others. Their young muscles simply couldn't maintain the pace they'd tried to set. Foelele and Matagi passed them. Tafola was still hanging back. The Nomads on the other hand looked to have gained another length on everyone. Jacob was feeling the temptation to paddle faster and catch up with the Nomads. Toa seemed to sense this urge within his crew.

"Easy, boys, keep to the pace. And breathe!"

Everyone took in air and tried to regulate their breathing. Fatigue was beginning to attack his muscles, forcing Jacob to fix his mind on each individual stroke in an attempt to block the pain. The Matagi canoe held its pace, but seeing that the Nomads had maintained their lead, the Foelele decided make a run at them. Markus increased the pace of his crew and they shot forward.

At about the 400 meter mark, the Foelele had drawn even and were battling it out with the Nomads for the lead. The Matagi were still a few lengths back and Jacob was beginning to wonder if they could catch up to the others.

"Ready," called out Toa as he observed the duel for first in front of them.

"Now!" he yelled. "Full speed!"

The strokers upped the pace and the Matagi canoe slowly crept up on the frontrunners. Markus and the Nomads were so busy jockeying for the lead that neither noticed the Matagi sliding up behind them.

Toa's order to focus on breathing and timing was paying off. Jacob had increased his pace and power, without noticing any increase in fatigue. He felt like a machine, part of a twelve- paddle torpedo that was heading for its target.

As the canoes hit the 450 meter mark, the Matagi had pulled even with the Nomads and Foelele. Markus glanced over and was stunned to see them.

Jacob could hear him yell "Power".

"Powa!" yelled Toa, "Go for kill!"

The Matagi boys grit their teeth, sunk their paddles in and drove the blades back. They streaked ahead. The Foelele and Nomads stayed with them for 20 meters. But the Matagi seemed to be getting stronger with each stroke. They kicked in their last reserves of strength.

The Nomads and Foelele had burned up their reserves fighting each other for the lead. The Nomads had nothing left. The Foelele had only a drop and though they paddled madly, it was too little, too late. The Matagi canoe crossed the finish line a meter ahead of them.

The sight on the Matagi steps was pure insanity. Moana was leaping up and down on her good leg. Everyone was hugging or high-fiving each other. Spectators along the seawall applauded loudly for the winners. Jacob looked across to Brigham and Tariq. Brigham was red-faced and gasping for air, but he flashed a quick thumbs-up. Tariq let out a howl.

A hand slapped down on Jacob's shoulder. He turned around and shook Toa's hand.

"You were right," gushed Jacob giddily. "You're a friggin' genius."

"Now you admit it!"

The Nomad canoe pulled alongside and congratulated them on the win. Markus' canoe also pulled up. Markus was exhausted, but a grin on his face.

"Good race, Toa. Looks like Teuila is yours again, but only by one point this time. I'm getting closer every year."

Toa nodded. "I guess I'll have to do something about that next year!"

Markus sneered as he and his crew paddled off. Toa wiped sweat from his forehead.

"He's right; they are getting better every year. But that's good, keeps everyone on their toes. That's the only way we'll build a half decent national team."

Jacob smiled. Toa had just won an incredible comeback win and he was already thinking of greater challenges ahead.

Toa steered the canoe past the steps as the Matagi crews sang a Samoan victory song. They then paddled the canoe back under the bridge and to the riverbank. They dragged the canoe up onto the bank then they marched back to the bridge and made their way up onto the road. A cheer went up as they rejoined their club mates.

Torch, Shaggy, Li and Chico bowed dramatically in front of Jacob, Brigham and Tariq. "We're not worthy," they chanted.

"Arise, you sniveling dogs," teased Brigham.

They shook each other's hands. Torch felt the biceps on Brigham's arms.

"See, scraping all those coconuts finally paid off!"

Brigham rolled his eyes. Jacob spotted Sanele rushing over to them.

"That was fantastic! What a finish!"

"Too bad we didn't have a video camera," moaned Chico.

Sanele smiled and pointed down the seawall, to the bend going into town.

"See that green landcruiser? That's TV Samoa. They filmed the last two races for the news tonight. You boys are going to be on national TV. I've a cousin that works there. I'll see if I can get a copy."

Toa hustled over to the group. Sanele congratulated him on the victory.

"Thanks," replied Toa. "Your boys showed a lot of heart out there. So we'll see you at the prize-giving tonight at Otto's Reef?"

The boys looked at each other, then to Sanele. He shook his head.

"Sorry, there are some things at camp that we need to attend to. Besides, I think asking for another night out might be pushing our luck. Maybe we can arrange for a barbecue or something another day."

Jacob nodded. "Fair enough, it's been a great two days."

The others were disappointed but nodded in agreement.

Sanele nudged Torch playfully. "But I think Suka might have fried chicken and ice cream on the menu tonight."

Torch's smile instantly returned. "Oh yeah?"

"Rumour has it," grinned Sanele. "So we better get going or by the time we get back, your campmates will have finished it all."

"Grab your bags, men, and let's go!" exclaimed Torch as he ran to gather his stuff. The others chased after him. Jacob stayed to talk with Toa.

"We'll miss you boys at the prize-giving," said Toa sincerely.

"We'll catch up with the gang some other time," replied Jacob. "But I gotta know one thing . . ."

"What?"

"You and Moana, are you . . . you know . . . talking?"

Toa looked at the ground, suddenly shy.

"I think so. Maybe tonight we can sort a few things out. We'll see."

Jacob nodded. "This is the one race you can't afford to lose Toa."

Toa looked at him.

Jacob continued. "You took a big chance letting me and my boys paddle in that final. You said it was because of fresh arms and lighter weight, but we both know that was just an excuse. You were going on your gut instincts. And it worked. I think you need to do the same with Moana."

Toa chewed on his lip then raised his eyebrows as if to agree with Jacob.

"You know for a palagi, you're not so stupid after all."

They laughed as they rejoined the crowd.

CHAPTER 49

"A report was made to the Blue Horizon Board of Governors, who earlier today made a ruling, given that it was not an isolated incident. The perpetrator of the incident has been asked to leave Blue Horizon."

The ride back to camp was a bittersweet one for Jacob. The sweetness was that the past two days had been so amazing. He had forged a friendship with six other misfits and they had beaten all the odds together. He had also gotten to know and respect Samoans like Toa, Moana and Sanele. All these good vibes almost made him forgot why he was even in Samoa.

The bitterness was in knowing that Big Sefo would be happy to remind him that he was still a bad boy. He dreaded the next few days. Sefo would be looking for payback for the past few weeks of special treatment the boys had received. Jacob knew he would be the favorite target. He wondered if he'd be setting any more records in the Cooler.

When the van pulled into camp, the sun was just setting. The sky was an incredible palette of baby blue, pink, orange and red. It seemed a perfect way to end a perfect day.

The boys tossed their bags into the dorm and headed straight to the dining hall. Torch sniffed the air.

"That's fried chicken all right!"

As they entered the hall, they were stunned to find the rest of the camp standing and waiting for them. Sanele stood at the staff table.

"Gentlemen, the fried chicken and ice cream you will be having tonight are courtesy of a little bet I had with the Honourable Joe Williams, the Minister of Justice. However, that bet was won thanks to your camp brothers who helped the Matagi Canoe Club win the Teuila Regatta. I suggest you show your gratitude for their hard work on your behalf."

The whole hall began clapping, whistling and cheering. Jacob and his crew walked proudly to a table reserved for them. Sanele held up his hand and everyone quieted. He said grace and then the chow line formed. The canoe team was allowed to go first. They stared at the succulent food in the trays. Not only were there pans of golden, crispy fried chicken, there were trays of chop suey, curried rice and home fries.

The boys loaded up their plates, Torch hoarding as much chicken as possible. The rest of the campers followed suit, eagerly filling their plates with the rare treats. The boys on serving detail came around and placed an ice-cold jug of pineapple drink on each table.

The hall was filled with the sound of smacking lips, crunching chicken bones and slurped chop suey. When everyone had eaten their fill, tubs of ice cream were cracked open.

The sound of spoons clinking and scraping the bowls punctuated the otherwise quiet hall. Torch licked his bowl clean and patted his stomach.

"I could do a week in the Cooler after a meal like that."

Jacob looked around, suddenly aware of something.

"Where's Sefo?"

They all looked around. Chico shrugged. "Probably ate in his room. I bet the sight of all us maggots having a decent meal would make him sick."

Li picked his teeth. "I hope he doesn't decide to make us do night chores. I'm dead tired, and with a full stomach on top of that."

Sanele stood up at the staff table and tapped his spoon on his glass. The boys looked up. "I have one announcement before we adjourn. As you know we had a bit of an incident here a couple of weeks ago. One of our rules is that we have a zero tolerance rule against violence or any form of bullying."

Jacob and the others looked at each other, completely baffled by what was happening.

"A report was made to the Blue Horizon Board of Governors, who earlier today made a ruling, given that it was not an isolated incident. The perpetrator of the incident has been asked to leave Blue Horizon."

The hall was filled with confused murmurs. Who had been sent home? Everyone scanned the room, trying to figure it out. Jacob smiled. He realized who Sanele was talking about.

"So," continued Sanele, "effective immediately I will be assuming full directorial control of the camp. Mr. Sefo has been sacked!"

Stunned silence . . . then a spontaneous cheer went up. Shaggy and Brigham high-fived each other. Jacob laughed. So this was the bonus Sanele had spoken of earlier in the day. They had finally pulled the plug on the big ogre.

Sanele tapped his glass again and the hall quieted. "Now, we will still have discipline and respect at this camp. Nothing changes as far as your duties or responsibilities are concerned. However, my hope is if you're all treated with fairness and dignity, you will respond in kind. This is an opportunity for each one of you to make Blue Horizon a stepping stone to a better life. Don't mess up."

The boys all nodded, taking the advice to heart.

"Oh," Sanele continued," and tomorrow after toonai, I'd like a volunteer to help me dismantle the Cooler."

Every hand in the hall shot up. Sanele suppressed a grin. He pointed at

Jacob. "Jacob, I think it would be poetic justice if you assisted me."

Everyone clapped their approval.

"That's all. Enjoy the rest of your evening."

The boys filed out of the hall, excited by the good news. The canoe team strolled toward the dorm. Brigham and Jacob hung back a bit. Brigham patted Jacob on the shoulder.

"I'm glad you talked me into staying, I sure would have missed out on a great time."

"I'm glad you stayed. I don't think things would have turned out as well if you hadn't."

"You know, without Big Sefo here for my last three months, I might actually miss this place when I go."

Jacob laughed. "Let's not get carried away. There's still the cockroaches, the humidity, Suka's cooking, centipedes and don't forget the crotch rot." He scratched his groin to emphasize the point.

"True, but now they seem a little more bearable."

They walked a bit in thoughtful silence.

"Do you think you'll ever make it to Australia?" asked Jacob.

"Maybe. I guess I still owe those Swedes a beer."

Shaggy stuck his head out the dorm door, looking for them.

"C'mon guys, like we're going to play reverse strip poker?'

"What's that?" Jacob asked Brigham.

"Just like it sounds. If you lose, you have to put clothes on."

"In this heat?"

"Exactly."

"You gonna play?" inquired Jacob as they reached the dorm step.

"Nah," winked Brigham. "Mormons don't gamble."

Jacob shook his head and laughed as they joined the others.

"We drove out to deliver a package. A leftover from the prize-giving last night," said Toa. Moana pulled a small trophy from the box. It had a small canoe on the top. She handed it to Jacob.

"Careful, those nails are rusty."

Sanele handed a short, heavy beam to Jacob. Nails stuck out from the ends. Jacob tossed it onto a pile. Next to it was another pile of roofing iron. The Cooler was all but gone.

"I'm glad to see this thing destroyed," remarked Sanele. "I wouldn't keep a pig in a pen like this. I told the governors that this is supposed to be a rehabilitation camp, not a retribution camp."

Jacob picked up a piece of scrap wood. "So why did they allow Sefo to get away with all that crazy stuff."

"I think they were intimidated by Sefo's claims that without harsh punishments the camp would become uncontrollable. Personally, I believe this camp works better without fear as the guiding principle."

He looked at Jacob. "I've seen a big change in you, Jacob. What caused that? Was it the fear, or something else?"

Jacob wished he could tell him about the escape plan, but he didn't think this was the right time. The irony was, fear had driven him to such a desperate act.

"No, sir, it wasn't fear that turned my thinking around. It was you. You believed in me, you took a chance on all of us on the racing team. I felt good knowing someone had faith in me."

Sanele smiled. That was what he'd hoped to hear.

"Malo galue!" someone called out.

It was Toa and Moana. They were approaching from the courtyard side. She carried a small cardboard box in her hands. Toa held her arm as she raised her artificial leg over the Cooler debris.

"Malo Toa. Malo Moana," replied Sanele.

"What brings you out to our little paradise?" asked Jacob.

"We drove out to deliver a package. A leftover from the prize-giving last night," said Toa. Moana pulled a small trophy from the box. It had a small canoe on the top. She handed it to Jacob.

"There was one big shield trophy for the winning club, but there were also trophies for each of the races. Everyone agreed you guys deserved this one."

Jacob read the engraving. "Teuila V12 First Place Champs. Wow!"

Sanele wiped his sweaty brow. "Between Suka's corned beef and this heat, I'm thirsty as can be. Can I get anyone else a cold drink?"

"No thanks," Toa and Moana said together. Jacob shook his head.

As Sanele headed for the kitchen, Jacob looked at Toa and Moana.

"Well?" he asked curiously.

Moana rolled her eyes. "Yes, we're back together and I'm not going to New Zealand, Mr. Nosey palagi."

Jacob smiled. "Well it took you two long enough to get it right."

"Malo Moana!" yelled someone from the kitchen. It was Suka.

She sighed. "Excuse me for a minute. I better be polite and say 'hi' to the aiga." She limped toward the kitchen.

When she was out of earshot, Jacob raised an eyebrow at Toa.

"So what happened?"

Toa grinned bashfully. "After the prize-giving, I walked her home along the seawall."

"Good move, very romantic," noted Jacob approvingly.

"We talked about the races and stuff first, then about her going to New Zealand. I didn't know what to do, then I remembered what you said and I just told her."

"Told her what?"

"The truth. About the accident, everything."

"Was she upset?"

"Yeah, at my family. And at me too, for not trusting her. But I calmed her down and we sorted it out."

Jacob shook his head. "You calmed her down? How?"

"I kissed her."

"Pepelo!"

Toa smiled. "Serious, man. I just grabbed her and kissed her. I think it was the first time I ever got the last word with her."

Jacob punched him lightly, "See, your gut instinct's never wrong."

"I can't believe how close I was to losing her." He shook his head. "Remember that first day we met? I mean, if someone had told me then that in a few weeks I'd be thanking that big mouth, hotshot palagi for helping me win back my girl, and a Teuila regatta . . . I'd have said they were crazy. But here I am, doing just that."

Moana walked back over to them. She stopped beside Toa and leaned on his shoulder. He put an arm around her waist.

"So, what have you two been gossiping about?" she asked curiously.

Jacob grinned. "Toa and I were just discussing how we'd like your

Matagi girls' team to wear uniforms like the Foelele junior girls."

Moana slapped Toa on the back of the head.

"Hey, he's lying," pleaded Toa.

Jacob nodded. "He's right, it was my idea. He said 'no' because you girls are too old and flabby."

She slapped Toa again, who laughed. He pulled her closer and they headed off. He looked back at Jacob.

"We better go before you really get me into trouble. We'll see you in two weeks."

"Two weeks?" called out Jacob.

Moana looked back, "We start training for the annual marathon to Savaii. You'll love the big water."

Jacob waved to them as they left. He looked at the trophy again. Hmmm, a marathon. It would mean more grueling training, extra chores on his off days and spending all his time with those other six knuckleheads on the Blue Horizon canoe team.

He smiled. It sounded like fun.

www.ingramcontent.com/pod-product-compliance
Lightning Source LLC
Chambersburg PA
CBHW060907250626
47159CB00008B/2902